MORNINGSTAR

The **PROMGEN** files
OPERATION: ABSOLUTION

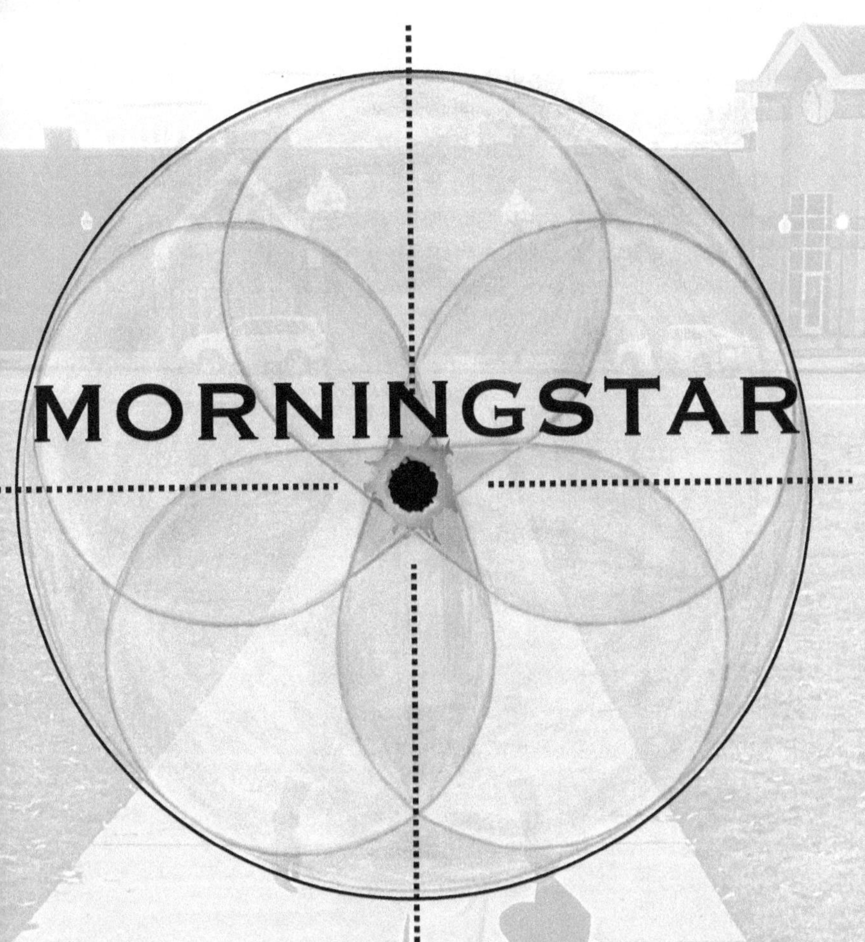

MORNINGSTAR

Aly Kay Tibbitts

BATTALION PRESS
BOUNTIFUL, UTAH

Library of Congress Control Number: 2021917405
ISBN: 978-1-955192-02-6 (Hardcover)
        978-1-955192-03-3 (Ebook)
        978-1-955192-04-0 (Paperback)

Any references to historical events, real people, or real places are used fictitiously. Names, characters, and places are products of the author's imagination.

The text type was set in Garamond and Copperplate.
Front cover image by Alyx Tibbitts.
Book design by Alyx Tibbitts.

Published by Battalion Press.

First Edition, Dec. 2021
Paperback Edition, Dec. 2022

To Ambri

You made editing enjoyable. Thanks for all the laughs.

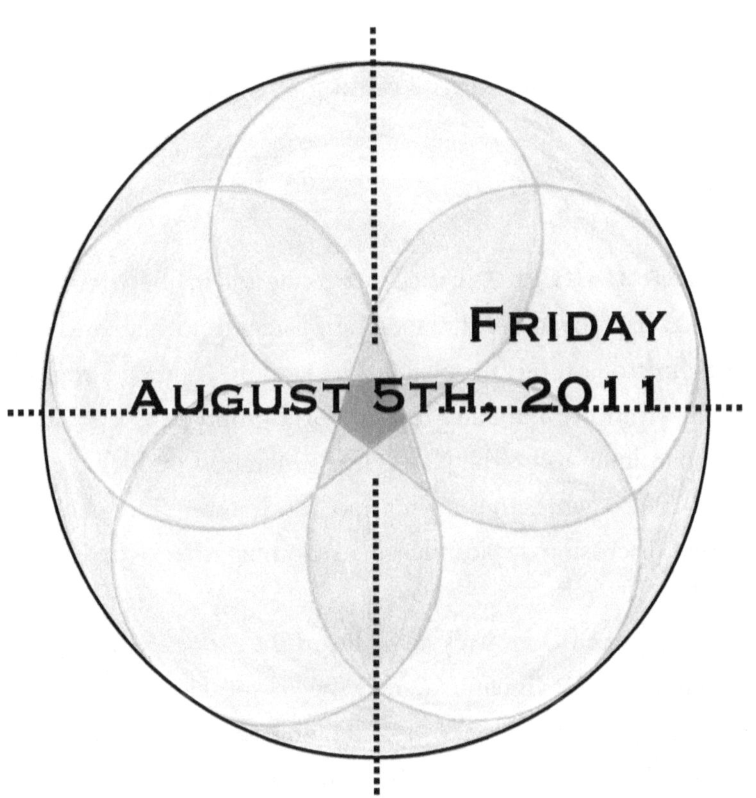

Friday
August 5th, 2011

11:54 PDT
Tracy, California
Promising Generation Training Program HQ

PETER CARLYLE drifted off as he sat in the room that should have been his dining room, listening to Nathan Levy, the director of the Promising Generation Training Program discuss various mundane topics. For a group that was meant to be training to be the CIA's next generation of highly qualified field agents, they spent too much time sitting in this room discussing topics that had nothing to do with field work.

Peter was drawn back as he heard the group's CIA liaison, psychologist Dr. Ignatius Wraith begin speaking. "The training division has given you a training mission of sorts. A BOLO has been issued for this young woman." Wraith used a remote to put an image of the young woman on the TV in the room.

Peter stared at the picture that was frozen on the screen. The image was clearly taken from a video, and may have been low-quality, black-and-white security camera footage, but he knew that the girl's eyes were a piercing blue. He knew, because he'd caught himself looking at them more than he would ever admit.

"Don't let her appearance deceive you. She attacked one of our guarded safe-houses in the Austrian Alps on the evening of July 11th. She put nine of our own in the hospital. She killed the tenth." Wraith paused, making eye contact with everyone at the table to ensure what he'd said sunk in. "Intelligence suggests that she is heading to somewhere here in the Bay Area next."

"And the training portion is what, exactly?" Cameron McKay asked. He was one of the oldest members of the group at 19, and was one of the few members who had actually completed training at the Farm. Technically he, as well as the director Nathan, and a handful of others, were graduated from the training program, but stuck around for reasons Peter couldn't even guess.

"It's a training in identification and observation. They want you to figure out who she is, where in the Bay Area she went, what she wants, and keep an eye on her until the CIA can decide how to proceed." Wraith reported.

Nathan finished the briefing. "You guys know the drill. If you see her, report it to Peter or I. We will decide where to go from there." He turned to Peter. "Is there anything you would like to add?"

Peter looked away from the frozen image, expending more effort than should have been necessary to pull his attention away from the girl. Her name was on the tip of his tongue. *Alyx McLean, age 16. She attends John C. Kimball High School. She's brilliant, if her grades in Algebra II are any indication.* But instead of rattling off what he knew about the girl, he decided to lie. "Nope."

Nathan nodded. "Ok. Meeting adjourned."

All of the members of the Promising Generation, who had been sitting around the table stood up, dispersing towards the door. Peter stayed seated, leaning across the table toward Wraith. "Can you by chance get me a copy of the video that picture was captured from? I'd like to analyze it to see if it can tell us any-thing else." Peter asked.

"The CIA already has their full time analysts on it." Wraith said dismissively, not looking up from the file he was pushing papers into. "Your time would be better focused on making sure you pass all the required exams so you can begin your mission immediately after graduation."

"School doesn't start for another week." Peter argued.

Wraith looked up at him. "Your French and Italian are flawless?"

"My French could admittedly use a little bit of work, but I've already been emailing with the French teacher at Kimball, and he has agreed to help me..." Peter replied, "Once school starts, which means I need something to do until then."

"I've given the Generation a task. Why don't you help with that." Wraith ordered.

"Yes. Identification and Observation. What if there is something in the video that could help identify her?" Peter insisted.

"I'll see what I can do." Wraith commented, then he too got up and left.

Peter went back to staring at the still image on his TV of Alyx McLean, the girl he'd sat behind two years before in Algebra II. She was intelligent, considering she'd been placed in a class for Sophomores and Juniors as a Freshman, and if that wasn't enough for her, she wasn't just in the top percentage of the class, but she was challenging Peter for *the* top spot. She was quiet, and observant, and used those traits to help her blend into crowds to the point where she almost disappeared. That was what had made him notice her finally. Her observation seemed to make her eyes this beautiful piercing blue that always portrayed constant thought.

He hadn't been able to stop noticing her since.

He'd chosen not to speak up during the briefing, because he felt like something was being held back, and the fact that Wraith evaded his request to see the footage only added to his suspicion. Fortunately, he knew her cousin.

There was only one question he wanted to know the answer to: What did Alyx McLean do this summer?

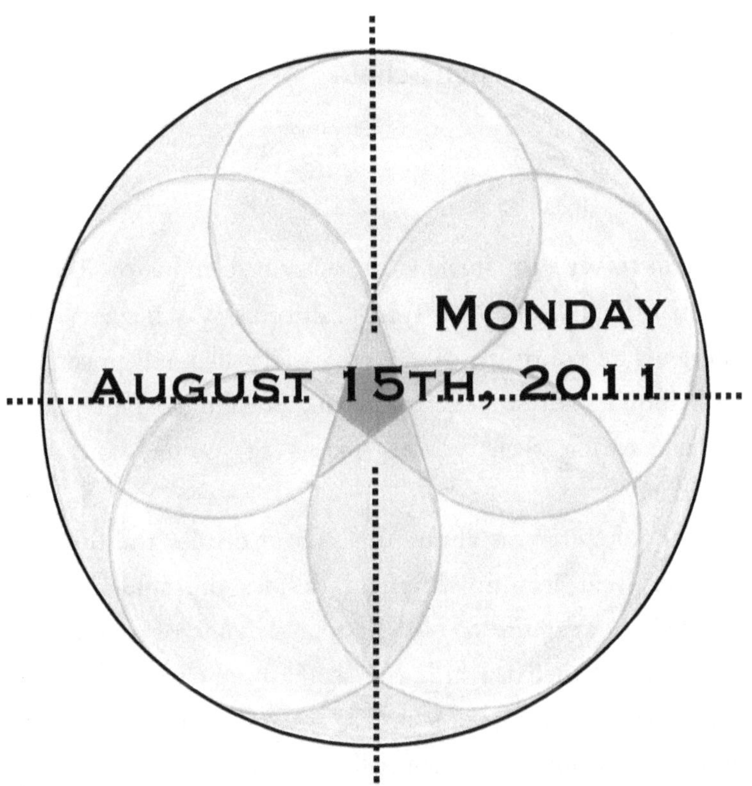

Monday
August 15th, 2011

10:57 PDT
Tracy, California
John C. Kimball High School

THE SPRAWLING, single story, outdoor campus of John C. Kimball High School in Tracy California was buzzing with energy. The courtyard of concrete sidewalks and grass hills was dotted with students displaying their exuberant school spirit, wearing their various pieces of orange and blue clothing.

School spirit was always on brilliant display the first day, and this year was no different. Besides the students who decided to wear the too-bright school color of orange, no one had lost their lanyards yet, so the bright icons were still visible around everyone's necks, and every Fall Sport was wearing their uniforms, especially the cheer and dance teams, who could be seen next to the orange polo shirts that represented the football team.

Having only opened three years before, this was the first time the school had seniors, and somehow that made everything about the first day of school better and brighter. Maybe, with Seniors, Kimball would finally have a formidable football team.

Alyx McLean walked through the crowds, feeling the energy buzzing. She felt like if she were to scream *Let's go Jaguars* everyone in the courtyard would respond to her call. The thought brought a smile to her face, but she let the thought come and go. Instead, she brushed past one of the Leadership kids, covered with school spirit from head to toe, and whispered the cheer in his ear. As she slipped into the cafeteria, she heard the fruits of her whisper sweep the students eating lunch outside, their voices rising above the sound of the music.

She may have taken a step into the spotlight at Fields Ball the summer before, but it was time to return to the shadows.

As she walked into the lunchroom, no one noticed that her backpack was already weighed down with textbooks. No one looked her way as she pulled her long, wavy, strawberry brunette hair out from under the strap. She was invisible, and she liked it that way. She was good at this. She was good at blending into the crowds, slipping through the shadows, but still leaving her mark, even if no one but her knew.

She arrived at a booth towards the back of the cafeteria, slipping her heavy bag off her shoulder, and sliding it under the bench of the booth. As upperclassmen, it didn't matter that it was the first day of school, because the habits of the previous two years returned, and they sat in the same spot they had everyday for the past two years. Despite there being two different lunch periods, with the classroom of each students' fourth period class determining whether they had first or second lunch, all four of Alyx' friends had managed to have the same lunch all three years they'd attended the school. As she slipped into her place next to her friend Savannah, she couldn't help but smile, and think about how the only reason she survived the shadows, was by having a strong group of people to tell her when she was going too far.

"What's wrong with applying to Delta College?" Thane asked. He was one of only two guys in their friends group. He was her next door neighbor when she had first moved to California. As an only child, she had been drawn to the brother-sister dynamic between him and his younger sister, Chelsi. Fortunately, he didn't mind her joining his friend group, where she had met Kaden, the other guy in the group, and Savannah, both of whom had gone to Wicklund, the K–8 school she had attended when she first moved to California four years before.

"Nothing, if you're a normal person." Carlie said. "I think Savannah was just hoping you would be applying for one of the CSUs she is applying for." Her reply caused not one, but two red faces to appear, but that wasn't good enough for her. "If you're Alyx, the only thing wrong with Delta is that it's not Oxford."

Alyx held her hands up in surrender. "Hey, I don't think there is anything wrong with Thane applying to Delta, so don't drag me and my choices into this."

"It's not that it has to be Oxford, it's the fact that it's not in London. If you haven't noticed, Alyx happens to be our resident Brit." Savannah corrected.

Alyx rolled her eyes. "That's what happens when I spent my entire childhood moving. I've spent more time in London than I have in any one city here in the US. London feels like home, and I think I have a decent shot at getting into Oxford, so why not?"

Savannah smiled, warning Alyx, too late, that she had just fallen into one of Savannah's traps. "And how was London this summer?" She asked Alyx.

While it might not seem like it from the outside, that was a dangerous question coming from Savannah. She was one of the more popular members of their friend group, with a propensity to participate in the school rumor mill, meaning she had either heard something from someone else, or she was hoping for something to add to the rather dull first-day talk.

The *last* thing Alyx needed was to be the subject of Kimball's juicy gossip. She was already being talked about in half of London's tabloids, albeit under the wrong name. She was enjoying the quiet of Tracy, and if one of her classmates decided to cash out on her after connecting the rumors to the tabloids, she could kiss any chance of a future in espionage goodbye.

Alyx shrugged. "You know, same old same old." She lied. "Actually, Kate has a twin, so that was new."

"Is Alyx telling you about her new boyfriend?" A boy

asked as he slid into the booth, squeezing Savannah and Alyx into the wall. Unlike the rest of his friends sitting in the booth, Kaden was wearing his class of 2012 shirt, with khaki shorts, and knee-high orange and blue socks. He, like Savannah, was quite popular, and heard most of the school's rumors, as was to be expected from someone in leadership.

"Boyfriend?" Alyx asked skeptically.

Both Savannah and Kaden nodded. "*The Daily Star* had quite an interesting article about Prince James' new girlfriend, Alex Feilds." Kaden told her.

"I read about it in the *Enquirer*." Savannah added. "I recognized you in the pictures. Nice dress, by the way."

Alyx knew she had made quite an entrance at Feilds' Ball. That had been the goal. She needed eyes on her for their plan to confuse Radford to work. And it almost had. What she hadn't accounted for was that she would draw the attention of the tabloids. If she was being honest, she didn't know anyone from the press attended. She knew Feilds' Ball for what it was; a celebration for the end of the Intelligence Conference, and only those who attended the conference knew of its existence. But Feilds' Ball? That was one of London's hottest events, attended by almost everyone with a title, so the world's intelligence officers could hide in the crowds.

Four sets of eyes settled on Alyx, waiting to hear what she had to say about the prince. But she had nothing to say.

"If I had known that all it took to get you to move on from your ridiculous crush on Peter Carlyle was a prince, I would have tried that two years ago." Carlie complained.

Alyx looked at her uncharacteristically quiet friends. "I'm not dating Prince James." She finally said.

With her denial, their booth erupted into a cacophony of arguments, the loudest of which being *prove it.*

She could prove it. She could tell them exactly what she had been doing that night, and by extension, what she had done the rest of the summer. The question was what rumor she would rather have circulating school: she was dating a prince, or she had saved her cousin.

Alyx glanced over at the table of football players in the center of the cafeteria, surrounded by cheerleaders, members of the dance team, and leadership kids.

"Exactly how much of the school has heard the rumor?" She asked distracted.

Carlie and Savannah shared a knowing look, recognizing the look on Alyx' face. Savannah reached across Alyx towards Kaden. "Pay up." She demanded.

Kaden sighed, pulling a five dollar bill out of his pocket. "How did you know?" He complained.

Savannah shrugged, handing the five back to Kaden. "But if you could go get me some pizza, that would be great."

Kaden rolled his eyes, but got up and walked toward the lunch counter.

Alyx just glared at Savannah. "You never answered my question. Who. Has heard. The rumor?"

"No one. Kaden and I like to borrow Emily's British

tabloids from time to time, so we saw the pictures. I told Kaden you were still hung up on Peter."

It was Alyx' turn to roll her eyes. Her aunt, Emily Hall, was a bit obsessed with reading the British tabloids, a habit she'd picked up when they were her only source of information on Ally, Alyx' mom's twin sister. Alyx should have know that introducing Kaden and Savannah to her aunt would be a bad idea, but these were the first friends that lasted more than a year, so she did. Now she was paying for it.

"So…" Carlie dragged out the word. Alyx could guess what was coming next, and Carlie's audible delay in asking it was filling Alyx with more dread than was fair, or necessary. "Are you going to explain why you were dancing with a prince, but you aren't dating him?"

"I dance with James every year." Alyx answered. "This year, someone simply caught it on camera."

Savannah shrieked. Carlie rolled her eyes. Kaden looked back and forth as he approached with Savannah's pizza.

"Alyx just calls him James." Carlie told Kaden.

"And she dances with him every year." Savannah added, her mouth full of the pizza she had grabbed off the plate before Kaden had a chance to sit down.

Kaden looked at Savannah suspiciously. "But she's not dating him. She still likes the football player she refuses to talk to, like a crazy person."

Kaden's question was answered by a chorus of nods.

"Why?" Kaden asked.

"We're friends, but he likes someone else." Alyx admitted.

"And he told you? Do you know who?" Savannah asked, too excited to wait until she was done chewing to ask her questions.

Alyx just drew her thumb and pointer across her lips in a zipping motion.

Thane raised an eyebrow interrupting before Kaden and Savannah started their loud pleas for Alyx to tell them. "I believe she is trying to distract us from the more important question." Thane observed. "If you dance with *James* every year, why is this year the first year the tabloids published the photo?"

Alyx shrugged. "Maybe they liked my dress." She suggested. "Oh, by the way, I may not be able to eat lunch with you guys this year. I'm supposed to study French with Mr. Martin during lunch. I'll find out today after school."

Carlie narrowed her eyes at Alyx. "Thane's right," Carlie said, "You're trying to distract us."

Alyx stared at her friend, neither of them breaking eye contact. Carlie was the one who finally broke, which was to be expected. She turned to Savannah. "What did Alyx' nice dress look like?"

"It was this gorgeous rose pink ball gown, paired with a cream pashmina. She had her hair in this elegant updo—I *almost* didn't recognize her." Savannah gushed.

"It was a sleeveless dress designed by Victoria Beckham." Kaden added. "How did you get her to design a dress? Since she launched her line, she's been a hot commodity."

"I used my uncle's name." Alyx said, shoving food in her mouth. She knew where Thane and Carlie were going with their line of questioning, and she wanted every excuse she could find for not answering them.

"If it was a custom dress, why was it sleeveless?" Carlie asked.

Alyx hated how perceptive her friends could be. She should have known Carlie would be the one to think the sleeveless dress was suspicious. While Thane had introduced her to Savannah and Kaden at school, she had met Carlie at church. Since she went to church with Thane and Carlie, they would be the ones to know her standards of modesty. If she didn't translate for her uncle, who was the master of evasion and obfuscation, she might be concerned about her friends breaking her.

"I was the distraction." Alyx said.

"Distraction from what?" Thane asked.

Alyx glanced at her watch, doing math to figure out how long they had left at lunch. Fortunately, it wasn't long.

"Well, you know, there was Kate, and Lynn. And Lynn is Kate's twin, but she just showed up and it was her introduction to the public, and they can be a bit intense. Plus there was Lyshiria, and—" She cut off as the bell rang. "Gotta get to class." She snapped the lid onto her container of food, shoving it into her backpack. "Finish this later?" She asked with a smile, tossing her backpack over her shoulder as she started walking away. As her head turned back toward the door, she caught sight of Peter Carlyle in his bright orange polo shirt as he stood up from the table he'd shared with his friends. Peter was laughing at something one of his teammates had said, but he turned and seemed to glance at the table Alyx had been sitting at. She could have sworn a frown crossed his face, but it was small, and disappeared.

Alyx turned away before he noticed her staring. Sometimes she wished she wasn't so invisible to certain people.

14:10 PDT
Tracy, California
John C. Kimball High School

PETER CARLYLE was grateful that Alyx McLean was as invisible as she was. Despite being in classes with half of the spies looking for her, Peter had made it through the day without any positive reports of seeing the girl in the photo. The longer it took the other members to realize that the girl they were looking for was right in front of them, the longer he had to figure out how to prove her innocence. Unfortunately, he doubted her invisibility would last. After all, he had noticed her for the first time when he was in the same Algebra II class sophomore year, and hadn't been able to stop noticing her since. It wouldn't take long for her intelligence to catch the attention of one of the seniors part of the Promising Generation, especially since she was a junior taking the classes a year early.

He knew the best way to help her, was to do everything he could to behave as normal. That meant he needed to prepare for the AP French test just like Wraith wanted him to.

With his football gear on for practice, and his duffle over his shoulder, he walked into Mr. Martin's room, causing the teacher to look up from his computer. "Bonjour monsieur Martin." Peter greeted.

"Bonjour Pierre," Mr. Martin replied, using the French version of Peter that he had chosen to go by the first year he'd taken French from the teacher. He reached up to the control panel just next to him on the wall, with buttons for the projector and speakers in the room, using the nob to turn down the volume of the French music he was playing. "Comment ça va?"

"Ça va bien." Peter replied. The classroom had the desks arranged the same way all of the language classrooms had them. The desks were in rows of four facing the center aisle, which allowed the teacher to walk up and down the aisle in front of the students as he taught. At the back by the door, Mr. Martin had a bookshelf with the classroom set of textbooks he kept available for students to use during class. At the front, the whiteboard spanned nearly from wall to wall, stopping just over Mr. Martin's desk in the opposite corner from the door. Peter made his way through the center aisle to the row of desks closest to Mr. Martin's desk, slipping into the third desk back so he was sitting right next to Mr. Martin.

"Bien." Martin replied. "You are not the only one who contacted me about preparing for the AP French test. The other student is also fluent, so I can imagine no reason why the two of you can't study together and do very well."

Peter nodded. "That sounds great to me. The only problem with that is I have football practice after school."

"I believe she has tennis. She should be on her way, so the two of you can work something out."

Alyx shrugged her bag of tennis rackets up onto her shoulder as she opened the door to the French classroom. Mr. Martin looked at the door with a smile. "Ah, elle est ici." He told the student sitting next to him. When Peter turned to look at the student he would be studying with for the next year, Alyx had a hard time forcing herself to keep moving. "Peter, meet Alyx."

Peter couldn't help but smile as he watched Alyx walk toward him, wearing her workout top and tennis skort. The only thing that gave her away as a tennis player instead of a cheerleader was the odd shaped padded bag that held her rackets. In her hand, she carried a bike bottle which, at the right angle, Peter could tell was full of water.

Alyx stopped at the end of the row of desks Peter was sitting in, giving an awkward wave in response to Mr. Martin's introduction.

"Both of you have expressed interest in taking the AP French test in May. You are both fluent enough, I don't think there is much more for me to teach you. What you most need is preparation for the test, such as practicing the written, verbal, and listening sections. That can best be accomplished by having you two study and practice together. I can give you assignments to keep you on track, and I'll meet with you once a month, maybe more often depending on how much help you need. How does that sound?"

Alyx tried to control a blush that threatened to color her cheeks. She had this curse when it came to talking to the boys she liked—it never went well—so she chose not to, unless it was completely necessary. She had been in Peter's Algebra II class for an entire year—all 180 school days—and she had said maybe 10 words to him over the course of that school year. Now she *had* to talk to him, in French, if she was going to get into Oxford.

"That sounds good to me," Peter answered. "We probably need to figure out when we can meet. I get done with football about 5:30pm, so I'm free anytime after 6:30."

Alyx shrugged trying to look and sound nonchalant. "I could do 6:30. Your house?"

"I mean my parents are never home…" Peter said.

"Probably not the best idea." Alyx admitted, mortified she'd just invited herself over to his house. The curse continued.

"What about the same time at your house?" Peter asked.

"My mom is in the trauma center until 7:00 tonight, and assuming my dad doesn't get called on a case, he won't be home until 7:00 at the earliest. I'll have to check to make sure." Alyx explained.

"Of course." Peter nodded his head saying he understood. "Mr. Martin, can I use a sticky note?" Mr. Martin handed him one. Peter took it and stuck it on the desk he was sitting at, pulled out a pen, and scribbled something on it. He peeled it off the desk as he picked up his duffle from under the desk and stood to leave. He handed the note to Alyx as he walked by. "Text me when you get an answer."

Alyx stared at the number in her hand, realizing as the door banged close that she hadn't said goodbye. How was she supposed to study anything with him if she was already distracted?

The problem wasn't him. It wasn't his well-trimmed blonde hair, or his piercing blue eyes. No, the problem was that she had imagined what it would be like if Peter gave her his number. It was a fantasy she sometimes indulged when the boredom of life got to her, but she had never let herself hope it might really happen.

"Thank you, Mr. Martin." Alyx said as she turned to leave. "I better get to practice."

Mr. Martin nodded. "Let me know if there is anything else I can do to help."

"I will." Alyx told him, then left through the door.

Oxford. Alyx thought as she walked to practice. *Oxford is the goal. And I can't let a cute football player distract me from that.*

SARAH MCLEAN watched as the garage door closed the last few inches before turning off the garage light and heading in the house. All three cars were lined up in their spots in the garage, telling her she was the last one home. She heard voices coming from the kitchen, and based on the words she heard, she guessed that was where Alyx was studying. Sarah smiled as she listened to the conversation. The young man speaking French with her daughter was quite talented. He spoke without an accent, and yes, he made some errors, but they were small, and mostly unnoticeable. Alyx, of course, noticed.

"J'ai étudie la langue pour presque tous ma vie, et ce n'est pas correct." She heard her daughter argue.

Sarah left the laundry room where she'd entered the house, turning right before turning left to walk down the hallway that opened up into the family room and kitchen. Sarah paused as she became visible to her daughter sitting on the left side of their breakfast nook table, kitty corner from a young man who was sitting at the end.

"Peut-être je peut aider." Sarah said as she plugged her phone into the outlet on the wall, setting it down on the countertop, far enough away from the sink it was unlikely to get wet.

Sarah noticed that, as usual, Neil sat on the couch, but the TV was off, probably so the news wouldn't distract their daughter. He looked up from his book, a look on his face that Sarah knew was regret. If Sarah knew her husband, he was thinking about how he should have studied French, so he could have prevented this situation: his daughter flirting with an attractive young man under the pretense of studying.

Sarah looked back over to the kitchen table. "I have been known to speak the language on occasion."

Alyx smirked. "Mom, this is Peter, the partner Mr. Martin assigned me."

Peter offered his hand to Mrs. McLean. "It's nice to meet you." He glanced at Alyx before looking back at her mom. "Do you speak French as well?"

"Bien sûr!" Sarah replied. "My mother emigrated from France before she met my father, and insisted her children know both languages. I can't tell you which language I learned first, because my dad spoke to us in English, and my mom spoke to us in French. We were all practically born bilingual." Sarah put her hand on her daughter's shoulder. "How can I help?"

Alyx shook her head. "It's fine. We can handle this. I'm sure you want to relax. It looks like you had a hard day."

Sarah glanced down at her blue scrubs which had smudges of a copper brown color that even Alyx knew could only be blood. Yes, she'd had a long, rough day. She had another set of scrubs she'd changed out of at work that had more stains than the set she was currently wearing. Once she changed, both sets would be thrown in the washing machine to try and salvage them. What her daughter didn't realize, was that after treating patients in the trauma center, most days she really just wanted to make sure her husband and daughter were ok, above everything else. Seeing her sitting at this table, and her husband reading on the couch helped her relax more than anything else.

"It won't kill me to answer a question first." Sarah insisted.

Alyx sighed. "Is it *Je connais Paris* or *Je sais Paris?*" She asked.

"Connais." Sarah answered. "As my mother explained, you know a city here" Sarah tapped her chest over her heart, "in *ton cœur*, like you would know a good friend. You know math, language, *knowledge* in your head—savoir."

"Told you." Alyx snarked to Peter.

Sarah just shook her head. "Have you eaten?" She asked.

Alyx shook her head. "Not yet."

Sarah nodded. "I'm going to go change and shower, then I'll be down to make something. Peter, will you join us?"

"Dad already ordered us some food." Alyx told her mom.

Neil got up from the couch and walked to join his wife in the kitchen. "It should be here by the time you're done," he told his wife. He grabbed her purse from her. "Everything is under control."

Without anymore words, both of Alyx' parents left the room.

"I didn't know your grandma was from France," Peter commented once they were gone. "That's really cool."

Alyx blushed. "Thanks. She's been teaching me French for as long as I can remember. I've always had a fascination with languages, and I can thank her for it."

Peter tapped his pencil on his notebook. "I have two questions then. Why are you taking the AP French test, and why did you ask Mr. Martin for help studying for it? It seems you would do better asking your mom or grandma for help."

"My mom works in the Stanford Trauma Center, so by the time she finishes her 12-hour shift and gets home, she's been gone for 15 hours. I'm lucky if I get a conversation from her like the one we just had. Usually it's some strangled combination of both languages. And since grandpa died, grandma has spent more time traveling. She was the daughter of a French diplomat, so her talent for diplomacy, and her citizenship makes her a priceless asset in DC and Paris. Plus it helps her keep her mind off of losing her husband."

"And the test?" Peter prodded.

"It's required for me to get into the course I want to follow at Oxford." She admitted.

Peter shook his head, looking down at his notebook.

"What?" Alyx asked.

"You just surprise me: Oxford, your ties to French and US politics through your grandma, plus the rumors I've heard about you having an uncle with a palace in London. You are connected Alyx McLean. Probably the most connected girl in Tracy. I can't believe you aren't the most popular girl in school." Peter commented, looking into her eyes.

He was fishing for information, and he knew it. He slipped in the bit about her uncle with hopes that she might confirm it, Maybe he could hear her side of what had happened in Austria. He'd heard the CIA narrative, and he didn't believe it. He just hoped it was coming off more like flirting than an interrogation. He had plenty of practice flirting. He had yet to use it to get information out of an asset. He tried to think of this as nothing more than practice, but the girl he was flirting with was the only girl he hadn't been able to stop noticing. And that was something considering the girl intentionally tried to blend in.

"I like my anonymity." Alyx replied with a smirk. *Oxford,* she reminded herself. She swallowed her smile and the warm feelings bubbling up within her as she talked to Peter—as he *flirted* with her. Even if Peter was flirting with her, she would be leaving the country at the end of the school year. It was pointless to start dating someone now, only to leave. "You can't believe everything you hear. But yes, I do have certain expectations and goals I hold myself to. Unless you want to continue this conversation in French, I would suggest we return to our textbooks."

Peter smiled slyly, looking back down at his textbook. The Promising Generation should be recruiting Alyx, not hunting her. She was exactly the kind of person who belonged in the Generation.

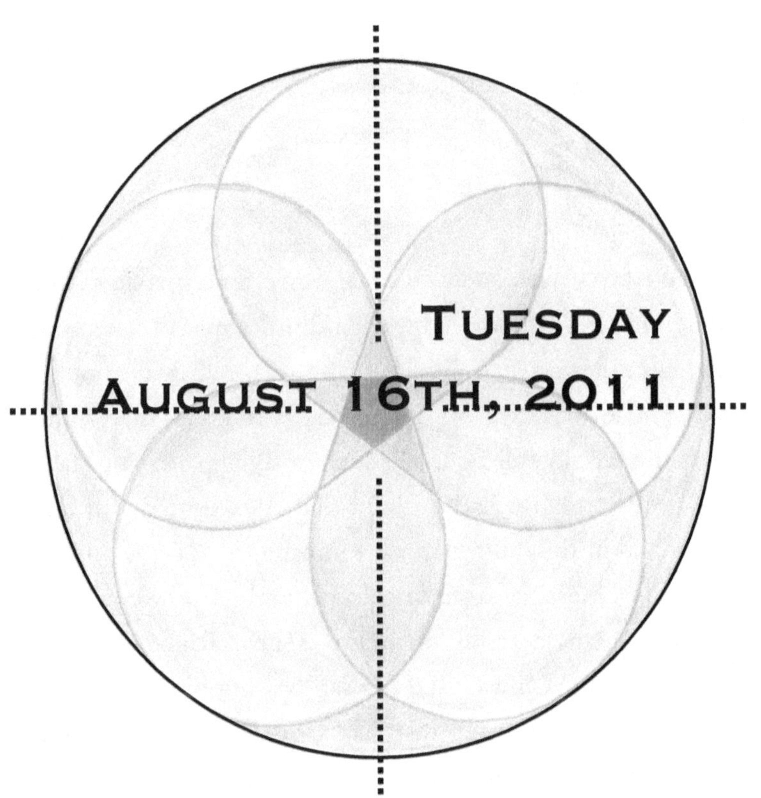

Tuesday
August 16th, 2011

07:10 BST
Twickenham, London
Feilds Palace

LYNN READ the coded email another time, making sure it really said what she thought, then did the math to figure out what time it was in California. She was still livid about the *official* MI-6 narrative of her rescue. She knew that without Alyx, she would still be a prisoner of Phillip Jackson, if not dead, and yet, MI-6 had decided that Alyx shouldn't even be mentioned in the report. It was almost as if MI-6 would have deleted her presence from London entirely if they could.

This email in front of her was her chance to set the record straight. Lynn closed her laptop, climbing out of bed. As much as she wanted to make that decision, she knew it wasn't hers to make alone. Kate, Stephan, and Lyshiria deserved to be part of the decision.

Lynn shoved her laptop under her arm before leaving her room. As she walked down the hallway towards the elevator, Lynn stopped by Kate's room, not knocking as she opened it because she knew Kate wasn't awake yet. She had no reason to be. Lynn walked across the room she'd gotten to know well over the last month or so since Alyx had brought her home before heading back to the United States. With Alyx gone and Lyshiria traveling back and forth between her home in Moscow and Feilds Palace, Lynn had spent much of her time trying to connect with her sister. If Lynn had learned anything about Kate since meeting her, it was that she did not like to be alone, so she welcomed Lynn spending so much time with her.

Lynn didn't even try to be gentle as she pulled Kate's blankets off. Kate did not respond to gentility, which was why she so easily slept in so late.

"Get up." Lynn ordered. "We have an important matter to discuss."

Kate just whined, her eyes still closed. "It's too bloody early to discuss important matters." She complained.

"If we wait too much later, the time difference with California will make us miss the phone call." Lynn informed her. "So get up now."

At the mention of a phone call with California, Kate shot up, all sleep lost from her eyes. "Alyx is calling?" She asked.

"Not exactly." Lynn muttered, leaving the room. She heard the soft thud of Kate's feet hit the floor: the sound of success.

Lynn stopped at the guest room door just past Alyx', which had become Lyshiria's when she stayed. She turned the lever, peeking in the door to see if Lyshiria was awake, and was met by an empty bed. Lynn had a guess as to where her cousin was. If correct, she would find out soon enough.

Kate and Lynn began their trek through the Palace to the west wing of the palace where there were small flats for the live-in staff. After what felt like an eternity, they arrived at Stephan's door, which they found open. Lynn smiled, knowing that it was proof that her guess about Lyshiria's whereabouts was correct. Stephan had the flat to himself, but since returning from Austria, he and Lyshiria had started dating, and in order to make sure he neither got fired by her uncle and his boss Michael, nor killed by her father Rafael, they left the door to his flat open when they were together.

From the door way, Lynn could smell the aroma of bacon cooking on the stove. Unfortunately, so could Kate, and if she hadn't been awake before, she was now, pushing her way past Lynn through the door.

"It just smells so good." Kate exclaimed as she plopped herself down in one of the chairs at Stephan's table.

Lyshiria just laughed at her cousin, seeming unperturbed by the intrusion. Stephan narrowed his eyes. "Don't you have cooks downstairs who prepare your breakfast."

Kate shrugged peeling a banana. "This one dragged me over here for some *important matter*. Apparently it can't wait because there is a phone call with California." She took a big bite of the banana, not bothering to make sure her mouth stayed closed as she broke up some of the bigger chunks it left in her mouth.

Stephan paused, looking at Lynn. "What did Alyx say?"

Lynn shook her head. "Not Alyx. I spent time in California after—I spent some time in California with Dylan and his family when I had some leave from MI-6." Lynn stated. "While I was there, I met the children of some of the best agents the CIA has. Apparently it is a training program of sorts."

"Promising Generation." Stephan said. "I've heard of it. Michael built them a school. He's still pissed his wife's legacy was taken away by the US government."

Lynn nodded. "They are in Northern California now. San Francisco Bay Area to be more specific."

"Where Alyx lives." Kate filled in. "Do they want to recruit her? Because they most certainly should."

"If you would let me finish." Lynn sighed exasperated. "I got an email from one of their leaders. He says the CIA has sent out a request for them to look for Alyx in connection to an attack on one of their safehouses. No name, just her photo from CCTV footage. He sent me the picture. It looks like the cabin she saved me from in the Alps."

"We knew it was Circle of Fifths." Stephan stated. "It makes sense that a group imbedded in the CIA would use a CIA safehouse." He paused. "But that does mean they know roughly where she's at. It is a big area. Even with the Generation's help, the chance they find her is pretty small."

"That's the problem." Lynn sighed. "He emailed me because he recognized her from school. He suspects something, which is why he reached out instead of reporting it, but he's not the only one at the school."

"I guess it's our turn to save her now." Lyshiria commented, breaking her silence.

Kate swallowed a laugh. "I'm sorry. I want to help. I do. But I know Alyx quite well, and she likes her school. She has some lofty dreams, and she knows she has to be in school to reach them. She won't leave, even if she is in danger."

Stephan nodded. "Kate's right. We can't pull Alyx out. We need to find another option."

"I might have one. My contact is asking for information. He believes if he can find proof the narrative is wrong, he can convince them to recruit her instead of arrest her." Lynn explained. "I'm still not happy about the way MI-6 rewrote what happened to remove her from the narrative. She saved my life. I want to fix this."

"So what's the problem? You tell him what happened. She saved you from the psychopath who killed our mum. Why did you drag me out of bed?" Kate complained.

"If Jackson is CIA, and he put in a formal request to use the safehouse, technically the accusations against her are true, regardless of who she saved." Stephan replied. "That's what makes the Circle of Fifths so dangerous. They know how to hide themselves within bureaucracy so anyone going after them have to break the law, thereby invalidating anything they do or prove."

"But the MI-6 report you and I wrote—"

"Would only tell the CIA she was working as an agent of the British government, who attacked a CIA safehouse. The Circle of Fifths have likely painted a narrative that paints her as an enemy of the United States who has now made her way to a large metropolitan area to execute an attack." Stephan interrupted. "We need to carefully craft a narrative that shows her as both loyal to the United States, and also explains why she did what she did."

"Or you tell him the truth." Lyshiria commented. "Because if we craft a story, or omit any details, once he finds out the truth, he will not only suspect her more than he does now, but he will no longer trust us. Trust is imperative if you want to continue working with him to help prove the CIA's narrative is wrong."

"And what if he decides to turn her in?" Stephan asked.

"MI-6 comes to you with compelling evidence that I want to kidnap Kate, again. Do you turn me in?"

"No, I'd want to look at all the evidence…" Stephan said slowly.

"He's not going to turn her in either." Lyshiria asserted. "He has already risked his job for her. There is only one reason he would have contacted Lynn rather than turn her in."

"You don't know that." Stephan argued.

Lyshiria nodded. "Alyx has herself an admirer." She grinned at her boyfriend. "Just like you admired me last summer, and you didn't turn me in."

"I threatened to make sure you went down with your father even though you were helping us." Stephan corrected.

"And why wasn't I already in a cell, being interrogated like he was?"

"That was Alyx, not me."

Lyshiria rolled her eyes. "The agent asking for info *clearly* likes Alyx. Telling him the truth of what we know will buy us time to figure out what to do next, so that is my vote."

"I'm willing to take the risk." Lynn said. "I trust the agent, and if anyone is able to find a way to convince everyone else not to turn her in, it's him."

"Hall is in California, isn't he?" Kate asked. She looked between Lynn and Stephan. "I know both of you have had contact with him so don't pretend like you haven't."

"Yes, Hall is home with his family for the foreseeable future." Lynn answered.

"We should do what we can to help the situation, but also let Hall know. He's closer and more help to her than we could be."

"I agree." Stephan set the spatula he'd been using down, walking over and grabbing something off of his bookshelf. He walked back over, handing it to Lynn. "Send him this."

"What is that?" Kate asked.

Lynn took the drive hesitantly. "Are you sure?"

Stephan took a deep breath, looking at Lyshiria. "Lyshiria is right. We need to give him as much of the truth as we have." He turned back to Lynn. "That includes giving him the security footage of *everything* that happened in that safe-house." He placed a hand on Lynn's shoulder. "You shouldn't have to watch the footage to send it to him. Or if you want, I can send it over."

Lynn shook her head. "I can do it."

"Has anyone told Alyx she's in danger?" Kate asked, trying to distract the room from the broken sound in her sister's voice—trying to distract Lynn from the flashbacks of what she'd been through in the safehouse she was rescued from.

"Have you met this family?" Lyshiria countered. "It's defined by layers upon layers of deception, added to a heathy dose of secrecy in the name of protection." She critiqued. "Of course no one's told her."

8:15 PDT

Tracy, California

John C. Kimball High School

PETER CARLYLE watched Alyx from across the cafeteria before school. He glanced at the notes in front of him from his phone call with Lynn. Apparently Lynn had been rescued from the CIA safehouse Alyx was accused of attacking, and she wasn't too pleased with the way Alyx had been cut from the MI-6 report, nor how she had been villainized by the CIA narrative. Peter, on the other hand, couldn't help but feel as if MI-6 had just handed him a gift. Lynn's anger resulted in him receiving the information he needed to prove that the CIA narrative was wrong. Even if he couldn't give Wraith the proof of her innocence, he could use what Lynn had told him to look for it. With what he'd learned, he couldn't believe that they hadn't noticed Alyx before. Lynn's description of her rescue portrayed Alyx as a spy with talent—and she had yet to refine it. Lynn had also sent him the surveillance footage MI:6 had gotten from the cabin, which he had yet to watch, but with what he knew already, he wouldn't be surprised if she was a better spy than Peter himself.

As the 6-minute warning bell for first period rang, Peter pushed his way to the front of the mob trying to get out the door. Until he found the information he needed to present to Wraith, Peter needed to make sure he dissuaded any Generation member who noticed Alyx from reporting it.

Peter waited just outside the cafeteria doors waiting for the first member he was concerned about. As Thane Hall stepped out, Peter fell into step beside him. "Hall, we need to talk."

Thane looked over at Peter, cautiously casting a glance behind him. Thane was a good spy, trained by his parents who just happened to be two of the CIA's best spies, but Peter could see the concern on Thane's face.

"You better hope Savannah doesn't see you talking to me. Not only will I never hear the end of it for being friends with you and not telling her, but who knows what rumors she might start." Thane hid his concern with a laugh.

"You are friends with Alyx McLean, right?" Peter asked.

Thane shook his head. "She's not the girl from the surveillance photo, if that's what you're thinking. She was in London all summer."

"You and I both know that's a lie. Lynn confirmed as much for me. But your attempt is noted. I take it I don't have to worry about you reporting her to Nathan or Wraith." Peter smiled.

"How long have you known and not told Wraith?" Thane

asked.

Peter couldn't prevent a goofy grin from crossing his face. "I recognized her the second Wraith showed us the photo. Something is wrong with the narrative. I plan on proving it. What do you know that I might be able to use to start?"

Thane just smirked. "To begin with, I can tell you that she likes you. She dances with a prince when she's in London, refers to him by his first name, and still, she likes you. Go figure."

"I'm pretty sure dating her would be a great way to piss Wraith off." Peter replied sarcastically.

"Screw Wraith." Thane interjected. "She's a genius who speaks more than a few languages, took five AP tests last year and scored a five on every one, is enrolled in another five AP classes this year, and has her eyes set on Oxford. You add her mental abilities to her athletic prowess in both Tennis and Track, and the martial arts training, you have an agent he could only dream of training. As it is, her dad is FBI and she has *unofficially* solved more of his cases than the FBI would like."

Peter glanced back to watch as Alyx left the cafeteria and began walking towards her first period AP Statistics class.

Thane smacked Peter with the back of his hand. "If you want to keep her safe, you should stay away from her. The second anyone sees you with her, she will lose all ability to stay hidden." Thane warned. He turned off of the path he and Peter had been taking to get to his own class. "And you know I'm right." He called. "It shouldn't be hard. It seems you've been admiring from afar, just like her. Leave it that way."

Peter contemplated what Thane had told him as he hurried to his own class, which was thankfully on the same side of campus as Thane's, not on the other side. While Thane hadn't shared any-thing particularly helpful in his mission to disprove the CIA's narrative, Thane had let two monumental pieces of information slip to Peter. First was that she liked him. If true, she did a really good job of concealing it while they had been studying. Second, Thane had revealed that she liked him more than a prince.

With a smile he just couldn't quite wipe from his face, he walked into class. Knowing she reciprocated his feelings only added to his motivation to help clear her name with the CIA.

13:46 EDT
Washington D.C.
International Spy Museum

PHILLIP JACKSON wandered the *Man Behind Bond* exhibit in the International Spy museum, shaking his head at tourists who gawked at every display. Clearly they had never worked in espionage. This was nothing new.

"We really need to find a better place to meet." A male voice said as he came up behind Jackson.

Jackson glanced at the man who came up next to him.

"Having a covert meeting in a museum where a bunch of wanna-be spies come seems like we're begging to be discover-ed." The newcomer explained.

"The emphasis on *wanna-be*." Jackson replied. "Now I might be concerned if we were having the meeting in the middle of Langley, but these guys..." Jackson gestured to the few people wandering the museum. "They wouldn't be able to pick us out as trading information even if someone ex-plicitly told them that someone was handing off classified documents."

"I still don't like it." The man said, his jaw clenching, moving his forehead where his close-cut blond hair framed his face.

Jackson shrugged. "Then act casual about it. Disguise what we're doing by acting as old friends would. We are, after all, old friends." Jackson paused. "So tell me George, how is your son?"

George clearly didn't appreciate Jackson using his name in such a public place, and the way his concerns were dismissed so easily was frustrating. But he played along. "Fine. As soon as he finishes training, he is being sent abroad. Soon we will have another agent in the field."

"Ah, yes. The ever growing force of agents the Nexus is building. Do you have the most recent list of probable targets for recruitment? Jackson asked, finally getting to the real purpose of the meeting.

George handed over a manila envelope, which Jackson knew was full of the names of the most current group of CIA recruits who were not only extremely talented at what they did, but also had something that made them easily corruptible.

"How is Kalen doing?" George asked, maintaining the appearance of normalcy as Jackson hid the folder by positioning it in the newspaper under his arm.

"He's still paying his penance for letting McLean get away last month." Jackson replied.

"What is your obsession with this girl? You know her

parents pulled her from her training program. She's not a threat, because she doesn't know about us, and even if she did, are you sure she's capable of toppling an organization that not even her grandfather could?" George criticized. "She's just another Hall that will try and fail to defeat us."

"She's already come closer than anyone to destroying us, and she was five at the time. We lost too many agents because of her, including my sister." Jackson replied. "If we don't get her on our side, we're done."

"Does the Nexus know that you're expending resources to try and recruit a 16-year-old girl?" George asked. "Rumor is that the director has appointed Dylan Hall to fill the vacancy for Deputy Director over Operations. They're going to want you to get as many agents as you can onto his team."

Jackson shrugged. "I plan to do just that. But that girl is guaranteed a spot on Hall's team, and she will be his best agent. Can you imagine what the Nexus will be able to do with that? And as long as it's not hindering my brother's campaign for President, they don't really care. Besides, if I can't turn her, I won't hesitate to eliminate her."

George just shook his head as he checked his watch. "Well, they'll be waiting for me at the Farm. We have young impression-able minds to train," he said with a smile, slipping away as easily as he'd arrived.

Jackson waited until George had left, then slipped out himself. As he got far enough away he was confident he wasn't being followed, he opened the envelope, slipping the list of names out. Maria Adams, Martin Armistead, Timothy Banthup, Alexandros Berzins, Xavier Bustos, Malone Delgado, Ada Humphrey, Patric Lavoie, Thiemo Moto, Jaqueline Nystrom, Katrine Rhodes, and Carl Scott. Now all he had to do was read their files, and decide which of them to turn.

11:50 PDT
Tracy, California
John C. Kimball High School

USUALLY, STUDENTS didn't receive the warmest welcome when they entered the councilor's office, and the students who were in there often enough to be recognized by the office staff most definitely did not, typically because it meant they were in trouble...*again*. Alyx knew the office staff just as well as the students who were office aides, but she wasn't like most of the office regulars who made the staff groan when they came in. As soon as they saw Alyx, they smiled and waved her back to the councilors' offices.

Alyx had been meeting with her councilor Ms. Maisley since her first week at Kimball, making sure she got the proper permissions, and took enough classes to graduate at the end of Junior year. Sure, Ms. Maisley had tried to talk her out of it at first, saying high school was the best four years of your life, but Alyx also heard the opposite. She didn't really care which one was correct, as she knew she could make her high school experience what she wanted, but she also didn't want to waste time. Fortunately she'd been able to convince Ms. Maisley she knew what she was doing. After this year, she would finally be able to study what she wanted to study, not what the state of California told her she had to study.

Ms. Maisley smiled when she saw Alyx peek in the door of her office, letting her come in and take a seat. She was always happy to meet with Alyx, because contrary to popular belief, high school councilors don't actually like doling out punishment all day. "Alyx! How are your classes? Are you going to be able to manage all of them?"

Alyx nodded. "Yeah, I think so. It was a good idea to be a TA for Mr. K. Thank you for suggesting I find an easy elective this year."

Ms. Maisley nodded. "No problem. So what did you want to talk to me about?"

"I was hoping you would be able to write me a letter of recommendation for Oxford. You know me and my academic standing just as well as any of my teachers here, maybe even better." Alyx asked.

"I'd be more than glad to!" Ms. Maisley agreed. "But let me suggest you still ask at least one of your teachers as well. Maybe one of your teachers can speak to your skill for the program you're applying for. I'm guessing it's something communications related, since that's the pathway you're in."

Alyx nodded. "Yeah. Oxford has a French and Linguistics course that I think will fit me perfectly." Alyx replied, excitement entering her voice.

Ms. Maisley nodded. "Then can I suggest that you ask Mr. Martin to write you a letter of recommendation. You've had him for two years, so he can speak to your habits as a student, but also to your skill in French."

"The problem is I'm already asking a lot from him. I asked him to help me study for the French AP test, since I need to pass that test to get into Oxford, and we don't offer the French 4 AP class this year."

Ms. Maisley shrugged. "It never hurts to ask. While it is one more thing for us teachers to do, it was one of the few things I never dreaded doing for my best students. Being asked to write a recommendation for a student like you always felt amazing." Ms. Maisley paused. "Now, when do you need the letter by?"

"Well, the application window opens the beginning of next month and closes October 15th. But technically it closes at 1800 British Summer Time, and we're eight hours behind them, so it closes at ten am here. I would probably need them no later than October 14th." Alyx rambled.

"You're a bit stressed about this, aren't you?" Ms. Maisley asked.

Alyx took a deep breath. "Maybe a little. It's only my future."

Ms. Maisley nodded. "I know I may not know a lot about the admissions process at Oxford, because not many students in this area apply there, and I know that this is the first time this school has had seniors, but I promise you I've helped students apply for college at other schools before Kimball opened. You'll be fine. You are a very impressive student, and if Oxford doesn't take you, which in my opinion just means they are not as smart as they think, you will have your pick of schools here in the states."

"Thank you." Alyx sighed.

"No problem." Ms. Maisley replied. "And I'll have my letter of recommendation ready by September 15th, how does that sound?"

Alyx smiled. "Relieving." She got up to leave, turning back once she was at the door of the office. "Thank you again."

Ms. Maisley nodded. "All of us councilors hope to have more students like you." Alyx smiled, turning out the door. "Oh, Alyx, I almost forgot!" She exclaimed, causing Alyx to pause and turn back. "Since you are graduating this year, we would like you to join us at Senior Sunrise on Friday. And any other senior activity we have this year." She added. "Basically, despite your ID saying 11, you can officially consider yourself a senior."

Alyx smiled. "I'll be there."

She needed something to take her mind off everything she still had to do to get into Oxford. Her future was waiting, but she was a bit impatient.

14:35 EDT
Langley, Virginia
Office of the CIA Director

DYLAN HALL read the proposal in front of him, before looking back up at the director. Hall knew that it would take some work and commitment to get himself placed as the CIA liaison for the Promising Generation, but he was starting to question his resolve.

"With all due respect, sir, what is the point of kidnapping the members of the Promising Generation?" Hall asked.

"Not any members," William McLean, the director of the CIA stated. "Only the members that your interrogations lead you to. I want to see how secure the Generation is, or, if one member falls, if they all are compromised." He pointed to the file. "The Training Division made a mistake placing a psychologist in charge of their training, but they need proof that Ignatius Wraith is providing them with inadequate training. If you want to have access to the Generation because you're concerned about the Circle of Fifths corrupting it, this is how we have to do it."

Hall nodded. "This should be interesting, but I can think of at least one problem. Some of them are still considered children. They will be reported missing, if not by their parents, than by their school. How do you want me to handle the local and or federal authorities who begin to investigate it?"

Director McLean smiled. "I believe we have an agent who left the CIA for the FBI. I'll make a few calls to make sure he's assigned to the case. We'll let the FBI know that it's nothing more than a training mission, but tell them to investigate as normal. We need to see how well they've been trained when it comes to police interference."

"Yes sir." Hall got up to leave, walking toward the door.

"Dylan," the director said, causing Hall to pause and turn back. "Don't forget that they're kids. I know how you can get in interrogations. Be effective, but careful. Get creative. See how little persuasion you can use but still get them talking."

Hall laughed. "You mean do my best to show how easy it is to get them talking—make Wraith look as bad as possible."

The director nodded. "That is certainly one way to put it."

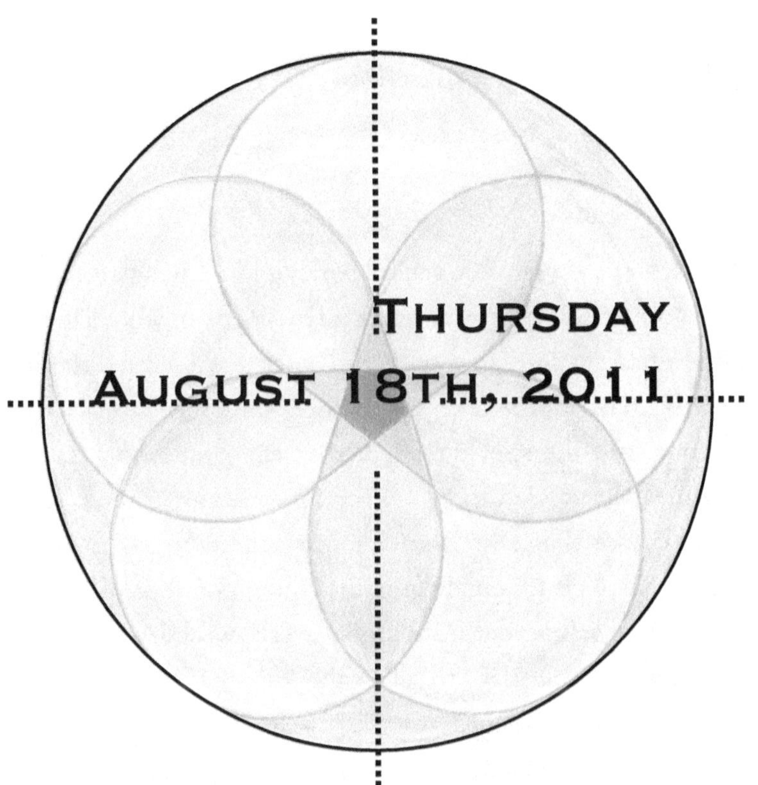

THURSDAY
AUGUST 18TH, 2011

7:25 PDT
Tracy, California
John C. Kimball High School

ALYX PULLED into the school parking lot, driving around to the student lot. She was the kind of person who liked to always park in the same spot, and since she'd started driving herself to school a few days before, she'd been successful, backing into the spot directly across from the doors of the Theatre. She tended to get to school earlier than most students because she came from Seminary, the religious class she took at the Chester building of the Church of Jesus Christ of Latter-day Saints before school every weekday morning, which got out at 7:30, to allow the kids that went to Tracy and West to get to their respective schools on time. Unfortunately, as she pulled up to back into her parking spot, she was met by a beat-up Mitsubishi Mirage LS coupe. It was supposedly sporty, as made evident by the rear spoiler, and only having two doors, but what had once been a beautiful deep blue color of paint was worn and fading. She reluctantly parked her gray 2011 Volkswagen Jetta GLI in the spot next to it.

She climbed out of the drivers seat and turned to close the door, noticing Peter leaning on the hood of the Mirage facing the theatre. Alyx rolled her eyes, holding the button for her trunk on her keys as she walked to the back of her car. As she got there, she helped the shocks open the trunk. "You know, just because their car is a piece of crap doesn't make it ok for you to sit on it. What would the owner say if they saw you there?" Alyx taunted Peter.

"*I* am the owner." Peter replied.

"Oh, so you're the one that stole my parking spot."

Peter gestured around the spot. "This is yours?" he asked incredulous. "I don't see your name on it."

"I park here every morning." Alyx argued. "That makes it mine."

"For three whole days? Because I don't think you were old enough to drive last year." Peter asked sarcastically.

"Yes. I believe three days is more than enough time to establish that this spot is mine." Alyx replied, ignoring the comment about her age.

"What if I told you this is my spot?" Peter asked.

"I'd ask you to prove it." Alyx replied.

"And if I parked here to get your attention?"

Alyx' cheeks flushed red, causing her to hide her red face by leaning into her trunk to grab her bag.

"You're a cute spy. You have my attention." Alyx mumbled as she reached into her trunk for her backpack.

Peter stood up. "Who told you I was a spy?"

Alyx finished throwing her backpack up onto her shoulder as she realized what she had said. She closed her eyes to her embarrassment. "I meant football player." She admitted.

Peter smirked seeing her red cheeks. "No. You meant something by it. If you hadn't thought it, you wouldn't have said it." Peter taunted.

Alyx could feel nothing but heat in her cheeks despite the relatively cool morning air. She turned to close her trunk, hoping she could avoid his question. The curse of the crush struck again. Only Peter could have flustered her enough. She had stories made up about the lives of all her classmates. Peter's skill in French, added to the fact that she had never been able to beat him for the top grade in Algebra II—even when she had 101 percent—led her to craft a story where he was secretly a spy.

"Come on McLean. Let me into that pretty head of yours." Peter prodded.

She didn't know why, but somehow, Peter using her last name deflated her, even if it was just a little. At the very least, it helped her hide her embarrassment with a confidence she had never felt before talking to Peter. "Can you prove to me you're not a spy? Because your knowledge of foreign languages paired with your physical skills tell a story..."

Peter turned it back on her. "Well you have exceptional language skills yourself. How many languages do you speak again?"

Alyx narrowed her eyes at Peter, trying not to let his not

so subtle flirting get to her. He had admitted that he was paying attention to her, noticing things like where she parked, which also meant he had taken the effort to figure out which car in the parking lot was hers. She'd had a crush on him since she'd started at the school, and she hadn't paid enough attention to him to know what car he drove. Having one of the cutest boys in school flirt with her was flattering, but she couldn't forget that she was leaving at the end of the school year.

"Are you going to move your beater so I can have my parking spot back?"

"My car is a beater?" Peter asked, feigned hurt in his voice. "I'll have you know this is a Mits—"

"Mitsubishi Mirage LS coupe from 1997. Yeah, not only is it old but the spoiler doesn't make it any more sporty."

Peter shook his head. "*Okay little miss spoiled*, but not everyone gets a brand new car for their birthday."

Alyx glanced around the parking lot. "I don't know, I've met some of the kids from Mountain House. I think they do." She teased. "But I'll have you know I paid for this car myself with the money I earn as a translator for..." She trailed off, realizing Peter had successfully pushed the right buttons, and she had gotten dangerously close to admitting something she really didn't like to. She had already revealed more to him than she should have.

Alyx spun without finishing her sentence, walking off before she revealed anything else to the blond football player with a sharp jaw. She pressed the lock button on her fob twice, hearing the car's cheerful beep in reply as she walked across the lane towards campus. *Oxford.* She reminded herself. Her goal to study in London was a good enough reason to keep away the one stranger good at getting her to reveal too much about herself.

"Wait!" Peter called after her. "I had a reason for getting your attention." He grabbed his backpack from the passenger seat, locking the door using the button on the inside as he shut it, before running after Alyx. "Why didn't you text me last night?"

"Was I supposed to?" Alyx asked.

"Well, I thought we were going to study, but I never heard from you." Peter replied.

Alyx sighed. If her future wasn't so dependent on passing the AP French test, she could just ignore him, and go back to admiring him from afar. "I have other things on Wednesday nights." Alyx said.

"What about tonight?" Peter asked.

Alyx shrugged. "Tonight might work, but starting next week, I have tennis matches Thursdays. If it's a home match it shouldn't matter too much, but if it's away, that's a different story."

"How about we worry about one week at a time?" Peter suggested. "And if you're concerned it might bring down your image being seen with me and my beater car, I might have a solution for that." He teased.

Alyx raised an eyebrow. "Are you sure it's not the other way around?"

Peter spun, showing Alyx his smile. "If you think I'm a spy, maybe we should be spies together." He taunted. "See how long we can keep up the clandestine meetings."

"And what might this solution be?" Alyx asked. He was definitely flirting, and she had to admit it. She'd had a crush on Peter Carlyle for two years. She was going to have a very hard time not caving to his flirtatious comments, when she'd been in love with his eyes and voice since she'd met him.

Peter's smile grew. "I guess you'll find out tonight." He strolled off, leaving Alyx to roll her eyes.

5:39 PDT

Tracy, California

John C. Kimball High School

PETER SLUGGED out to his car, his duffle bag heavy with his football equipment. Practice had been rough, but that was to be expected. The coach was trying to whip the team into shape for their first game the following Friday. Since the school had only been open for three years, it was the first year they had seniors, and there were high expectations for how they would do. As one of those seniors, his classmates expected a lot from him, which meant the coach just pushed them harder.

He shook his head when he reached his car to find Alyx sitting on the hood like he had been this morning. "Just because you think my car is a beater doesn't make it ok for you to sit on her!" He called as he got closer.

"You were sitting on it this morning," she argued.

Peter shrugged. "Mira and I go way back though. She knows I do it out of love."

"Mira?" Alyx asked. "You named your car Mira? Like

Princess Mira Nova from the Adventures of Buzz Light-year?"

"It was either that or Mitsy, and that didn't quite seem to fit her. Plus she's blue just like the character, so it works." Peter replied. He used his keys to unlock and open his trunk. "What's your car's name?"

Alyx slid off the hood of his Mitsubishi, pointing at her Jetta, her eyebrows raised in a question. "My Jetta doesn't have a name." She finally said as she walked up next to him, watching as he put his duffle bag into an amazingly organized trunk.

"Sure it does," Peter replied. "What do you call it when you're talking to it?"

Alyx rolled her eyes. "I don't talk to my car. I'm not a crazy person."

"Then you haven't been driving long enough." Peter stated, closing his trunk. "What do you know about brush passes?"

"And you wonder why I think you're a spy." Alyx commented.

"I've heard the rumors this school likes to spread." Peter told her, getting close enough that Alyx almost couldn't resist the magnetic force urging her to put her hand on his arm. "How would your anonymity fair if suddenly the school is saying you are dating a football player."

Alyx turned red. "We're not dating." Alyx whispered.

Peter smirked. "And that means no one will see us

studying, and decide to tell the school we are."

Alyx bit the inside of her lip. He was too close. Way too close. *Oxford.* She tried thinking about her goals to distract her from the cute way his eyes conveyed he was completely serious about protecting her from his reputation while his smile tried to tell her he was joking. Instead, her brain decided to justify it—and it made sense. Peter Carlyle needed to pass the AP French test just as much as she did, otherwise he wouldn't have asked Mr. Martin for help studying for it. The more time she spent studying with him, the better she would do on the test. Dating him would give her *plenty* of time to study for the test.

"So that means brush passes would be a good way to plan our study sessions without anyone figuring out we know each other." Peter explained.

Alyx gave a quick nod, backing up so her brain could think of something other than him. "How much do you know about brush passes? Because I'm betting I know more than you do."

Peter smiled. "Who is saying things that makes it seem like they're a spy now?

"Maybe I know some spies. Practically grew up surround-ed by them. I've picked up a thing or two." Alyx admitted. "You pointed out Monday I'm connected."

Peter shook his head at the amount of pride he heard in Alyx' voice. She was better than even the CIA had tried to convey. But she didn't seem to be connected to any agency.

She resorted to a child-like state of excitement when asked to talk about the skills she'd acquired associated with espionage. If she'd been formally trained, it would be expected, not something worth getting excited. "Show me." He challenged, showing her a small folded piece of paper in his hand.

Alyx brushed past Peter, her hand expertly stealing the paper from between Peter's fingers with a smirk on her face as she walked around to her driver's door.

"You didn't do it." Peter called after her.

Alyx gave Peter a confused face, holding the folded piece of paper up. "What's this?" She asked.

Peter shook his head, a small smile forming. She was good. "Are you going to Senior Sunrise tomorrow?" Peter asked.

Alyx nodded. She suddenly turned her head to the side, her smile becoming a frown. "Wait. Why would you think I was?"

Peter smiled. "You might be invisible to our classmates, but teachers talk. Besides, don't think I haven't noticed you are in senior classes. That number on your ID is a technicality."

Alyx narrowed her eyes at Peter, not quite believing that he, a cute football player, payed enough attention to notice what classes she was taking.

Peter laughed. "Anyway, I want you to pass your schedule for next week off to me at Senior Sunrise. I will then make a list of the times that work for me and fit in your schedule and pass it off to you during the passing period between fifth and sixth. We pass each other going to class."

Alyx shook her head. "You should try to challenge me." She said, sliding into her car, deciding to ignore the fact that he had noticed that his fifth period class was in the same building as her sixth. Of course she had noticed yesterday, three days in, but it was because she liked him. She had an almost supernatural radar when it came to locating him. The fact that he had noticed said something else, and made her wonder if maybe they passed each other because he left his class late enough to see her. In a moment's notice, Alyx could see them using brush passes to pass off notes during their passing period, schedules turning into love notes, love notes into inside jokes. She could imagine it becoming a daily occurrence, an opportunity to brush hands at school. She could already feel the thrill of everyone surrounding them, but no one knowing.

Alyx shut her car door, sliding her sunglasses on to interrupt the flow of imaginary situations that felt within reach. Unfortunately that was the problem. The attainability of her dream of dating Peter Carlyle meant it was going to be much harder to come up with reasons why it could never happen. And apparently Oxford wasn't working. She could justify that one.

She was going to need a better distraction.

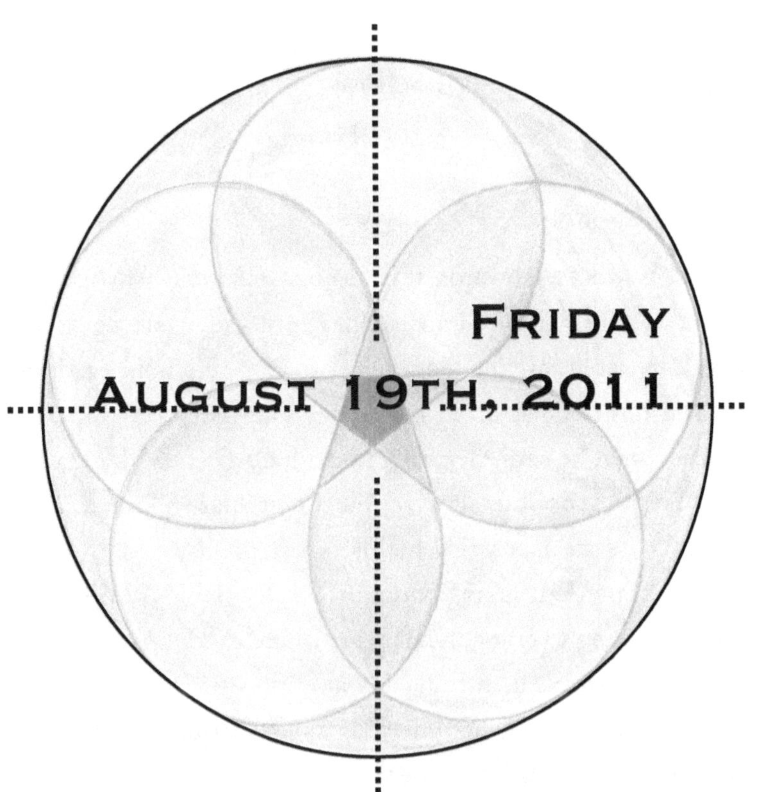
FRIDAY
AUGUST 19TH, 2011

7:40 PDT
Tracy, California
John C. Kimball High School

ALYX WALKED towards the football field, the chosen location of the Senior Sunrise. She saw Kaden sitting at the check-in table by the entrance of Don Nichols Stadium, decked out once again in his orange and blue class shirt. He smiled when he saw Alyx walk up with Carlie and Thane.

"So the school finally decided you are part of the class of 2012!" He stated, crossing her name off the list.

Alyx nodded, taking a donut off the table. "Absolutely, and I'm going to enjoy the perks and free food."

Kaden smirked, turning his attention to the next group of students walking up, checking their school IDs to check them off the list as he let them in.

As Alyx walked into the stadium full of celebrating seniors, she felt a jumbled mess of emotions. She was excited to be here, afraid the seniors would view her as an imposter, and nervous. She was overly aware of Carlie and Thane behind her. *Pass a note to Peter without letting Carlie and Thane see.*

That was her objective. But as she inexplicably felt her gaze drawn to Peter, she couldn't help but wonder if she was as capable as she knew she was.

To calm her mind, she decided to think about how glad she was that Savannah hadn't found them yet, because while Carlie and Thane may have been more observant than Savannah in most things, when it came to boys that Alyx liked, Savannah always noticed them first. She also tended to pay more attention to what they did, probably so she could find a way to help Alyx get their attention. She was a good friend that way. But that good friend would be the one to notice Alyx pass the note off, and with the way she liked to talk to everyone about everything, if Savannah saw, the whole school would know before lunch.

Alyx could feel her pulse vibrating through her chest. This was the most excitement she'd had since she was running through an Austrian forest to escape an assassin and save her cousin. She would be lying if she said she didn't enjoy the feeling, and hadn't missed it since she'd returned home. And while she was nervous, she knew it only added to the rush. She was about to hand a piece of paper with her schedule on it to a boy she had a crush on. Maybe it wasn't a literal life or death situation like it had been a couple months before, but it was figuratively, as pertaining to her social life.

After what felt like an eternity, Alyx finally caught Peter's attention, a knowing wink telling her he'd seen her. He casually lined up his path to intersect with hers, drawing closer in the crowd. Alyx made sure Carlie and Thane weren't paying attention in a way that seemed as if she was trying to make sure they were still behind her, then casually brushed Peter's fingers, letting the paper impercievably pass from her hand to his. She bit her lip to prevent it from forming a smile that tempted to betray the covert act that had just transpired.

Now she just had to wait until 6th period to receive his reply. It was going to be nearly impossible to pay attention today. *Please give me something to distract me from Peter before he distracts me from my school work.* She sent the silent prayer heavenward with one last glance in Peter's direction.

PETER UNFOLDED the piece of lined paper that Alyx had handed off to him this morning. She had talent. She had effort-lessly completed a brush pass without her friends noticing, even though they were just behind her. One of those friends had been Thane, who had been trained to notice exactly that sort of covert activity.

As he read Alyx' careful script outlining her schedule for the next week, and the times that would work best for their study sessions, he couldn't help but shake his head. She hadn't been exaggerating about her schedule being crazy.

MONDAY: Scrimmage @ Edison High until 6pm.
Study session 7:30pm.
TUESDAY: Practice. Study @ normal time.
WEDNESDAY: Mutual (church activity) @ 7pm.
Sorry. Can't study.
THURSDAY: Match against West (Home). Study @
normal time.
FRIDAY: Match @ Edison. Same as monday.

Peter checked his schedule to see when he could study with her. His was surprisingly empty comparatively. Football didn't have games until the following week, and even then it was only one a week. She'd also let slip that she got paid to be a translator, which wasn't on her schedule, and that added to the homework he was sure her course-load had, as well as the time she spent helping her dad solve FBI cases, he didn't know how she had any time to sleep. How was it that she could have so much more than him, when he was the teenage spy?

Peter hurried and refolded the piece of paper as one of his buddies from football, Trevor, sat down next to him at the table, focusing his attention on the food in front of him.

"Whacha got there?" Trevor asked, trying to snatch it from him.

Peter thankfully kept hold of the paper, shoving it deep into his pocket where he knew Trevor couldn't get it. "Nothing." He lied. "Just some notes from class."

Trevor rolled his eyes. "That was definitely not your handwriting. It looked like a girls handwriting."

"Handwriting is handwriting." Peter claimed, even though he knew that traditionally, female handwriting was much nicer than male handwriting, though he knew exceptions. He had even been present when Dr. Wraith had shared some theories as to why he thought that was the case. But he knew if he could get Trevor to explain his own statement about the handwriting, he could more easily make him forget about the note.

Sure enough, Trevor took the bait. "Handwriting *is not* handwriting. Girls handwriting is all neat and organized, and usually more bubbly, and honestly, more readable, where as our handwriting looks like random marks on the paper, that can be deciphered as letters upon closer inspection."

Peter had to prevent himself from laughing at Trevor's description of handwriting. "Don't you think decipher is a little harsh?"

"I've had to grade your assignments. No. It's not." Trevor asserted. "So who's the girl?"

"No one I want to tell you about." Peter admitted. "Hey, you run track, right?" Trevor nodded. "How many meets do you have in a week?"

Trevor shrugged. "Usually only one. Well, two. We have a league meet during the week, and typically an invitational on Saturday. Why?"

"The tennis team has three matches next week." Peter replied distracted. "Sounds to me like tennis players might be more dedicated athletes."

"So the girl plays tennis." Trevor teased. Disappointed when he didn't get anything more from Peter, he prodded. "Come on. I've introduced you to every girl you've dated. Screw that. I've introduced you to every girl you *know*."

"Not this one." Peter corrected. He smirked. "You would probably say she's not my type."

"Your type is female." Trevor corrected.

"What?" Peter scoffed.

Trevor shrugged. "You have dated *every* girl I've introduced you to. I was suspicious, so I started introducing you to girls so far outside what I pegged your type as, and guess what, you still dated them."

"That's not true." Peter argued.

Trevor squinted his eyes at him. He turned to one of the cheerleaders they ate with. "Hey Scarlett. How many of your friends has Peter dated?"

Scarlett turned her head to look at the two boys she considered to be friends and rolled her eyes, but answered anyway. "Am I counting just my immediate friends, or all of my friends and acquaintances? And by dated do you mean one date, two dates, the oh so rare more than three dates, or the *I got dared to kiss you at this party, we made out, I feel guilty, so let me take you to dinner?*"

"Fine." Peter conceded. "What did you peg as my type?"

"Hard to describe." Trevor answered. "I would say perfect. Athletic, academic, attractive. You know, someone that doesn't exist."

"Isn't *perfect* everyone's type?" Peter asked.

Trevor shrugged. "Fair." He thought for a moment. "You know the girl on the track team that I complain about. Track Star McLean. She is totally your type."

Peter rolled his eyes as his stomach did flip flops at the mention of her name. "What makes you say that? You just said you complain about her."

"Yeah, because she's perfect. Besides, she's a challenge, and you love challenges." Trevor replied. "Totally your type."

Scarlett nodded. "And I'm pretty sure you are hers."

Peter fell quiet, withdrawing to his thoughts. He'd dated lots of girls, using Trevor to introduce him to his next thing. They never lasted long, and they never got serious. He'd grown up with absentee parents whose goal was to make him the perfect spy: emotionally detached. He'd always thought he couldn't love anyone because he didn't know how to.

Alyx had always been different. He noticed her wherever she went. He'd even found himself tuning out his friends at lunch as he watched her from across the cafeteria. For the first time, he wondered if the reason he'd never made an effort to ask her out had something to do with a fear that he would be just as apathetic towards her as he had been with other girls.

He smiled, glancing at her as she argued with Thane about something, textbook open in front of her. That fear told him he already cared more about her than he had anyone else.

15:50 PDT
Langley, Virginia
CIA Headquarters

DYLAN HALL looked at the file in front of him before look-ing at the agent he was interviewing. His stats were quite high, especially for someone so young. In all honesty, this agent reminded Hall of himself when he had first joined the CIA. That was the reason why he was here. If he was going to be successful, he needed agents around him who were motiv-ated, and willing to protect their country.

"So tell me Timothy Banthup, why do you want to work in Operations?"

"I have—"

"Let me stop you. You don't have to convince me you belong here." Hall interrupted. "You're here."

"So what are you asking?" Banthup asked.

"You have the talent to work in any number of jobs. Why did you chose Operations?"

Banthup thought for a moment. "You." He finally ans-wered. "You aren't here for the politics. You are here because you care about the country, and you want to do what you can to protect it from this office."

Hall shook his head. "I wasn't asking for flattery."

"I was only being honest sir."

Hall took a deep breath. "If that's so, I have an assignment for you. It might not be what you were expecting, but I can promise it will make a difference."

Banthup sat in silence waiting for Hall to tell him what the assignment would be, concern growing the longer Hall took to tell him.

"I want you to go back to high school."

"I'm sorry sir, but I'm afraid I'll have to ask you to—"

"You heard me correctly. The Director has asked that we test the effectiveness of the Promising Generation's training. In order to do that, I will need you to try to get close to them and help me identify the members so we can capture and interrogate." Hall paused. "This will be a gateway to more prestigious assignments."

Banthup nodded. "Where am I going?"

Hall smiled. "Tracy, California."

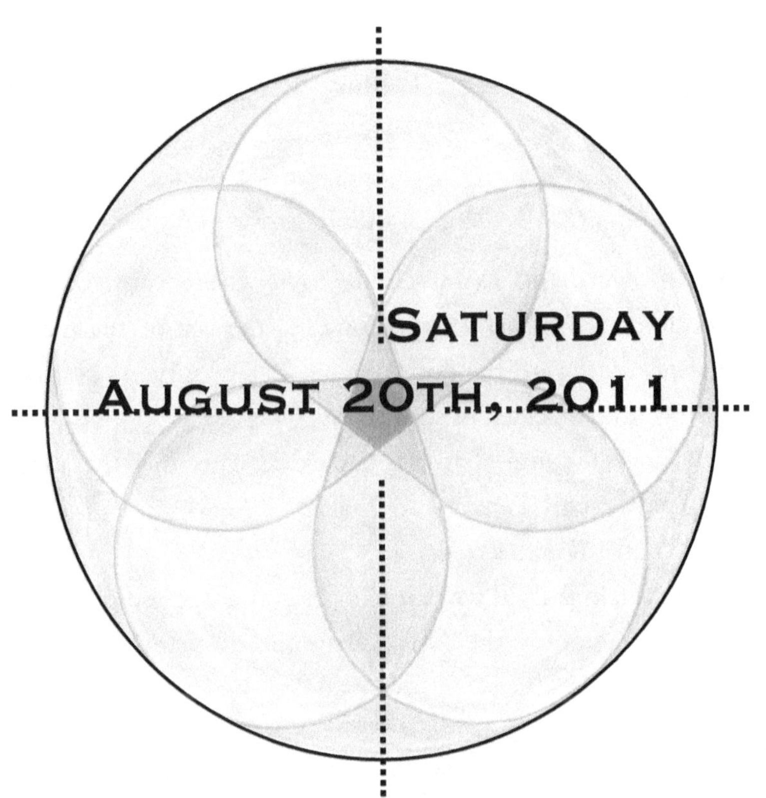

SATURDAY
AUGUST 20TH, 2011

12:57 PDT
Tracy, California
Promising Generation Training Program HQ

PETER WATCHED as his dining room cleared out, waiting until he could talk to Wraith alone. As the last of the members walked toward the door, leaving just Wraith and Nathan with Peter, he decided to speak.

"The safehouse that was attacked, who was the asset being protected?" Peter asked Wraith.

"What?" Wraith asked.

"You said the girl we're looking for attacked ten guards at a CIA safehouse in the Alps, killing one of them." Peter reminded him. "The safehouse wouldn't be guarded if they weren't protecting someone."

"That wasn't included with the BOLO." Wraith dismissed, looking back down at his papers as he gathered them up to leave.

Peter looked at Nathan. "Come on, I can't be the only one who finds the lack of information being provided by the CIA suspicious."

Nathan shrugged. "Peter makes a point."

Wraith sighed. "I can look into it, but I won't make any promises. It makes no difference. She killed one of our agents, and the CIA would like us to find her."

"I already looked into it." Peter replied. Lynn had given him enough information to search the CIA files he had access to, which had given him information he was hoping he could use. "The safehouse hasn't been used. At least it wasn't authorized to be used. And the video surveillance that the CIA has—"

"How did you get the surveillance footage?" Wraith asked.

"That's beside the point." Peter said. "The video shows that the girl used a knife to fight the team. The CIA didn't have an autopsy report for the agent you told us was killed, but the one that the Austrians' have said the agent killed was killed by a bullet. She didn't kill him."

"It's not our place to assign guilt, only keep an eye out for the girl." Wraith retorted.

"So the fact that we're being lied to doesn't bother you?" Peter asked.

Wraith just smiled. "We're spies. Of course we're being lied to." He stood up, placing his files into his bag. "The BOLO remains. If you see her, let me know."

Wraith left the room, leaving Nathan and Peter alone.

"Do you know—"

"No." Peter answered the question before it was asked.

Nathan shook his head. "When you answer before I finish asking the question, you admit you're lying."

"Something is wrong with the BOLO." Peter asserted. "We should be recruiting her, not hunting her."

Nathan stood up from the head of the table. "I hope for your sake you find more proof. I would start by figuring out who placed the BOLO."

Peter took a deep breath. He knew who had placed the BOLO. He just didn't want to make the phone call to find out why.

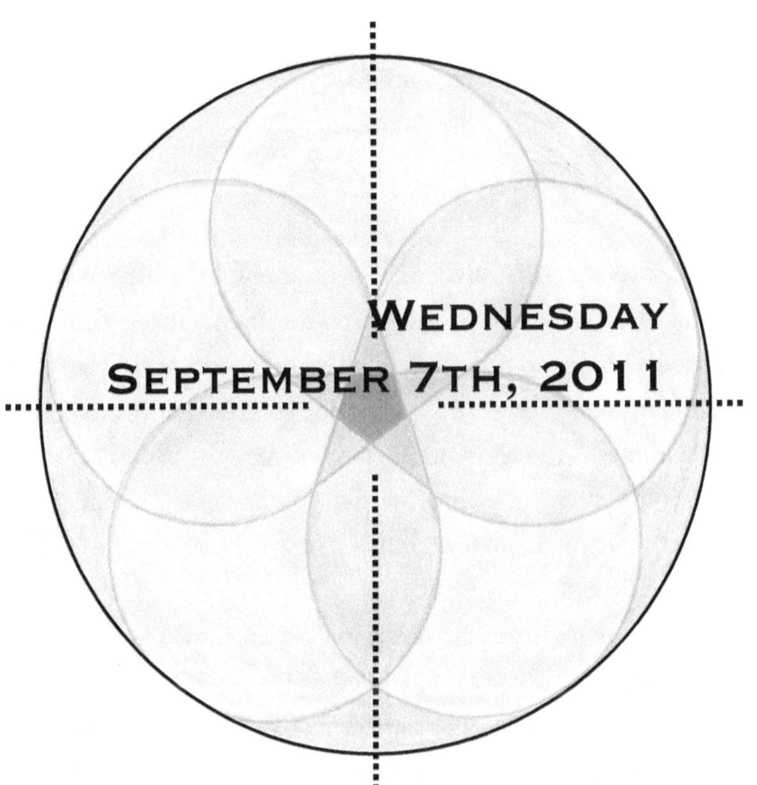

WEDNESDAY
SEPTEMBER 7TH, 2011

18:12 PDT
Mountain House, California
Hall Residence

HALL GAVE a frustrated sigh as he threw his research down on his desk. He had to give it to the Generation: they had learned a thing or two from their parents. He suspected that the older members would be the ones who would have access to their files—the most important secrets the group kept. If he got them to give him access to those, he would have proved their inadequate training. The problem was he had to find them first.

Hall got up from his desk, wandering out to the family room, rubbing his eyes. He smiled as he saw his daughter laying on the floor with her laptop in front of her. If for nothing else, he was glad he was finally home to be able to spend more time with his family. Too often his job and the fact that he was trying to track down his sister's killer kept him from watching his kids grow up. He felt like it was just yesterday that Chelsi was born, and now, she was a Freshman in high school.

Hall walked over to her and reached down to tickle her side. She scrunched up with a strangled giggle. "Stop it!" She pleaded.

Hall peered over her shoulder. "What are you doing?"

Chelsi shrugged. "I'm on Facebook."

"Facebook?" Hall asked, trying to get a closer look. "What's Facebook?"

Chelsi rolled her eyes. "It's a social media site. I post stuff, and people who are my friends can see it and reply."

Hall looked at Chelsi's Facebook wall. "You post stuff about your life on the internet?" He stood back up. "I'm not sure how I feel about that."

Chelsi gave her dad a dirty look. "Mom told me it was ok. You can't just disappear for two years and expect to override her decisions. Besides it's how I keep in contact with half of my friends."

Hall looked up at his wife as she walked into the room. "You're ok with her posting stuff about her life on the internet?" He asked his wife.

"I'm friends with her, so she knows that I'll see anything she posts."

"But on the internet." Hall emphasized yet another time. "For everyone to see?"

Addy shrugged. "It's the new normal, Dylan." She walked out of the room, hollering over her shoulder. "Maybe you should get used to it."

Hall returned his attention to Chelsi. "You said half your

friends are on here?"

Chelsi shrugged. "Well, I mean, most everyone either has a Facebook, Instagram, or Twitter, so yeah."

"So if I'm looking to see if one of my agents is posting something that might compromise their position in the Agency, could you show me how to find it?"

Chelsi nodded. "The best option for that would be twitter, since everything you post is available to the public." Hall watched as his daughter typed the website into the domain bar. The website loaded, and Chelsi showed her dad the search bar. "Then you can just type the name of the person you are wanting to find in here, so as long as they are using their real name, you can find them." Chelsi typed *Tom Cruise* into the search bar, bringing the popular spy actor up. "Just like that."

Hall kissed his daughter's head. "You may have just solved my problem." He told her, leaving the room to walk back to his office.

SARAH WIPED her hand on her apron as she heard the doorbell ring. "Alyx, dinner is just about ready. Can I get you to clear off the table, clean it, and set it?"

Alyx nodded, her attention barely leaving the French book in front of her.

Sarah sighed exasperated as she left the room. "I'll just tell Emily you don't want to see her then."

"I was just finishing the chapter." Alyx whined. "I'll get everything done."

Sarah just shook her head with a smile as she opened the front door. Emily stood on the porch with a store bought cheesecake.

"Sorry" She apologized. "I had to buy something on my way over."

Sarah just shook her head, giving her little sister a hug around the cheesecake. "It's fine. All I care is you made it. I take it Bryan couldn't make it."

Emily shook her head. "Nope. He's backed up at the lab, so he's putting in overtime. He promised he'll try to make it next time."

"You've said the same thing the last three times you've been here." Sarah critiqued. "Just tell me he's afraid of me and avoiding me, and my feelings won't be hurt. It's not the first of your boyfriends I've scared off."

Emily laughed. "See, I wondered why I wasn't married yet. I didn't know I had you to blame."

"Absolutely!" Sarah joked. "Now if I could scare off boys just as easily for my daughter."

Emily stared at Sarah. "I didn't know that Alyx had a boyfriend."

Sarah nodded toward the kitchen. "He's in there with Alyx." She smirked, telling Emily she was up to no good. "Hey, why don't you go in there and introduce yourself. Make sure to mention your job, and your boyfriend's job. I'm going to go tell Neil dinner is ready."

Emily shook her head as she walked around to the kitchen. She smirked as she saw Alyx setting the table, a young man she didn't recognize packing his book into his bag.

"Emily!" Alyx exclaimed, setting the plates she was carrying down on the table before running to meet her aunt on the threshold. "You made it!"

"Of course I did! Where else would I be?" Emily replied as her niece wrapped her arms around her. "Hang on a sec, I swear you've gotten taller somehow." She complained, pushing Alyx out. "You're taller than me!"

Alyx giggled. "I have been. You just haven't admitted it." Alyx looked around the wall. "No Brian?"

"Nope. Just me. Is that good enough for you?" Emily challenged.

Alyx smirked. "Even better. You know, he might be attractive, but I don't quite like him."

Emily shook her head. "You just don't want any competition for my attention. It's ok to admit it."

"Maybe." Alyx replied with a sly smile.

Emily nodded toward Peter. "Are you going to introduce me to your boyfriend."

Peter looked up, watching the interaction with amusement. They interacted more like sisters than aunt and niece, and based on the way Alyx' cheeks started to burn red when Emily asked to be introduced to him, he couldn't help but think that Emily definitely knew how to tease Alyx the way a sister would.

"Not my boyfriend, but this is Peter. He is also taking the AP French test, so Mr. Martin assigned us to be study partners."

"Oui?" Emily asked. "Et est-ce-qu'il parle français bien?"

Alyx nodded, the red in her cheeks becoming more and more evident. Emily was trying to embarrass her, and she knew exactly what buttons to push.

Emily stepped closer to Peter, extending her hand. Peter stood up, meeting her hand with his and a firm shake. "I'm

Emily, Vee's aunt. And just fair warning, I am a Police Officer with the Santa Cruz Police Department. So you better treat my niece well."

Alyx rolled her eyes. "Mom put you up to this, didn't she?"

"Oh, and my boyfriend, which Alyx apparently doesn't like, is a Forensic Scientist for the department, so I know enough about murder to get away with it. The only way I would know more is if I'd taken a forensic pathology class in college."

"Remind me. What did you minor in again?" Alyx asked.

"Forensic Pathology." Emily replied.

Alyx gestured at her aunt. "And this is what it looks like when my parents get my aunt to intimidate my friends."

Peter laughed. "I'm going to go wash my hands, then come help with getting dinner on the table."

Alyx waited until he'd left the room before glaring at her aunt. "Come on. Really? He already has to deal with dad wearing his service weapon on his hip while he's here."

Emily threw her hands up in surrender. "Your mom asked. What else was I going to do?" She washed her hands in the kitchen sink while Alyx set plates in front of five chairs. "Is he the same Peter you've mentioned before?"

"Yep." Alyx answered.

Emily dried her hands, smiling at Alyx. "Look at you finding an opportunity. You know French is the language of love."

"Trust me, I know." Alyx sighed. "He keeps flirting with me, and it's getting harder to pretend I don't notice."

Emily popped Alyx with a towel. Alyx spun to see her with wide eyes. "Why on earth would you pretend not to notice that the cute football player you've been gushing about for two years is flirting with you?"

"Oxford." Alyx said.

Emily rolled her eyes.

"What?" Alyx crossed her arms at her aunt. "I've heard you echo the same statement I get from my parents all the time. *Don't let short term wants and desires prevent you from achieving your long term goals.*"

Emily rolled her eyes, disgust emanating from her facial expression. "First, never quote me back to myself. It's weird. Second, that mostly applies to things like, I don't know, getting pregnant, doing drugs, you know the things that could permanently alter your future."

"You didn't date in high school." Alyx accused.

Emily pointed at Alyx. "Yeah, well I was a little busy raising you."

Emily grew silent, preventing Alyx from continuing their banter. Whenever the topic of Emily's senior year of high school came up, she always shut down. Alyx felt bad for bringing it up. She didn't remember much from that period of her young life, but she knew Ally, her mom's twin, died about that time, and it had altered Emily's life plans.

"Vee." Emily said the nickname she'd given Alyx softly,

and almost as if she was pleading for Alyx to reply. "Don't make the same mistakes I did. If you want to date Peter, go for it." She paused. "You deserve to be happy."

"Does Brian make you happy?" Alyx asked her aunt.

Emily smiled. "He does." She looked at Alyx. "Not that I need a man to make me happy. I've gotten there on my own. But it's nice to be able to have someone to share the happy times with."

Peter re-entered the room. "Ok. I have to ask." He looked at Emily. "What is up with Vee?"

Emily smiled, causing Alyx to groan. "So you see..." Emily walked over to Alyx, throwing her arm around her shoulder. "I was twelve when she was born. So as a teenager, I was naturally lazy. Alyxandrie was just way too long, plus it was my mom's name. Too weird. Alyx was cute, but everyone called her that. And this little one was always such a ray of sunshine, even in my darkest times, so I thought of her as my morning star, staying with me through the sunrise. But again, I was a lazy teenager, so morning star was too long. Venus was shorter, but Vee was perfect." Emily let go with a shrug. "It just kinda stuck."

"Vee." Peter repeated. "I like it. So meaningful."

Alyx glared at Peter. "No more English." She ordered. She continued with a smirk. "I want to hear nothing but French from you through dinner."

"Come on!" Peter complained. "That's just cruel."

Alyx shrugged. "It's not like you're not fluent. Besides,

the only one who doesn't speak the best French is my dad, and at least he will be understand most of what you say." She whispered to him as he came up alongside her, putting spoons on top of the napkins Alyx was placing next to each plate. "Maybe you should stop prying for information."

Peter shook his head. "Jamais."

Alyx blushed, moving away to place a napkin at the next setting. Peter couldn't help but watch as she did. He knew she was special. He cared. Maybe it was time he admit as much, even if it was only to himself. The only question was if he cared enough to do the one thing he'd sworn never to do: call his mom. She alone had the power to tell him why there was a BOLO on Alyx McLean, and if he played the right cards, he might even be able to get her to retract it.

THURSDAY
SEPTEMBER 8TH, 2011

20:15 PDT
Tracy, California
Hall Base of Operations

THANE SLIPPED in the door of the house at the address his dad had given him. The house was a flurry of activity you wouldn't expect looking at it from the outside. He noted an agency team wiring the house with cameras, and another team bringing in cots and interrogation tables. When his dad mentioned he needed his help with an operation, he wasn't kidding.

Thane walked around the different teams of agents, heading towards the door that looked like it was the center of activity, which meant his dad was likely there, giving orders. He opened the door, peeking in to see his dad with two more young-looking agents. Dylan Hall looked up, waving his son into the room.

"Come in and close the door." Dylan told Thane. "Thane, meet Timothy Banthup and Derek Stevens."

Thane nodded at the two gents he'd just been introduced to. He recognized one of them as being on the football team at West High School a few years before. If he remembered correctly, he'd been pretty close to Peter.

"Director McLean has authorized me to test the training of the Promising Generation. While I will handle the interrogations, I want the three of you to work on identifying members and strategizing how to capture them. I have picked the three of you to simulate possible real life scenarios." Dylan explained. "Thane is a member of the Generation, so he is your inside source." Dylan turned to Thane to address him directly. "Be careful how you help. Try to maintain a plausible cover with the Generation, while also working to help this team undermine them for the purpose of this training mission."

Thane nodded at his father, acknowledging he understood. He never thought he would be betraying his team, but it was a training mission, and his father had explained what was at stake. If he happened to identify members that connected Alyx with the BOLO, and recommend their capture, preventing them from reporting Alyx, he was only supporting his mission.

"Derek Stevens is going to be doing research, both to help me discover the weaknesses of the members we interrogate, but also to identify members based on their digital footprint. And Timothy Banthup is undercover at the high school. His job is to watch the members we identify, analyzing who they interact with to try and connect more members that way."

Dylan paused, looking at each of the young men he had selected for this mission. He had chosen each one deliberately. Thane had actually come to him, concerned about a BOLO the CIA had sent out for Alyx McLean. Using Thane provided him the opportunity to contrast his training with the training of the rest of the members. Banthup had shown the ability to cultivate assets, so Dylan suspected he would do well developing a network at the high school. Stevens already had connections, as well as the technical know-how to be able to find the members on the internet a lot faster than he would. In fact, he had already found the first member.

"Our objective is to gain access to the classified files of the Promising Generation. But first, we have to figure out which of the members have access, which means identifying members. Fortunately, Stevens has already found a name for us: Adison Levy." Dylan told the group.

"What's the plan?" Banthup asked. "I start at Kimball tomorrow. Should I befriend him to start figuring out who else belongs to the group?"

Thane smiled. "I say we kidnap him."

Banthup and Stevens started debating the efficacy of waiting.

"I may not be able to tell you who has the files, but I can tell you the protocols. If it is deemed that the Generation and its secrets are at risk, the Director of the program and the member with access to the files are meant to go to ground. If we kidnap Adison, we can throw the generation into emergency protocols and see who runs." Thane explained.

Dylan's eye's lit up with pride for a second before he extinguished the emotion. "I think that is a solid plan of action." He turned to the other two. "What do you think?"

"It's a risk." Banthup admitted. "Do we have a way to guarantee they know they are under attack?"

Thane's smile grew, knowing he had information that the others didn't. "His brother is the Director."

Stevens nodded. "I think it will work." He shrugged. "One weakness everyone falls victim to is family."

Dylan smiled. "Then I'll leave it to the three of you to decide how to proceed. Bring him here, and I will start interrogations." He walked out of the room, closing the door behind him.

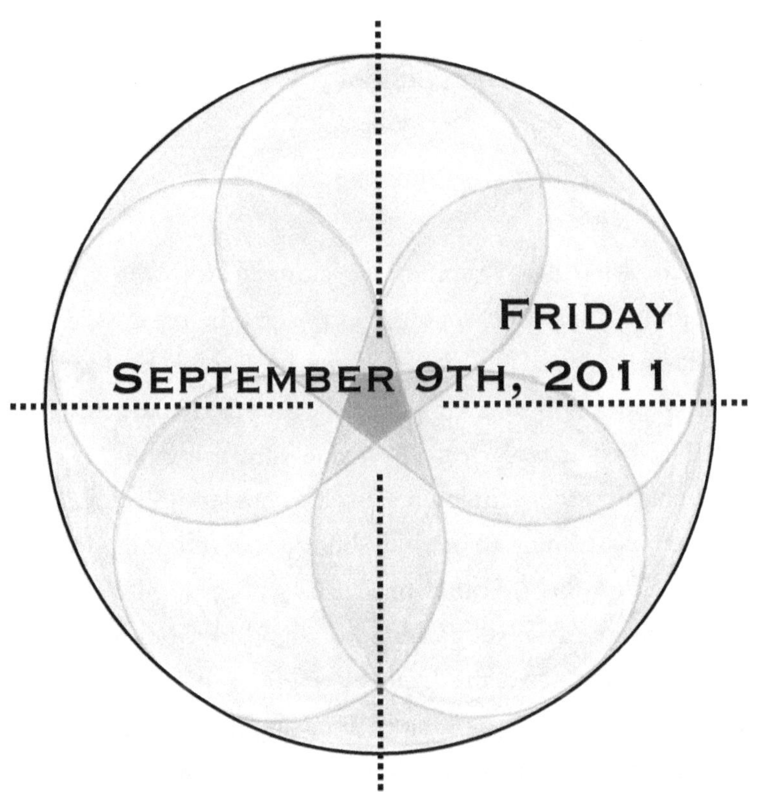

FRIDAY
SEPTEMBER 9TH, 2011

11:34 PDT
Tracy, California
John C. Kimball High School

ADISON FINISHED running the cleaning cloth through the foot joint of his flute, setting it in the case before moving on to the body joint. He inspected the head joint, pushing the cloth into the top to try to get the last drops of moisture out. Satisfied that it was clean, he made sure everything was in place in the case, snapping it shut. He checked his phone. His brother was coming to get him, but he was still going to be a bit. Small groups of other musicians gathered, talking excitedly about the football game. Sure, they'd lost, but it was the first year they'd had the band playing as a pep band in the stands. There was something exciting about knowing that you were the reason the crowd didn't lose hope even as the score made it seem hopeless.

Adison left the room alone. He was a freshman, so he didn't know anyone else, and so far all they'd done was learn the Pep band songs, and auditioned for their chairs. There was something about knowing that you were in competition

with the student next to you that prevented easily making friends. He adjusted his binder under his arm, standing awkwardly on the sidewalk by the pick-up lane in front of the
theatre. He watched as various students decked out in their
orange and blue walked back to their cars, speeding out onto
the deserted midnight roads, keeping an eye out for the
headlights that indicated his brother's car.

A group of band students walked past him, their black
shirts with the blue music logo disappearing into the parking
lot. It was just him and the football players left at the school,
and the football team was across the campus changing in the
locker rooms. Adison couldn't help but feel small in his band
shirt, waiting for his older brother to come pick him up, especially as he watched as other students climbed into cars and
drove off. It was weird, going from big-man on campus, back
to the bottom of the food chain.

"Hey Adison!" A voice called. He turned to see Thane
waving at him as he pulled up in his car in the pick-up lane.
"Do you need a ride?" He offered.

Adison shook his head. "Nathan should be coming."

Thane nodded. "OK. Do you know how long he's going
to be, because if you need me to, I can wait for him to get
here."

Adison checked his phone. It had been twenty minutes
since Nathan had told him he was leaving, and he still wasn't
here. "He should be here any minute." Adison told him. "I'll
be fine."

Thane nodded. "OK." He paused. "Banthup now."

Adison turned too late to see another young man coming up behind him. Adison dropped his flute and binder to the ground, trying not to damage them the best he could as he got prepared to fight off his attacker. Unfortunately, Adison's under developed body was no match for the other young man's strength. Before he could get a punch in, he found himself in the back of the dark sedan Thane was driving as it sped out of the parking lot.

PETER WALKED out to his car from the locker room with Jacob, excitedly talking about the plays that had gone well in their game against the school where they'd once played football. Sure, they had lost to their rivals, but somehow all of their small victories when they'd scored a touchdown, or prevented West from scoring counted so much more. They would learn from this game and throw everything they had into next week's game, no matter what.

Peter couldn't help but think about Alyx, and what it would be like to celebrate with her. He'd seen her at the game tonight, watching from the stands with Thane and the rest of her friends. With all of the time he'd been spending at her house studying, it felt weird not to acknowledge her at school, but he hadn't been able to bring himself to call his mom, so he kept his distance. The last thing he wanted was the Generation noticing her.

Peter was pulled from his thoughts as his phone buzzed.

He dug it out of a pocket in his bag, interrupting Jacob in the process. "Hang on, it's Nathan." He told him.

Jacob shrugged, pausing his thought to let Peter answer his phone. He was used to Peter taking calls from Nathan. He liked to think of himself as Peter's best friend, as he was one of the people who spent the most time with him, between football, and being in the same grade, but Peter held a leadership position in the Generation, which meant Jacob was always sharing Peter with Nathan or Wraith.

"What's up?" Peter answered.

Jacob watched as Peter got a quizzical look on his face.

"Slow down. Jacob and I are almost to my car. Can you tell me when we get over there?"

Peter hung up, starting to jog over to the student parking lot where his car was. Jacob followed on his tail. As they reached the flagpole on the corner of the campus by the library and had a clear view of the parking lot, they saw Nathan crouching by his car in front of the theatre building.

Nathan looked up as he saw them coming. "Please tell me Adison is with you." He pleaded.

Peter shook his head. "Why would he be?"

Nathan let out an exasperated string of Russian words, some of which Peter and Jacob could only assume were swear words. "Adison asked me to pick him up, but when I got here, he's no where to be found." He picked up a thin black plastic hard case from the ground as he stood. "But I found his instrument and music binder."

A drop of sweat rolled down Peter's back, a cold feeling wrapping its' spiny tentacles around his spine. *This can't be happening.* Peter had trained for this kind of situation, but now that it was actually happening, he didn't want to recognize it for what it was. Adison wouldn't have willingly left his instrument on the ground. He was attacked. And he lost, which suggested his attacker had training—more training than Adison. And his attacker wasn't after money, otherwise they would have taken the flute.

Adison was targeted. And that meant the Promising Generation was being targeted. He and Nathan were supposed to disappear. But looking at Nathan, Peter could tell that he wasn't ready to admit that this was a targeted attack either. Nathan would do everything he could to find his brother, fighting protocol as he did. But if Nathan wasn't going to enact protocol, neither was Peter. Disappearing meant cutting all ties, including from Alyx. He wasn't sure he was ready to do that.

"Let's go back to my house. We can activate the GPS in his phone." Peter suggested.

Nathan took a deep breath, putting the flute and binder on his passenger seat as he climbed into the car. Peter waited until Nathan had driven off, then pulled out his phone, sending a text to an encrypted group chat.

If they were going to find Adison before Wraith forced him and Nathan to disappear, they were going to need all the help they could get.

Saturday
September 10th,

03:40 PDT
Tracy, California
Hall Base of Operations

NEIL MCLEAN watched the young man through the camera. "You don't think you could have warned me?" He turned to look at Dylan Hall. "This is more than a small favor." He complained.

"It's been cleared by your bosses." Hall defended. "Technically, it's nothing more than a training exercise. And it's not like I'm asking you to break any laws. Their parents are aware of it, and will help you and I in any way we need. All I need is for you to do your job: investigate. We need to see how they respond to police interference."

Neil narrowed his eyes at Hall. "You asked for me by name, didn't you. That's why I'm here. You called in a favor."

"Technically, your dad called in the favor." Hall admitted.

Neil shook his head. "I hope you realize that Alyx loves to try to solve my cases. It's a game to her. She tries to solve it using nothing but google, while I work the evidence."

Hall rolled his eyes. "Of course I'm going to have to stay

in front of Alyx again." He sighed. "Can you do your best to keep her away from this case?"

Neil laughter. "Yeah, telling her to stay away is a sure way to get her to look into it." He told Hall. "But I'll do my best." Neil folded his arms, returning his attention to the video feed. "So how long are you going to let him sit there?"

"How long would you let a suspect you were interrogating sit there?" Hall returned.

Neil huffed. He knew Hall was avoiding his question. FBI interrogations were all about getting a confession that would hold up in court. CIA interrogations were not the same, and Neil would know as much, as he'd worked for both agencies. He turned away from the video feed, walking toward the door without saying good bye. If he was good at his job, and he was, he might get more information out of Adison's family and friends than Hall got out of Adison. After all, he was there to help them find Adison.

8:16 PDT
Tracy, California
Promising Generation Training Program HQ

PETER BLINKED several times, trying to clear the gravel feeling from his eyes as he opened them, lifting his head off of his laptop. After he hadn't been able to track Adison's cell phone the night before, Nathan had insisted they start searching for him right away. Peter hadn't disagreed, because if they found Adison, he wouldn't have to go into hiding. So while Nathan and Jacob chased down leads, Peter used his access to the CIA database to find more. At some point, he had clearly fallen asleep.

Out of reflex, Peter checked his phone, feeling guilty that he'd wasted time in the search for Adison by succumbing to sleep. He had three missed calls with voice messages. He listened to the first two, quickly deleting them. Nathan had called, ordering Peter to wake up and help find Adison. As if he didn't feel guilty enough. He would call him back, but first he had another voice mail to listen to.

The third wiped all sleep from Peter's mind. Wraith knew.

Wraith knew. He and Nathan had intentionally kept Wraith in the dark about Adison's kidnapping, because he would insist on en-acting protocol. But someone had told him, whether intentional or not didn't matter at the moment. Wraith knew, which meant he was going to make Nathan and Peter go to ground.

Peter sent a quick text to Nathan, apologizing for falling asleep, and explaining the situation with Wraith. Fortunately, Nathan told him he would be back at the house in minutes, already on his way to drag Peter out of bed. Within minutes, Nathan was in the house.

"How did he find out?" Nathan asked out of breath.

Peter shook his head. "I have no idea." He glanced a-round to make sure Nathan was alone. "Someone must have let it slip."

"You know what this means. All the evidence we've found suggests that he was targeted. Wraith is going to enact protocol." Nathan finally voiced his concerns.

"I know." Peter told him. "I don't want to disappear any more than you do." He took a deep breath. "I may have a solution, but I need your permission. Jacob isn't here is he?"

Nathan shook his head. "No, he's still chasing down leads."

Peter nodded. "Good." He sighed. "I know the girl from the CIA BOLO."

"That's not important right now. Right now we need to be —"

"Her name is Alyx McLean, and I've been studying French at her house a couple nights a week." Peter admitted.

"If I weren't trying to find my brother right now..." Nathan trailed off in an exasperated way that told Peter he didn't even know where to begin with criticism.

"I know. But I've had my doubts about the BOLO. Remember when I asked Wraith who was being protected at the safe house?" He waited only long enough to see Nathan nod. "I'd already asked and gotten the question answered, just not through official channels. Turns out, Lynn Feilds was being held, against her will, at that safe house. Alyx is her cousin." Peter told Nathan.

"Adison is friends with Lynn. They spent a lot of time together while she was staying with Thane and Chelsi." Nathan admitted. "Do you think the same people kidnapped Adison?"

Peter shook his head. "I don't know," he sighed. "The point is Alyx attacked that safe house to rescue her cousin. Not to mention she found her in the first place. Lynn was taken from Feilds' Ball, and was rescued from the safe house in the Austrian Alps."

Peter let the implication of what he was saying sink in. Nathan shook his head. "No. You want to ask a *fugitive* of the CIA to find Adison. Absolutely not."

"We don't need to give her any details. Her dad is FBI, and from what I've heard, she's solved more of his cases than he or the FBI would care to admit." Peter insisted. "We prove she's worth recruiting, and we find Adison so you and I don't have to go to ground."

Nathan narrowed his eyes. "Exactly how much time have you spent with this girl?"

"Enough that I know what nickname her aunt calls her, but not enough to call my mom. Turns out she's the one that called in the BOLO."

Nathan whistled. "Trying to decide if you like the girl enough to overpower your hatred for your mom. Must like her quite a bit." He took a deep breath. "But do you trust her?"

Peter nodded. "Absolutely. I'm telling you, she deserves a place in this training program."

Nathan turned to leave the room. "Let's try it." He turned back as he continued walking. "But Peter, call your mom. We're going to need to get Wraith on our side if we're going to keep our jobs after this."

Peter spun his phone in his hand. He hadn't talked to his mom since he was seven, and she had taken off. He'd tried calling at first, to ask why she'd left him with his father, who only gave him enough attention to feed him, but she never answered. Once his father had gone back to DC, leaving him to take care of himself, she started calling, but by then, he didn't care anymore.

He grabbed his keys off of the table next to him and headed for the door.

9:49 PDT
Tracy, California
McLean House

ALYX STIRRED, her eyes opening to glance at the clock. She felt a moment of panic, her body shooting upright as she forgot it was Saturday. She fell back on her pillows when she realized her mistake, letting out a sigh. She hated when she did that.

She twisted her feet off the side of her bed, padding over to her desk. She was already up, so she might as well put her time to good use. As she looked at the time again, she paused. The house was awfully quiet for being almost ten on Saturday. Usually her dad would be downstairs watching something on TV as he cleaned his service weapon, and that was if he hadn't asked if Alyx wanted to go with him to the range, or go play a round of tennis at the park. If she didn't hear the echos of the TV, and he hadn't asked Alyx if she wanted to join him on errands, or father-daughter bonding time, it meant he was on a case.

But usually he let her know he was leaving, especially

when her mom was working.

Distracted, she wandered downstairs to confirm her suspicion. She checked the kitchen and living room, finding them empty, before wandering back to the laundry room. She walked past the washer and dryer to open the garage door, where she found two empty bays where her mom's Audi TT, and dad's Honda Civic belonged. While Alyx wanted to shrug it off and enjoy the time she had to herself, she suspected something. If her dad left on a case without telling her, it meant he didn't want her to know.

She smirked as she walked into the living room, turning the TV on. Fortunately she had other sources. Her dad served in the Criminal, Cyber, Response, and Services Branch where he handled various criminal cases. That meant, usually, his cases were important enough, and big enough in the relatively quiet area of California they lived in, they made the local news. Alyx had all of the local news stations memorized, so it didn't take very long for her to get to one of the stations. Her search for information was over almost before it had begun. There on the TV in her living room was her father, answering questions at a press conference in front of the Tracy Police Station.

Her dad did have a case. It was local. And he didn't tell her.

Alyx tossed the remote onto the couch, leaning on the back of it from the hall way as she fumed at her dad through the TV. Gone were all notions of doing her homework, replaced with an insatiable desire to solve her dad's case before him, again, just to spite him for not telling her.

While the FBI authorized press release didn't reveal anything about what leads they were following, or who they suspected, they did reveal just enough about the time, place, and victim, to try and get the public to come forward with what they may have seen. It helped the FBI actually get a conviction if they had multiple witnesses.

For Alyx, the press conference almost always gave her enough information to begin her own investigation. The headline at the bottom of the screen told her a Freshman playing in the pep-band at the Kimball High game was missing. She knew Freshmen. She also knew students in the band. Someone had to know the student that was kidnapped. And in the name of curiosity, she could conveniently talk to those students, getting information that her dad would never be able to coax out of them.

What could she say? Teenagers didn't really like authority figures.

She ran upstairs, leaving the TV on so she could hear if her dad inadvertently gave her any more information, and grabbed her laptop and phone from her room. Between google and her surprising large collection of casual acquaintances, she was pretty confident she could have the case solved before her dad got home.

Alyx started by texting Savannah. If any of her friends had heard about a kidnapped freshmen, it would be her.

Hey, I just heard that a freshmen was kidnapped last night. Have you heard anything?

not as much as u. ur dad is on the case! Spill.

That's the problem. He didn't even tell me he had a case.

srsly

Yep

I heard his name is Adison Levy, he plays flute. Apparently he dropped it when they got him.

With the information she got from Savannah, Alyx decided to text Chelsi, figuring she would be the best source of information for another freshmen student.

Hey, do you know Adison Levy? He's a freshmen like you.

Hes in a few of my classes. y?

He was kidnapped last night after the football game.

rlv?

Chelsi read Alyx' message again and again, closing the conversation with Alyx to open the secured group message between all of the Generation members. Sure enough, the thread was full of at least a hundred messages from the night before, all of them talking about Adison being kidnapped, and the Generation's efforts to find him.

She pulled herself out of bed, annoyed not to be sleeping in longer. She unlocked her phone again, opening her chat with Alyx. If anyone besides the Generation was going to find Adison, it was going to be her.

r u helping ur dad?

No. He didn't tell me it was his case. I might be trying to investigate on my own tho.

Can I come over? I can help.

I will always accept your help. Should I pick you up?

Yes pls.

Chelsi went to her closet, pulling out a shirt to go with the pair of jeans she pulled from her dresser drawer. She grabbed her phone when she finished getting dressed, running downstairs.

She knocked on Thane's door, planning on telling him that she was leaving, but she wasn't surprised when she found his room empty. He was always more responsive to calls to help the Generation, but it made sense, since he was one of the older members. She padded downstairs, finding a note from her mom saying she'd gone shopping. No one dared to enter Chelsi's room when she was asleep, not any more. Not after the incident. While she appreciated the opportunity to sleep, it meant that if she had wanted to go shopping with her mom, she wasn't given the opportunity to.

Chelsi knocked on her dad's office door, one last attempt to tell someone that Alyx was coming to pick her up. When she didn't get an answer, she pushed, sure he was in his office because he never left it unlocked when he wasn't in there, and definitely not open. She looked in, staring at the computer screens straight across from her, seeing her dad in a video on screen, him walking into what looked like an interrogation room. As her dad sat at the table, she watched as the person he was interrogating lifted their head off of the table— Adison.

She immediately recognized the young man who she knew from more than just a couple of classes. He'd been one of her best friends in the Generation. Curious, Chelsi dared to enter a little more. Her dad had a sticky note postulating that social media might be a weakness of the Generation. Chelsi's heart fell. She had shown him how to find people on social media, and had even suggested that Twitter was the best site to use. She pulled out her phone, looking up Adison's twitter. He had more than one tweet that he had signed with *#spylife*.

Chelsi spun, preparing to make her swift exit, when her dad's computer dinged, telling him he had a message. She paused her exit as she read the notification from her uncle, updating her dad on the press conference he'd just finished.

So her uncle Neil was helping her dad too. This was going to be interesting.

She left her dad's office, closing the door so it was exactly as she found it, heading out front to meet Alyx before she texted.

HALL WALKED into the room that he had turned into an interrogation room. Adison Levy brought his head up off the table, giving Hall a tired look.

"Good." Hall smiled. "You're tired. I don't think anyone understands the extent to which exhaustion affects our filters. I've found it works better than truth serum."

"Truth serum is a myth." Levy slurred, placing his head back on the table.

Hall shook his head. There was such a thing as pushing exhaustion too far. "All I have is one question, and then you can sleep." He offered. "I'm looking for the Promising Generation files. Who has access?"

Levy just mumbled his reply into the table. "I wouldn't know. Why don't you ask the perfect brother of mine?"

Hall shook his head, wondering if Levy knew what he had just admitted. It hadn't been hard to break him. "That would be Nathan." Hall said.

"Mom and dad's perfect son. He can do no wrong. He wouldn't find himself here. That's sure."

Hall knocked on the door behind him. Banthup answered the door. "Take Levy here to his cot. I believe we're done."

Banthup nodded, grabbing Adison's arm, lifting him out of the chair and escorting him out the door. Hall smiled. Maybe he was going to find the intel he needed before it was too late.

JACKSON SET another personnel file to the side from the new batch he'd gotten from his contact. They all had great potential talent, but he wasn't sure how many of them he could turn, or, if once he had turned them, they would be willing to do the things the Circle of Fifths required them to do. Recruiting had slowed since the surge of patriotism that had been sent through the country after 9/11 brought a new group of idealists to the agency. He, however, had remained the COF's number one recruiter, as his position as a black-site interrogator for the agency had given him the opportunity to exploit the internal battle many of his fellow interrogators felt. Personally, he found them weak, but his job let him play on their insecurities and turn them.

It was his ability to recruit agents that kept the Nexus, the Circle of Fifth's leadership, from discarding him when the Agency discharged him. When the collective conscious of the country had grown weak as it pertained to interrogation techniques, it was deemed he was no longer necessary, and the CIA discharged him. Fortunately, his ability to recruit agents for the Circle of Fifths was unmatched, proving loyalty and usefulness to the Nexus. His cultivated network of contacts within the agency also helped, allowing him to maintain access to classified data, although no longer direct.

The apartment's door made a noise as someone unlocked it from the outside. Jackson looked up at his nephew Kalen walked through the door he had just opened. Jackson turned his attention back to the file in front of him, considering how the young agents he turned now might be more useful agents than his nephew, who every day seemed to become more and more like his mother, who had started to question the Nexus before her untimely death.

"Thought your objective was clear." Jackson scolded. "You aren't to come back here until you bring me actionable intelligence telling me where McLean is, since you lost her in Austria."

Kalen boldly approached Jackson. "And who's to say I haven't?" Kalen asked, handing Jackson a file. "Alyx McLean appeared in an article covering local high school matches in Tracy, California. Not only do I know which city she lives in, but I know which High School she goes to." Kalen paused as Jackson opened the file.

Jackson looked up at his nephew as he read the name in the articles. "McLean. Are you sure this is really her?" Jackson asked, his excitement barely slipping into his voice.

"One of the articles included pictures of the girls during their match." Kalen reached over the desk, flipping pages of the articles to find the one with pictures. He pointed to the color photo he had printed from the newspaper's online database. The girl he pointed to was wearing an orange tennis dress that was clearly the uniform for her high school team. "She keeps winning her matches." Kalen stated. "And I would recognize that look of determination to win anywhere."

"What high school?" Jackson asked.

Kalen smiled. "John C. Kimball High School. Home of the Jaguars."

"Hall went home to protect her." He muttered. Jackson looked up at Kalen. "Pack your bags. You're going to Tracy."

14:21 PDT
Tracy, California
McLean Home

ALYX OPENED the front door revealing Peter's smirk. She shook her head as she opened the door wider inviting him in. "I thought Saturdays didn't work for you."

Peter shrugged. "I snuck away from work."

"Really? You have a job?" Alyx asked incredulously.

"How else do you think I was able to buy my car?" Peter retorted.

Alyx smirked. "I don't know, but probably not by sneaking away when you should be working." Alyx taunted.

Peter looked at Alyx seriously. "Well, it wasn't a problem until I met you."

Alyx' heart started pounding in her chest, and her cheeks began burning red. "Oh yeah?" She tried to sound as if she was still indifferent, but her voice wavered.

Peter smiled sweetly. "Yeah."

Alyx shook her head, turning back towards the kitchen to hide her bright red cheeks. "So did you bring your textbook, or were you just planning on flirting with me and not studying? If so, I will make you flirt in French."

Peter scoffed as he followed behind her. "Are you accusing me of flirting with you? I assure you I am here for nothing other than flirting—I mean studying."

Alyx smirked, proud of herself for finally making Peter flustered enough to make a mistake. "Then where's your textbook?" She glanced back at Peter, pointing at his empty hands.

Peter opened his mouth to argue, but then looked at his hands, as if noticing for the first time that they were empty. "I left it in the car."

Alyx nodded. "Yeah. Totally here to study." She mocked.

Peter turned toward the door. "I'll be right back."

Alyx took a deep breath as Peter walked out the door. She hadn't realized how little oxygen she was getting. Apparently she was hyperventilating, *just a little bit.*

Peter's trip to the car gave her time to come up with an excuse as to why Chelsi was sitting in her kitchen. Alyx walked into the kitchen, immediately addressing Chelsi. "We need a cover for why you are here. Now."

"You're tutoring me?" Chelsi offered.

"What subject?"

"I don't know."

"Is there a subject you need help in?" Alyx asked.

"Not really." Chelsi replied.

Alyx paused as she heard the front door open and close.

"Well we better have something fast." She urged.

"Maybe I just came over because no one was at my house, and I wanted someone to do homework with." Chelsi suggested.

Alyx nodded. "Works for me. I'll be right back." She promised, then ran from the kitchen where they had been working to the dining room before Peter came down the hallway between the kitchen and living room, created by the couch. She used the formal living and dining room to sneak up to the landing that acted as the entry way, so she could get upstairs without Peter seeing.

Peter entered the kitchen; his forehead creased as he saw Chelsi sitting at the breakfast nook table, not Alyx.

"What are you doing here?" He asked.

Chelsi crossed her arms. "I could ask the same of you."

"Alyx and I have been studying for the AP French test." Peter replied. "Your turn."

Chelsi smirked. "Alyx is like a big sister. No one was at my house, so Alyx offered to pick me up so the two of us could do homework." She looked at Alyx as she strolled back into the room, French book in hand. "You didn't tell me that the football player you have a crush on was coming over."

Alyx turned bright red. She may have done her share of flirting with Peter since they'd started studying together, but having Chelsi just straight up say—in front of him, no less— that she liked him was the definition of embarrassment.

Peter smiled. "Has she told you as much?" He asked

Chelsi.

"It may have come up. Besides, she told Thane, Carlie, Savannah, and Kaden that she dances with a prince every summer, and she still likes you." Chelsi said.

Alyx ran to sit next to Chelsi, covering her mouth. "Clearly, Savannah talks too much." She looked at Peter. "I promised Chelsi that we would do homework, so I can only study with you for like an hour or so."

"I'll take any time with you I can get." He admitted. "You're not the only one with a crush."

Alyx' already red cheeks somehow turned an even deeper red, and she forgot to breathe. She'd been pretty sure that Peter had been flirting, but here he was openly admitting as much.

This is what death felt like.

PETER WAITED until Chelsi had left the room to go to the bathroom before looking up at Alyx. He couldn't help but notice how cute she was when she was being studious. She bit the inside of her lip as she transcribed one of the questions they'd been working on. Chelsi had been the second person to tell him that Alyx liked him, but everything she'd done had made it seem like the opposite was true.

He had to know. He had to hear it from her. "So, what Chelsi said, about you liking me... Is it true?"

Alyx looked up from her workbook, her face gaining color. "Français."

Peter raised his hands in surrender. He had broken too many of their study sessions with his questions, and since dinner with Emily, she had enacted the *no English* rule, which meant almost all of their conversation took place in French. "Est-ce-qu'il vrai?" He asked again.

Alyx sighed. "Maybe."

Peter stared at Alyx. "I thought you said French only."

"That rule only applies to you." Alyx teased. She looked at him, her smile disappearing as she bit her lip. "What would you do if it was true."

"I don't know." Peter admitted quietly. "Not distract you from homework."

"What do you mean?" Alyx asked.

"You have lofty aspirations. The last thing I want is for you to not reach them because you spent too much time with me. I noticed you were doing homework the other day before school, so obviously just studying French with me is taking up too much of your time." Peter admitted.

"If you had my friends, you would do homework too. Any opportunity to ignore them is a blessing." Alyx blushed. "Besides, studying with you is helping me prepare for a test I have to pass to be able to reach those goals."

"Yes, but me taking you on a date wouldn't help with either of those things." Peter mumbled, a smile playing on his lips.

Alyx cocked her head. "Did you just say date?"

Peter looked up at Alyx with a cocky smile. "And what if I did?"

"I would ask what you meant by it." Alyx said.

"My reply would be that I want to take you on a date, no matter what our classmates might say." Peter stared at Alyx, waiting for her to reply.

"What? Flirting wasn't enough? You want to taunt and

tease now too?"

Peter shook his head. "I'm serious."

Alyx took a deep breath. "We study together just us all the time."

"Studying is not a date." Peter insisted.

"Fine." Alyx conceded. "I will go on a date with you."

"Why does this sound like I'm trying to coerce you to go on a date with me?" Peter teased.

"Peut-être je t'aime, et je... I don't want to get attached and end up hurt when I leave for Oxford." Alyx admitted quietly.

Peter nodded. "I guess we won't know unless we try." He grabbed Alyx' hand. "I think your goals are amazing and will never try to hold you back from reaching them." He smirked. "Besides, don't you think you are assuming quite a bit. All I asked for was one date."

Alyx shook her head with a small laugh. "Fair point." She slyly pulled her hand from his as she heard Chelsi coming down the hallway. "Espions?" She said the French word, hoping Peter would understand. Fortunately he nodded, a smile on his face.

Maybe we should be spies together.

15:28 PDT

Tracy, California

Promising Generation Training Program HQ

NATHAN WALKED into Peter's house, hoping to get another update from him about Adison, or even what Alyx was able to contribute to their search, but instead of finding Peter in the family room, he found Dr. Wraith. Nathan froze, thinking about possible escape routes, all of them failing when Wraith turned and saw him before he was able to retreat.

"Adison has been kidnapped," Wraith started. "And you didn't think I should know. Why?"

"We're handling it." Nathan told him.

Wraith pointed at Nathan. "You don't get to handle it. Protocol states you go off the grid, and coordinate the search from a safehouse where you can't be targeted."

"I'm more use here." Nathan argued. "I know where Adison might go, and I can identify the clues he might leave."

"The same can be said of your sisters. You are the leader of this program. What happens to the search for Adison if you are captured? What happens to the Generation?" Wraith

133

asked.

"Yes, but if you're going to enact protocol and make Peter and I disappear, who is going to lead the Generation when we can't make contact? You? Because you don't have the authority. You're nothing more than a liaison."

Wraith clenched his jaw. "Fine. But Adison being kidnapped most likely means they are after you. Peter can stay to run the Generation in your absence, but I want you to leave, as per protocol."

While not ideal, Nathan had to admit Wraith's proposal made sense. It had crossed his mind many times that day that Adison was being used to get to him. And when Special Agent Neil McLean from the FBI had questioned him, he couldn't help but feel guilty. Adison was missing because of him. Whether it was because he hadn't gotten to the school fast enough to pick him up, or because he was being used to attack Nathan, it didn't matter.

"I'll let Peter know." Nathan conceded.

"Where is Peter?" Wraith asked.

"I don't know." Nathan admitted. "He mentioned something about a possible asset we could use to find Adison faster. Maybe he went to see if they could help."

Wraith nodded, leaving the room. "When you talk to him, let him know I would like to talk to him too."

Nathan took a deep breath, looking around Peter's family room. He took in the table that he sat at the head of during their weekly Generation briefings. Despite being in college, and having the opportunity to take on a role at the Langley during his studies, he'd chosen to stay here. This was his family, and he hated to leave them. But if he really was the target, Wraith had a point. If he was captured, he could identify all of the other members. He needed to leave to protect them. He knew they were capable. They could find Adison and eliminate the threat. And when they did, he could return. With one final look around the room, he pulled out his phone, sending a text to Peter.

PETER SMILED as Alyx walked him down the driveway to his car. He looked at her, noting the way she had her arms folded around her, pulling her sweater tight around her. The brisk Californian air was making her cold, yet she was braving it for him.

"I'm pretty sure I'm supposed to walk you to your door. You're not supposed to walk me to my car." Peter joked.

Alyx smiled. "Yes, but we literally just came from inside. I'm just being a good host." She replied with the same light tone. "Besides, maybe I want to just spend a little longer with you, without Chelsi eavesdropping."

"Fair." Peter nodded. "We still need to plan that date of ours. Maybe over brush pass this next week." He offered.

"You better plan on it." Alyx' eyes sparkled, reflecting the streetlight from above them. The thing about her eyes was that they didn't need a light source to shine. Her eyes carried a happiness with her, a smile that never quite left, at least not that Peter had ever seen.

Peter gestured toward the house with his head. "Go inside before you freeze. I don't want you to get sick so I can't see you Monday." Peter teased.

"I thought the proper thing to do was for you to offer me your jacket." Alyx replied.

Peter shrugged his tee-shirt clad shoulders. "Yes, but I don't really have many layers to share." He faked a brrr.

Alyx rolled her eyes. "You'd never survive London."

Peter shrugged. "I've never been, so I'll have to take your word for it." He unlocked his car, reaching into his backseat to pull out his Senior hoodie. He handed it to Alyx. "Here."

Alyx took it, pulling it on over her sweater. "Thanks." She pulled her hands up in the sleeves, wrapping them up to keep her fingers warm. "So you know an awful lot about me. Why don't you tell me a little about yourself?"

Peter shrugged. "What do you want to know?"

"You mentioned that your parents are never around. What do they do?" Alyx asked.

The question he dreaded. His parents. "They are instructors. They, um, care more about their research and their students than me." Peter said.

Alyx gave Peter a sympathetic frown. "I'm sorry."

"It's ok. I prefer it that way." Peter lied. The lie came naturally. He only told himself the same thing every day."

Alyx' mouth slowly slipped into a smile. "Fine. What are your plans after high school?"

Peter shook his head. She was persistent. "I want to serve my country in whatever way I can."

Alyx lifted her eyebrows, the corners of her mouth turning up. "A spy maybe?"

Peter rolled his eyes. "You can't assume you have everyone figured out."

"Then why don't you tell me what you want to do with your life?" Alyx prodded.

Peter sighed. "If I'm being honest, my parents have always expected that I would follow in their footsteps. I'm supposed to be just like them, and my entire life, I've just followed the path they told me to take. Now, I'm starting to think maybe there is another path I might want to take." Peter admitted.

"Like what?" Alyx prodded.

"An engineer." Peter joked. "I hear they make good money."

Alyx rolled her eyes. "I told you what I want to be."

"Did you?" Peter asked. He stepped closer to Alyx. "Because all you've told me is that you want to go to Oxford for some fancy degree."

Alyx bit her lip. "Well I mean, that fancy degree will help me be a better translator."

Peter nodded, a smile twitching at his lips. "Uh-huh. Just what every genius teenager wants to be. A translator."

"You are avoiding my question *Mister I-want-to-be-an-engineer.*"

Peter shrugged. "It's not so much the profession as what it represents."

"And what's that?" Alyx asked.

"Stability. And family friendly." Peter replied.

Alyx shook her head. "You are such a sap. Who knew? Peter Carlyle, high school jock, is a romantic sap."

"Hey now," Peter whined. "I blame this on you."

"Me?" Alyx asked.

"Yes you. The more time I spend practicing *the language of love* with you, the more I become like this." Peter teased.

They were interrupted as Peter's phone began to ring.

Peter turned the sound on his phone off. "It's nothing. Probably just some crisis at work that they think only I can fix."

"Well, with the way your phone has been buzzing since you got here, I think it's probably safe to say they've tried everything now. They might actually need you." Alyx replied. "Take the call." She insisted, starting to take the jacket off.

"Keep it." Peter told her.

Alyx paused. "Keeping your jacket seems like a little more than just one date."

Peter shrugged. "Maybe I see this going past one date too."

Alyx smiled, biting her lip. "See you Monday." She promised, walking back toward the house. "She turned as she transitioned from the driveway to the sidewalk leading to the front door. "Answer your phone!"

Peter held it up to her, showing that he was doing just that, watching as she went inside as he put it up to his ear. She was definitely special enough that he could put his hatred for his mom aside long enough to call her.

NATHAN PUT his phone on speaker, throwing it on his bed next to the bag he was packing. He'd gotten comfortable. He should have had a bag ready to go, so he could have left by now, but it was too late to prepare for a fast departure. He was there already.

"I thought you would have left by now." Peter answered his phone.

Nathan shook his head, despite knowing Peter couldn't see it through the phone. "Yeah, well, I got comfortable." Nathan admitted. "I didn't have a go bag. That's not why I called."

"Then why did you?" Peter asked. Nathan could have sworn he heard irritation in his voice. That wasn't normal for Peter.

"Alyx McLean. When you said that name earlier, I knew it sounded familiar. I finally realized why. Director McLean had a granddaughter that went by the same name. She was part of the Generation when she was five. If I'm right, and it's the same girl..."

"She's already part of the program. I don't need to recruit her. Just reactivate her." Peter finished. "You said had. Past tense."

"Yeah. Rumor was she died. Supposedly all of his grandkids died. It should be in our files. Look her up. If I remember right, the incident took place in 2000. But like I said, that's assuming it's the same girl."

"McLean as her last name would mean her dad is the Director's son. Was his son's name Neil?" Peter asked.

"I don't know." Nathan admitted. "Her personnel file would tell you though." Nathan looked at the clock. "I wish you luck, but I've got to go. I'm leaving my phone here, so I'll pick-up a few burners and check-in when I can." He promised.

"I hope to have some news for you by then." Peter told him, then clicked off. Time was of the essence. There was no time for goodbyes.

ALYX CLOSED her bedroom door, opening her laptop. Between her and Chelsi contacting their contacts, they seemed to have a pretty good idea of what had happened the previous night. After the football game ended, Adison had wandered back to the band room with the rest of the pep band, carrying his flute and his music stand. Once in the band room, he texted his brother, letting him know the football game was over and he could come pick him up. He then removed the tape keeping his music on the stand, putting it back in his binder before he cleaned his flute and put it in his case. Despite the large number of kids hanging out in band room, Adison left to wait for his brother outside. A group of kids saw him still waiting for his brother ten minutes later.

Alyx did a google search for Adison Levy and didn't find much. She found his Twitter, Instagram, and Facebook pages, and scrolled through each of them to try and find anything of interest. The one thing that stood out to her was that his most used hashtag on twitter was *spylife*.

Alyx decided to read how he used the hashtag, scrolling through pages and pages of tweets. His life seemed pretty boring, so the hashtag seemed to be used ironically. But obviously his life wasn't as boring as it seemed, because he'd been kidnapped. Then again, the most important thing to figure out was whether he was targeted, or if he was a victim of opportunity.

She knew it probably made her odd to know so much about victimology and how to investigate a kidnapping, but her father *was* an FBI agent, and she had definitely borrowed his handbook, and read it, and she retained just about everything she read. But her knowledge came in handy sometimes, especially when she needed a distraction from cute boys distracting her from her future. If she was honest, after finding Lynn the summer before, she'd been a bit bored. School didn't keep her attention the same way it used to.

If someone did a google search on her to dive into her life, what would they see? They probably wouldn't find the uncle with a title in London, and they definitely wouldn't find out that she'd chased Dylan Hall across Europe after he'd kidnapped her cousin. If Adison did have a life that was more exciting than she'd found, she wasn't going to find it on google.

She sighed, opening a new window, this time typing *kidnapping at Kimball High, Tracy California* into the search bar. If Adison was targeted, the news reports of his kidnapping might have a few important details that she'd missed during her dad's press conference. She had, after all only caught the end of it.

The news reports were shockingly void of many more details than she'd already gotten from her network of acquaintances at school. The FBI wasn't releasing very many details about the case. Besides the time and location of the abduction, little was said about the victim, other than he was a freshman, and played in the pep band, and his brother was supposed to pick him up. The reports didn't say anything about what had happened to Adison's instrument and music binder. The flute fit into a fairly small case, and the kids in the band that she and Chelsi had talked to insisted that he'd taken it with him. While the flute he played likely wasn't very expensive, whether it was taken or was left might indicate whether his attackers were after money, or him. But none of the reports mentioned anything about it. All she had to go on was Savannah's gossip that it had been dropped and left behind in the kidnapping.

Alyx really wanted to know who this brother was. He seemed like he might be the key in figuring this out. He would have been the one to report his brother missing. But there were some other things about Adison's brother that she wanted answers to. Why was his brother picking him up, and not his parents? If his brother could drive, why wasn't he at the game? Was he older than a high school student? While Adison was too young to be a CIA agent, like his twitter suggested, his brother wasn't. Maybe Adison was kidnapped to get to his brother.

Alyx clicked back to Adison's Facebook page, hoping his brother might show up in his friends list. She opened his friends list, noticing that Chelsi showed up right at the top, because she was a mutual friend. Chelsi had admitted that she knew Adison, but hadn't mentioned that she knew him well enough to be friends on Facebook. She tried to not let Chelsi's picture distract her as she clicked on the search tab, typing his last name into the search bar. Three people popped up: Nathan Levy, Stephanie Levy, and Christy Levy. She immediately clicked on Nathan's profile.

Nathan only had one picture, which was his profile picture, but looking at it, Alyx could clearly see the familial resemblance. This had to be the brother that kept being mentioned. She scrolled through his profile, reading anything that he had available to the public, which was sadly not much.

She opened another window, typing *Nathan Levy* into the search bar, hoping for better results on google. She looked through the first few options, not finding much of interest. Finally she came to something that piqued her interest, so she clicked on it. Nathan had been tagged in a post that a student at Hampton University had posted to her Facebook page. It was obvious looking at it that the girl cherished her online following, and nothing on her page was private, which was why the photo had popped up. Alyx clicked on the photo, reading the geotag that the poster had been all to happy to share: *Hampton University.*

It looked like Nathan was a student at the university, which was odd, because Alyx hadn't heard of it, and it seemed like Nathan lived at home, otherwise, why else would he pick up his brother from school? She opened yet another window, this time searching *Hampton University*. The results pulled up the page for the school, as well as a map showing where it was located. Alyx clicked on the map, finding that the school was located in Virginia. As she panned across the map, she saw a name that stuck out to her: Camp Peary. Alyx had read classified briefs as part of her job as a translator for her uncle, so she knew the importance of Camp Peary.

If she was right, Nathan was CIA. He'd been training for the CIA at Camp Peary—AKA The Farm—and had attended Hampton University while there, probably as part of a cover. That was most likely the reason Adison had been kidnapped. Someone was after his brother. Knowing that Adison was targeted was just the beginning. Now she would know how to proceed with her investigation.

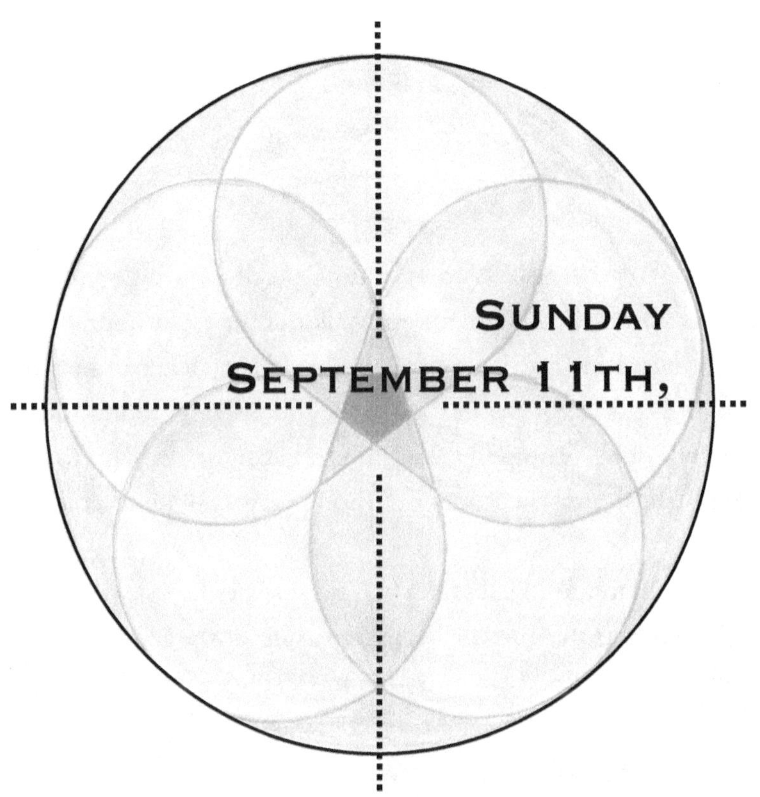

SUNDAY
SEPTEMBER 11TH,

BANTHUP SNAPPED to attention, picking up his phone as his as he watched Nathan Levy walk out the front door, heading toward his car. Levy threw a duffle bag that Banthup recognized as his *go bag* in the trunk, and walked around to the driver's door, prompting Banthup to make the decision to call Hall. He started the car as his phone rang, waiting to connect to Hall.

"Talk to me." Hall said when he answered.

Banthup put the car in drive, easing out a good distance behind Levy. "Sir, Levy is on the move. He's running."

"Follow him. I'll get a team together."

"Yes, sir." Banthup replied.

"And Banthup, try not to lose him. He's trained; he's paranoid." Hall warned.

"Understood." Banthup hung up, keeping his eyes on the silver Toyota Camry in front of him as he selected another contact. Banthup knew that he wasn't going to be able to continue following Nathan for very long. Not very many people were out on the roads at 2:30 in the morning, so it wasn't a matter of *if* Nathan spotted his tail, but a matter of *when*. He was just glad that Jackson had provided him a number of tracking devices, even if their purpose had been to track McLean once he found her.

"Call my uncle." A voice on the other end of the line answered with tired anger in his voice. "I'm not his answering machine."

"I'm not calling to check in. Although if you want me to call Jackson and tell him you are refusing to do your part to find McLean, I'd be more than happy to. Then maybe he would have me take the kill shot when the time comes." Banthup taunted.

"What do you want?" Kalen snapped.

"I need you to check to make sure that the tracking device I planted earlier is active and transmitting." Banthup replied.

"You've found McLean already?" Kaden asked groggily.

"No. But Jackson wants me to gain Hall's trust, and to do that, I need to follow this kid. So I planted a bug on him. I need to make sure it's transmitting his location before I lose him."

Banthup could hear rustling as Kalen got out of bed and signed into his computer. "I only have one tracking device assigned to you transmitting." Kalen reported after a pause.

"I've only activated one, so as long as it is showing it on

Corral Hollow at 11th, we should be good." Banthup said.

"And what if the one that's been activated is with you? You're following him; you are within the margin of error." Kalen said.

Banthup took a deep breath. "What do you suggest then?"

"Activate another one of the trackers so I can see both of you. That way if you do lose him, I can tell you where you need to go to find him again." Kalen suggested.

Banthup sighed, taking his eyes off the road for a second to pull one of the tracking devices out of the center console and turn it on. "Done."

"It looks like they're both working." Kalen replied.

Banthup smiled. "Good." He turned on his signal making a right-hand turn onto Lowell.

"Um, he's going straight, why did you turn?" Kalen asked.

"Levy has had training. Had I continued following him, he would have realized I was following, and then he would have started evasion techniques." Banthup replied. "Where does it look like he's going to you?"

"I don't know. I've been in Tracy less than a day. He turned left onto Grant Line Road." Kalen replied. "You figure it out."

Banthup smiled. "My bet, since he's running, is that he's getting on the freeway. Let me know if he goes east or west."

"And where might you be going?" Kalen asked miffed.

"I'm getting on the freeway another way. Levy won't think

I'm following him if I get on elsewhere." Banthup postulated.

"You think too much of yourself." Kalen criticized.

"You're only concerned about Jackson trying to replace you with me." Banthup laughed.

"No one can replace me. I'm his nephew. I've been training under him since I was eight. I was literally born into this. You, on the other hand, were just recruited." Kalen argued. "Levy is heading east."

"I told you." Banthup commented.

Kalen watched the progress of the two dots on his screen in silence, listening to the engine of the car Banthup was driving through the phone. Kalen was so tired, and the purring of the engine was so soothing, especially when accompanied by the soft blinking lights on the computer screen, that Kalen started dozing off. He was doing everything he could to maintain consciousness, and still, he nearly missed it when Banthup got on the freeway before Levy passed that entrance.

"Where's Levy at?" Banthup asked.

"Behind you still." Kalen mumbled. Your brilliant idea wasn't as brilliant as you thought."

"Are you asleep McKenzie?" Banthup asked.

"Well, let's see, until I got your phone call just before three in the stupid morning, yeah, I was asleep. And I'll have you know it's rather uninteresting to sit and watch two blinking dots." Kalen mumbled again.

"So you start dozing off?" Banthup asked incredulously. "Is that the superior training Jackson trained you with."

Kalen sighed. Banthup hadn't even been on the team one month, and already he was playing on the insecurities he felt as it pertained to his uncle to get his way. It was pathetic really. "I'm sure he would love you waking him up in the middle of the night to complain about me waking up in the middle of the night to help you with something that isn't technically our objective." Kalen said. "Now, why don't you keep your eyes and focus on the road, and I'll speak up if I see anything."

Kalen didn't wait for Banthup's response to mute the mic his phone and start blasting music. If Kalen wanted to take the shot that would redeem him for letting Alyx best him the summer before, he had to remain perfect in his uncle's eyes, and unfortunately that meant staying awake to help Banthup. That wasn't going to happen if he kept listening to the white noise coming from Banthup's phone call.

Nathan pulled into the parking lot of a lodge. Banthup pulled up on the street, watching as Levy got out of the car, running inside to check in. Banthup smiled. If catching the leader of the Promising Generation was so easy, how easy would it be to catch McLean? Jackson hadn't told him much about the girl he was after, but what he did know was that she was sixteen, and she had never had any formal training. So if he had just been able to find a nineteen-and-a-half-year-old trained spy, what did that tell him about being able to find McLean?

"Thanks McKenzie, but I think I've got it from here."

Banthup said, ending the phone call with Kalen. He scrolled through his contacts, hitting the contact he'd named *McLean's uncle*. He pulled a camera off the passenger seat, using the lens to zoom in and watch as Nathan came out of the Lodge office, and walk up to the room he had just paid for.

"Talk to me." Hall said when he finally picked up the phone.

"Levy just checked into Oakhurst Lodge." Banthup reported. "He's in room 18."

"Sit tight. The extraction team is on its way." Hall ordered, then the line went dead.

2:57 PDT
Oakhurst, California
Oakhurst Lodge

NATHAN CLOSED the door behind him, go bag in hand, despite only staying long enough to send an update to Peter. He tossed the bag onto the bed, then pulled out a prepaid burner phone he'd picked up at the grocery store on the way out of town, and dialed Peter's number out of memory.

"Pacific Gold Tutoring," Peter answered.

"This is Semargl. I made it to my first client. I will call when I reach my second." Nathan reported. When Peter referenced Nathan's contingency plan recorded in the Promising Generation files, he would know where he was, so if he didn't report back in, he knew where to start looking. "My appointment with them is in three hours.

"Understood. Call if you need assistance." Peter replied.

Nathan hung up, tossing the phone onto the nightstand. He would need a new phone by the time he made it to his next stop, so there wasn't much point in being careful with it. He pushed through the room, heading towards the bathroom.

He may have paid for the room through the week, but he wouldn't be staying. He was going to find a new car and move onto his next stop: a secluded cabin in Yosemite. Once he used the bathroom, he would be gone.

Nathan splashed cold water on his face, hoping it would help him stay alert. Leaving in the middle of the night helped him identify cars that might be following him, because roads were deserted, but the fatigue he felt because of it was his enemy. He hadn't gotten much sleep at all since Adison had been kidnapped, so he was running on fumes, and he couldn't help but feel as if he was missing something.

As he heard a car door slam outside, he knew he had. Someone had been following him, and now they were right out front. He moved silently to the window. He hadn't turned on any lights because he wasn't planning on staying, and now he was glad. He watched as shadows moved closer to the window. Whoever was after him wasn't taking any chances. There was an entire team of professionals moving in on his room.

He had seen a window in the bathroom when he'd been in there. That had been part of the reason he had chosen this hotel. It had more than just the one escape route. He moved back to the bathroom, grabbing his bag off the bed and prayed the window was big enough to let him escape. As he opened it, he knew it wasn't ideal, but it should work. He pushed his bag through first, climbing through after. As he landed on the other side, he saw Thane Hall, a smug look on his face. "Told you he would climb out the window."

Another young man not much older than Nathan stepped up along side him. "Another point for team Hall." He mumbled.

Nathan shook his head, the betrayal by Thane registering, but he couldn't acknowledge it if he wanted a chance to survive this. He knew he had to be quick if he wanted any chance of escape. Thane was good, and his companion had the advantage of more experience than Nathan, but he still liked his odds fighting these two better than the team of agents on the other side of his door.

Nathan attacked, aiming his body for the agent with Thane, figuring if he could eliminate the stronger attacker first, his chances got much better. And despite being outnumbered, he had the advantage of studying this lodge before choosing it as the first step in a disappearing act. Unfortunately, his attackers had the advantage of a taser. After throwing a couple of well placed punches, Nathan felt the unmistakable jolt of electricity running through him.

Banthup wiped a trickle of blood from the corner of his lip as he looked down at Nathan. "He also warned me that you were a better fighter than your brother." He held up the self-defense taser he'd acquired. "I thought I should come prepared."

Nathan just groaned on the ground, the shadows he'd seen out front appearing above him, two of them picking him up off the ground and dragging him to the van.

PETER SCROLLED through the files that Nathan had suggested he look into. Alyxandrie Madelyn McLean was born June 2nd, 1995, the third child of two of the CIA's best agents. The McLeans started the Promising Generation to give their children the skills they needed to protect themselves, but also train to eventually be spies like their parents if they wanted to. Both of her older siblings had chosen to join the program when they turned five and started school, so when she turned five in 2000, she did too. Although she was only part of the program a short period of time, she seemed to learn very quickly, which was probably the result of practicing with her older siblings.

The incident Nathan had referenced happened a few weeks after she'd officially joined the program. Apparently there was a house of enemy operatives just around the block from her house, which she identified, and despite only being five, she'd decided it was up to her to do something about it.

Her brother and sister couldn't let her go in alone, so they went with her. And it got them killed. The report didn't specifically say anything about what happened to Alyxandrie. She just kind of disappeared from the program. It did however, give him the code names of her parents, which thankfully let him find their agency files. They'd been deactivated, but they were still classified.

Peter had the clearance.

Alyx was Alyxandrie. She was Director McLean's granddaughter. And suddenly everything made quite a lot sense.

Peter sighed, backing away from the computer. He rubbed his eyes looking at the time. He did a double take on the time, certain that the one he'd seen was wrong. It wasn't. Nathan was late for his check-in. That only meant one thing—he'd been captured.

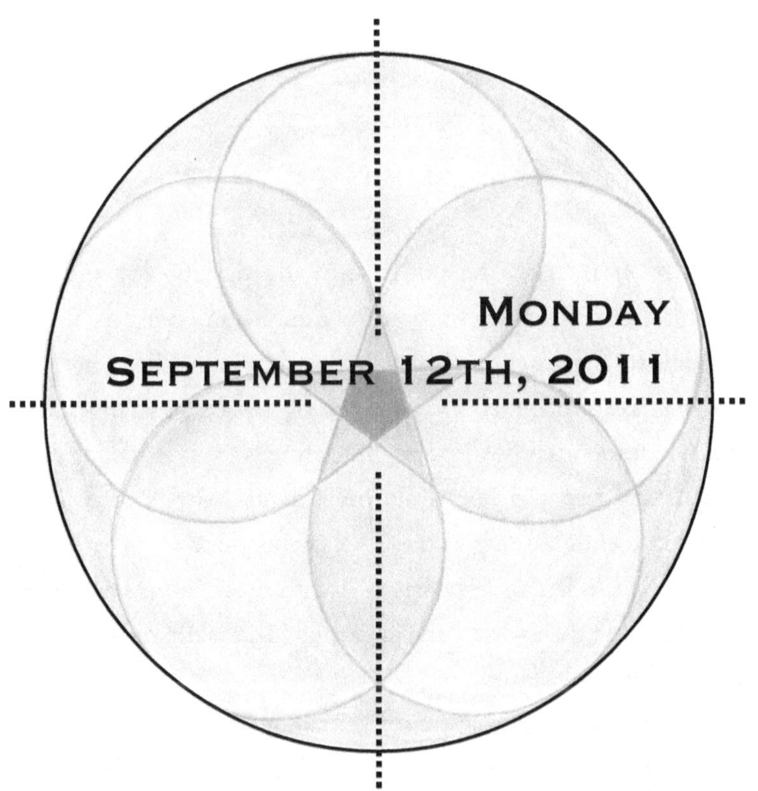

Monday
September 12th, 2011

7:51 PDT
Tracy, California
John C. Kimball High School

PETER SMILED as he pulled into the parking lot and saw
Alyx in her usual spot, waiting for him. Seeing her was almost
enough to forget about his missing friend and the weight of
his new responsibility. He got out of his car, smiling at the
girl he desperately wanted to be dating. It was amazing how
just seeing her and her smile melted his worries into just a
dreaded feeling lurking at the back of his mind.

"Good morning," she greeted with more enthusiasm than
was possible so early in the morning, and with more energy
than Peter could mimic.

"Why are you so happy this morning?" He asked.

Alyx frowned. "I'm trying to distract myself. If I keep
telling myself I'm happy, eventually I will be."

"And why might the happiest girl I know need to
convince herself that she's happy?" Peter asked.

"I don't quite remember." Alyx admitted. "Is it cheesy to
say that seeing you makes me happy?"

Peter smiled. "No. But I bet I was happier when you admitted you like me." He smirked. "Or did you say you love me, because you know you said it in French, and it means both..."

Alyx turned red. When she'd said *je t'aime* on Saturday, it was because she couldn't think of anything to say in English, and for some reason, saying it in French gave her more confidence. But she knew Peter spoke French too. She should have known that he would recognize the double meaning of her statement.

"If I remember right, either interpretation is null because I said *peut-être* first. *Maybe. Maybe* I like you. *Maybe* I love you. You have no proof of either." Alyx argued.

"I'm pretty sure you were the one who said you didn't want to get hurt." Peter teased. "So I'm pretty sure that's proof of you at least liking me. Maybe more." He smirked.

Alyx shook her head. "You are such a flirt. I can't believe you don't have a girlfriend." Alyx grabbed her backpack off her backseat as an excuse to turn and hide her blush from Peter.

"Whether or not I have a girlfriend is entirely up to you." Peter smiled as Alyx turned around with a bright red face.

"First you say you want to take me on a date, now you're implying that you want me to be your girlfriend. I'm not sure I will ever understand you Peter Carlyle." Alyx gushed.

"I did give you my sweatshirt Saturday." Peter prodded. "What's your answer McLean?"

"My answer is that I'm not technically allowed to have a boyfriend. Mais je t'aime, alors si mes parents ne savent pas... I think I'll say yes." Alyx replied.

Peter shook his head. "Alyx McLean, little miss perfect, willing to break the rules for me. I'm honored." Peter teased.

Alyx rolled her eyes, closing her door and starting to walk away. "What can I say? You're a bad influence."

"Where are you going?" Peter asked following her.

"Well, if this is going to work, my parents can't know... my friends can't know." Alyx glanced at him. "Espions, remember."

Peter nodded. "I mean that makes sense. And you're sneaky. I'm sneaky. This will totally work." He glanced around to make sure the school was as deserted as he hoped. It was still early enough, it was. "But wouldn't it make sense to hide in the parking lot, at least a little longer?" He asked.

"No, for three reasons. One, anyone coming to school can see us. Two, if I don't make an appearance in the Cafeteria soon, my friends will start to ask questions. Three, I desperately need to finish my Stats homework before class and I should probably read enough of the novel we're reading in English that I can fake it if we have a reading quiz. I'll see you for our brush pass." Alyx promised, then picked up her pace, leaving Peter behind.

Something was wrong. If she'd spent Saturday doing homework with Chelsi like she'd said, how had she not done her homework for her first two classes. She had also admitted to needing to convince herself she was happy. He'd had enough strained conversations with his father to recognize evasion. He wanted to be happy that she had said yes to being his girlfriend, but he couldn't help the foreboding feeling that was developing in the pit of his stomach. He needed more information about her.

8:11 PDT
Tracy, California
John C. Kimball High School

THANE SLIPPED into the passenger side of the blue '97 Mitsubishi Mirage in the parking lot like he'd done it countless times before. He looked over at Peter as he had closed his door. "Do you realize you're parked next to Alyx?" Thane asked.

"No." Peter lied. "It's a strategically perfect place to park."

Thane rolled his eyes. "Why am I here?"

Peter took a deep breath. "While I would love to harshly ask why you chose not to inform me who Alyx' grandfather was, and that you are her cousin, I will be content asking if you knew anything about the time Alyx spent in the Generation just after she turned five."

"Who told you?" Thane asked.

Peter gripped his gear shift tighter. "Saturday morning I read Nathan in on the Alyx situation. I thought she might be able to help with Adison. Before he went off the grid, he called me. He recognized her name and told me to look for her in our files." He sighed. "I remember a cute little girl that seemed to be better than me at everything, but she was only in the program for three weeks, so I wouldn't have connected her to the young woman she is now. But once Nathan told me to search the files, and I found it... How did she survive?"

Thane shook his head. "I don't know. That day affected the Generation more than we can ever possibly know, and it changed the course of her life, which is why you better not have brought her in to help find Adison. Searching for Lynn already jeopardized enough."

"No, I chickened out." Peter said. "But you better explain."

Thane shrugged. "After Cole and Analyn were killed, Alyx was pulled from the program, and her mom and dad quit, leaving the program without a leader. That was when the CIA assigned us Dr. Wraith. Don't the files say anything about that?"

Peter shook his head. "Why did searching for Lynn jeopardize Alyx?"

Thane shifted in his seat, turning to face Peter. "You really care about her?" He asked. "Because I know your reputation at school. You claim it's a cover, but I know how you were raised."

Peter shook his head. "This isn't about me. This is about your cousin. The BOLO is bogus, but the more I've looked into her, the more I seem to find evidence that nothing about her life is as it seems." Peter commented. "I just want to make sure she's safe."

"Alyx is a target. She was pulled from the program because her parents took her on the run." Thane told Peter. "The same people killed my Aunt Ally. It scares my parents. It scares her parents. She should be scared, but she keeps running straight into danger. She ran into that house, and somehow survived, even though she lost her siblings. She saved Lynn from them, and survived. The people after her are afraid of her. And the rest of us are afraid for her, because she doesn't know fear. And they will stop at nothing to make sure she never joins the CIA." Thane started to get out, leaving Peter to contemplate what he'd said.

"Does she know?" Peter asked before Thane closed the door.

Thane shook his head. "She was young, and it was traumatic. When she started to forget the trauma, she started to forget her siblings. Her parents thought that was best for her." He smiled. "You and I might know our parents have their share of secrets from us, but it pales to the secrets her parents are keeping from her. What she doesn't know about her past can't hurt her." Thane told Peter. "It also makes it easier for us to protect her."

"Does it?" Peter asked.

Thane shrugged. It wasn't his decision. He was only repeating what he'd heard his parents say.

Alyx had saved Lynn, putting herself in danger as she had. Maybe she wouldn't have if she would have known. But what scared Peter was the fact that she was getting into something now. He hadn't told her about Adison, but that didn't mean no one had. Chelsi had been at her house, and he suspected it wasn't to do homework.

17:40 PDT
Tracy, California
John C. Kimball High School

"OK GIRLS. Listen up!" The tennis coach yelled at the end of practice. She waited for the team to gather around her to continue speaking. "In light of the kidnapping after Friday's football game, the Athletics department has decided that we need to do what we can to make sure something like that doesn't happen again. That means starting today, I won't leave until everyone either leaves or gets picked up. I want you girls to be safe."

All the girls nodded. By the time sixth period had gotten out, they had all heard about the kidnapped freshman, if they hadn't heard about it already. It was nice to know that the school was taking precautions to keep them safe, but it felt like a little too little, a little too late. Who had been waiting to make sure the freshman was getting home safe?

"I have four empty seats in my car." Alyx offered. "I am more than happy to give anyone a ride so you don't have to wait."

The coach smile at Alyx. "Thank you." She looked around at the girls. She had been coaching the tennis team since Kimball had opened, and if she had learned one thing from those years, it was that the Tennis team was a tight knit group of girls. With spots for only nine girls—three singles players and three doubles teams—plus a handful of alternates, the team was easily small enough for all the girls to know one another. Just a few games into the season and already they had developed a habit of going out for frozen yogurt after their games.

"That said, tomorrow we are playing East Union. They're good, so I need you girls to try and do the best you ever have."

"Yes coach," the girls said in unison.

She nodded, satisfied with the team and the preparation they'd made for their match the following day. "Alyx, will you lead us out?"

Alyx nodded with a smile. "Ok girls," all the girls put their rackets in the middle of their little circle. "Jags on three! Jags on three!" She yelled, quickly moving into the count, "One! Two! Three—"

"JAGS!"

Their voices and rackets rose into the air in unison. Their cheer complete, they split out of the circle, putting their tennis rackets away in their cases. Alyx grabbed her tennis racket and duffle bags, swinging them onto her shoulder as she grabbed her keys from out of the outside zipper pocket on her duffle.

"Hey Alyx," Chelsi said. "Would you mind giving me a ride home?"

"Of course." Alyx frowned. "Isn't Thane supposed to take you home?"

"He's busy." Chelsi replied. "But he told me you would take me home."

"He did?" How wonderful he told me!" Alyx couldn't keep the sarcasm from her voice. "What are we going to do with that brother of yours?"

Chelsi shrugged. "Thane does this all the time. I would walk home, but..."

The kidnappings. While it was never said, the words held a haunting presence in the air. Alyx nodded to say she understood what Chelsi was talking about. "It's way too far to walk, especially after practice." Alyx added. She probably didn't need to cover with that, but it was just as true as the kidnappings. "Come on, let's get my car." She led Chelsi off of the tennis courts, onto the sidewalk behind the M building.

Chelsi was oddly quiet on the walk to her car, but Alyx didn't blame her. She could imagine how Chelsi was feeling, knowing Adison. She had felt the same way the summer before when Lynn had been kidnapped. No one really ever expects someone they know to be kidnapped, yet it happens, and then they have to find some way to deal with it. For Alyx, that just so happened to be searching for them. And with how eager Chelsi had been to come over and help her on

Saturday, she suspected Chelsi was the same.

"I won't let anything happen to you." Alyx promised Chelsi. "I am officially adopting you as my little sister."

Alyx glanced at the very quiet girl that was walking next to her. Most all of the other players moved their cars so they were over in the parking spots closest to the tennis courts, but Alyx liked leaving her car over by the theatre, partially because it gave her an excuse to see Peter. He'd asked to be her boyfriend this morning. She couldn't help but smile at that.

"Are you ok?" Alyx asked, the antagonizing silence too much for her.

"I lied to you on Saturday." Chelsi said quietly. "I know Adison better than him just being in a couple of my classes."

"I'm sorry." Alyx said softly.

"I mean, it's one thing knowing him, but it's another to... I don't know. I want to wait until we get to your car."

"Okay." Alyx said reassuringly, then continued walking in the silence.

"It's not that I don't want to tell you, because I do, but I don't want someone to overhear."

"I understand." Alyx commented. She looked across the parking lot. She could see her car sitting next to Peter's and the football team slowly migrating down from the football field.

"I messed up. I mean I should have known. I could have warned him." Chelsi rambled.

Alyx handed Chelsi her keys. "Why don't you put your stuff in my trunk. I need to make a call, but then you can tell me all about it while we go get some In'n'out."

"Are you serious?" Chelsi asked, eyes wide.

Alyx nodded. "You are obviously down, and I don't know about you, but I think I need calories after the workout we did at practice today."

Alyx handed Chelsi her keys, and Chelsi kept heading toward the car. Alyx paused, giving her enough space from Chelsi she could make the phone call to Peter. She pulled her phone out of her duffle, selecting Peter from her list of favorite contacts. She held the phone up to her ear as it started to ring. She watched as across the parking lot, he pulled out his phone, looking at it before looking across to her and smiling.

"You know, you could wait just a couple of seconds and talk to me in person." Peter teased.

"Yeah, well, I have Chelsi Hall in my front seat, and her mom is my mom's best friend, so..." Alyx replied.

"Ah, I see." Peter pretended to be hurt. "You didn't really want to be my girlfriend. You were just too nice to say no."

"Or maybe, I'm trying to cheer up a freshman by taking her to In'n'out and I was letting my boyfriend know that I'm going to be late for our study date." Alyx replied.

"Studying is not a date." Peter insisted.

"My mom asked if you wanted to stay for dinner and games." Alyx smiled. "What do you say? Double date with my parents?"

"I say that's more weird than you think, but I'll be there." Peter smiled. "Anything to see you."

Alyx awed, "Such a roo-maan-tic." Alyx smiled as she saw Peter shake his head, the two of them about at their cars.

"You tell anyone I will deny I know you." Peter whispered. He opened his trunk and threw his football gear in the trunk. He hung up the phone and looked straight at Alyx, then stomped his foot three times.

Alyx bit her lip to keep from laughing, remembering that she'd told him that Kate had done that after saying *serious* when she was younger.

He went and climbed into the drivers seat before driving off. Alyx shook her head, trying to get control of her blush as she threw her bags into the trunk, then texted her parents to tell them she was going to be home later than anticipated. Alyx slid into the driver's seat, taking her key from Chelsi as she did. She used the little metal button on her key fob to flip the key out, then stuck it into the ignition, starting the car.

"We're alone." Alyx commented. "Would you mind telling me what's your fault?"

"Dylan Hall is the one responsible for kidnapping Nathan and Adison Levy." Chelsi told Alyx.

"I'm sorry, did you say Dylan Hall? As in the agent that convinced my cousin, I still don't know why she trusted him, to come with him, and because he'd removed her from MI:6 safety and protection, she ended up being kidnapped by some psychopath? You mean *that* Dylan Hall?" Alyx rambled.

"Yes?" Chelsi questioned.

"Good, just thought I'd make sure." Alyx paused, glancing at Chelsi as she turned out of the parking lot. "You dad is good at his job, so how exactly do you know?"

Chelsi looked down at her hands. "There are things I probably can't explain to you..." Chelsi drifted off. "Wait, what do you mean my dad is good at his job?"

"Your dad is Dylan Hall, am I right?" Alyx guessed. She'd never actually met Chelsi's dad. No matter the number of times she'd been over to Thane and Chelsi's house, he was never around. But when Chelsi stared at her, her mouth hanging open a bit, Alyx assumed she was right.

Chelsi stuttered for a second. "How did you know—"

Alyx shrugged. "I mean your last name is Hall—I know because that is what everyone at church says your last name is, despite the fact that all of our teachers at school seem to use your mom's maiden name of Hayes when they're taking attendance, and I know that Dylan is a spy who would probably take precautions to make sure his kids aren't connected to him—so that was a dead giveaway. That and since getting back from London after facing Hall last summer, I've noticed that Thane looks like a younger version of Dylan."

Chelsi sighed. "Long story short, my dad left his office open, and I saw video feed of him interrogating Adison. And I'm pretty sure I helped him find Adison on the internet so he knew who to kidnap. I know you're already working on it,

176

so I want to help you figure it out."

Alyx eased off the clutch as she turned right onto 11th. With the way she was focused on the road, Chelsi couldn't tell if she'd heard anything she'd just said.

"I know your dad is working the case, but I'm pretty sure he knows. He's working with my dad. And while that makes me want to think that they're safe..."

"Do you have any new information for me?" Alyx asked. "Because the FBI is releasing even less information than usual."

"It involves spies." Chelsi admitted.

Alyx nodded. "Figured that much out on Saturday after you left. Your dad must have kidnapped Adison to get to Nathan, which I'm guessing worked, because my dad was gone all day yesterday, which I can only guess means someone else was kidnapped since he didn't find Adison." Alyx took a deep breath, glancing across the car at Chelsi. "Stupid question: Is your dad my uncle?"

Chelsi nodded sheepishly. "Should I even ask how long you've known?"

Alyx laughed. "Well, I figured it out over the summer." She sighed, realizing she was about to tell Chelsi something she hadn't told anyone. She'd never planned on revealing this particular secret. "I know where one of Ally's secret rooms at Feilds Palace is. She had a photo in there of she, my mom, Emily, and Dylan Hall. That and going on visual evidence, have you ever noticed how similar we look? If we wanted to, we could pass as sisters."

"You're taking this better than I thought you would." Chelsi commented,

Alyx shrugged, checking her mirror and blind spot before changing lanes. "I'm sure it wasn't your idea to not tell me we're related. Now my parents, your parents, Thane... I'm bound to give any one of them a piece of my mind about not telling me. Then again, I like knowing, and them not knowing I know."

As Alyx turned into the In'n'out drive-thru, she smirked.

"Maybe we should ask your brother for help looking into this." Alyx suggested. "I mean, having both of you should help us figure out what your dad is after a little faster."

"Why does that suggestion sound like I'll regret it?" Chelsi asked cautiously.

"Because I would love to give your brother a piece of my mind." Alyx admitted.

Chelsi shook her head in the passenger seat as Alyx pulled up to the drive through window. She may not have known Alyx as well as Thane did, but she'd learned that you don't cross Alyx McLean. She was known to be a bit vindictive, and could serve revenge faster than a tennis ball.

THANE WALKED out to Alyx' car as Chelsi walked in with her shake from In'n'out, her burger finished not long after they'd left the drive through. "Where's my In'n'out?" He complained.

"I didn't get you any." Alyx replied. "You left your sister stranded at school. Plus she's terrified because she has a class with the freshman that went missing."

Thane looked back at the house. "I didn't know that."

"Yeah, well, if you were a better brother, you might have paid attention to your sister. She's been asked to keep enough secrets, don't you think." Alyx chastised.

Thane narrowed his eyes. "What did she tell you?"

"Nothing." Alyx said. She smiled. "What I figured out on the other hand..." Alyx let her words drift out as threat. "You know, I may not have a younger sister, or any sister for that matter, but I like to think I've been a pretty good sister figure to Kate, and while I find him highly annoying, Stephan has been a pretty good brother figure to me, I mean he's never left me stranded anywhere. Or asked me to lie to my friends."

Thane put his finger up. "First, Stephan is Michael's Chauffeur. It is *literally* his job to give you rides where ever you want to go." Thane folded his arms. "Second, I really don't like what you're insinuating."

"Good." Alyx replied. "How long have you known I was your cousin?" She asked. "And don't lie to me, because I'm liable to fight you."

"I'm gonna kill her." Thane muttered.

"Again, she didn't tell me. Your looks, however, did. You should also remember that I *do know* my mother's maiden name." Alyx drew in the air with her finger. "Sarah Hall, you look like Dylan Hall. Dylan Hall was in a picture with my mom. All the dots connect."

Thane sighed. "I've known a while. There. I said it. You happy?"

Alyx shook her head. "No. Chelsi, as I already said, told me nothing. But I want to know why she's friends on facebook with the kidnapped kid, who's older brother is CIA. Dylan Hall is CIA. I'm thinking that's not a coincidence. So how, exactly, does Chelsi know Adison?"

"You're serious." Thane commented. "Training. And that's all I'll tell you."

Alyx smiled, getting back into her car. "That's fine. I'll figure it out."

ALYX SHOOK her head gently with a small smile as she drove around the bend on her street revealing Peter parked on the street in front of her house. As she pulled around his car, checking to make sure the street was clear of approaching traffic, before turning her car into the street to back into the garage, she saw Peter smile and start getting out of his car. Peter watched from the side of the driveway as she lined her tires up with the marks on the floor in the garage.

"I'm impressed that you are able to get it lined up so quickly." Peter commented when Alyx got out of her car.

Alyx handed Peter an In'n'out bag. "I told you I was going to be late."

"And yet you brought me food." Peter replied with a smirk.

"I hate to break it to you, but you're kind of predictable." Alyx replied with a smile. "Also you just got done with football, and if you're anything like me after tennis, I figured you'd be starving. I just ate, and knowing my dad, he's going to work late because of his case, so we won't eat for another hour or two."

Peter stepped in close. "Now look at you being the thoughtful girlfriend."

Alyx smirked. "Yeah, well, it's not every day that someone like me gets to date someone like you." She replied. He was close enough it unnerved her, but not as much as it had in the past. She knew why he was so close now. "Maybe I want to make sure I'm a good girlfriend so you don't have any excuses."

Peter just shook his head, lightly placing his hand on her arm. "Trust me, there isn't anything you could do to get me to forget about you." He gazed into her eyes, waiting to see them soften, to see her open up. But before he did, the garage door started to open, causing Peter to take a step back.

"Are you coming in?" Sarah asked her daughter. She smiled when she saw Peter. "Ah. Since when has studying been moved out here?"

"It hasn't." Alyx replied. "Peter pulled up as I was getting out of my car. I decided to wait for him."

"Well you better hurry." Sarah warned, heading back inside.

Alyx waited until the door closed. "The food is also an apology." Alyx told him. "I still need to shower, so you are going to be alone with my mom."

Peter shook his head. "And here I thought I could whisk

you away for a date."

"Not tonight," Alyx smiled, "but maybe after your game."

"What's your curfew?" Peter asked.

"Who said I have a curfew?" Alyx asked innocently.

Peter rolled his eyes. "You expect me to believe that you don't have a curfew?" He held up is thumb as if counting. "Not only have I been threatened by your parents," he put up his pointer finger with his thumb, "but I've also been threatened by your aunt on behalf of your parents."

"Fine." Alyx conceded. "Midnight."

Peter shook his head. "I don't think a date is going to happen after the football game then."

"I have a church dance Saturday night." Alyx offered.

"That might work." Peter smiled.

Alyx nodded. "Good."

Peter caught her arm as she turned to walk into the house. "Are you ok?" He asked.

"Why wouldn't I be?" Alyx asked, confused.

Peter dropped his hand, realizing he was still holding her arm. "It's just, you told me Saturday that you couldn't study French very long because you were doing homework with Chelsi, then this morning you ran off early because you had to do your homework for first and second period." Peter sighed. "And your schedule isn't leaving us much time to spend together either. If you hadn't said yes to being my girlfriend this morning, I might be concerned you were trying to get away from me."

Alyx froze. She'd forgotten that she'd told Peter she and Chelsi were doing homework on Saturday. If she would have remembered, she would have used another excuse to finish her homework earlier. She looked down at the ground. If she was going to come up with a believable excuse as to why she couldn't spend so much time with Peter this week, she needed to make sure it wasn't homework.

"I translate for my uncle, you know, the one with a title in London." She started. She hoped starting with a truth, and giving him more information about herself than she usually did, she could convince him it had nothing to do with him. "And he just sent me a new batch of documents to translate." The second part was a lie, but there was no way he could check that. Not without access to MI-6's database. "That's why I don't have much time to study." She smiled at Peter. "But it'll make seeing you all that much more special."

Peter smirked. "You're a flirt McLean, and you accuse me of interrupting our study sessions." He shook his head and started walking into the garage. Alyx kept pace beside him. When Alyx stopped at her trunk to grab her bags, Peter stopped, helping her carry in her backpack while she grabbed her tennis bag and duffle. As the two of them walked to the door, Peter's pointer finger brushed the back of Alyx' hand. She looked over at Peter a small smile on her lips. Peter looked over at her as she slid her hand into his.

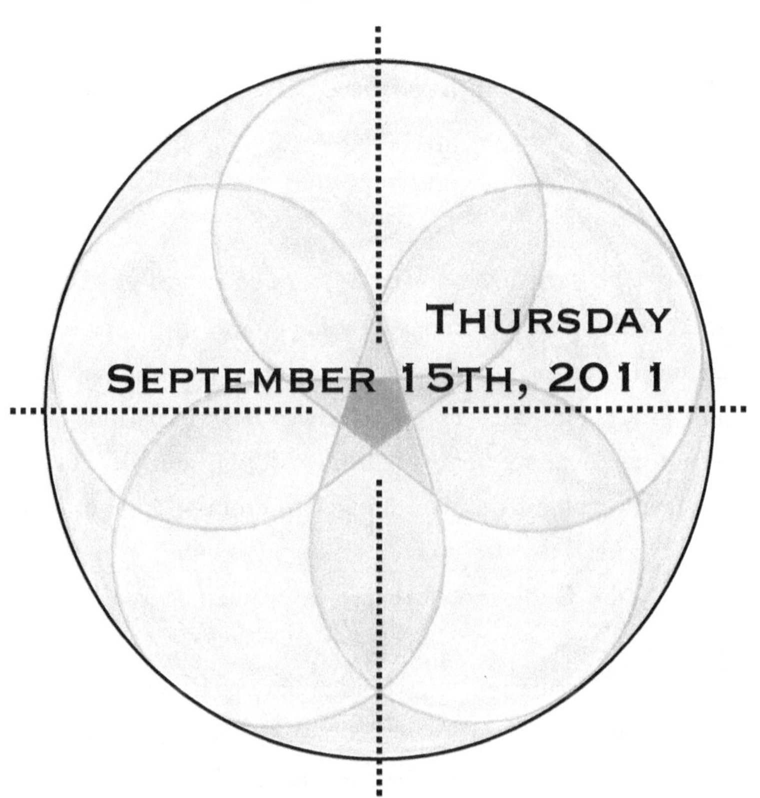

Thursday
September 15th, 2011

18:21 PDT
Tracy, California
John C. Kimball High School

PETER LOOKED down to the bottom corner of his laptop, checking the time. Alyx was heading home from her tennis match. He was half tempted to text her and ask if he could come study. He didn't care if she was busy translating files. Just sitting next to her while she worked, and he did his homework would be a nice change from not seeing her at all since Monday. But he couldn't keep neglecting his job and duties to the Generation because he wanted to see his girl-friend.

"If you recruit her, you wouldn't have to decide."

Peter looked up from his computer to see that Christy and Josh had let themselves in, no doubt using the key Nathan had given to Christy before he'd left. "What do you mean?" He asked.

She shrugged. "You're checking the time. I assume it's be-cause you know the girl from the BOLO, and you know her schedule because of the research you've done. If you recruit her, you don't have to decide between her and us, because she would be one of us." Christy explained.

"That's the reason I've dated Christy so long." Josh added. Christy backhanded him. "The only reason Christy and I have made it work for so long," he corrected. Christy smiled.

"Assuming the girl I know is the girl from the BOLO, don't you think the BOLO is a good reason why recruiting her is a bad idea?" Peter replied.

Josh shrugged. "She's proved herself. Anyone who's able to do what she did is an asset, and obviously she's not a threat, because otherwise you would have told Wraith by now."

Peter sighed, closing his laptop. "What brings you by? I assume it's not dating advise."

"We hit a dead end looking for Nathan and Adison. We came to report." Josh said.

"Also, the FBI agent assigned to the case is being annoying. He's scheduled yet another interview with my family, and has requested I be present. It's getting really hard to sneak out and look for them with the house swarming with FBI." Christy reported.

"Using school as an excuse still works, right?" Peter asked.

"For now." Christy replied. "That, and Josh and I have found that PDA makes the FBI agents rather uncomfortable, but I guess we'll see what *Special Agent* McLean has to say about us using that tonight."

Peter turned to Josh. "Are you going to the meeting tonight?"

Josh shrugged. "Might as well. McLean has asked Ashley to be there, and I'm there often enough that I think we've convinced them I'm family."

"Good." Peter nodded. "The more members we have there, the better. Let me know if the FBI has any leads that we're missing. I don't know how they're jumping on this so fast, and we *have* to find them before they do."

Christy smiled at her Josh. "I think we can help with that."

Peter watched as they left, considering how easy it would be for him to use his connection to Alyx to find out how much her dad knew. He could even ask for her help. But he couldn't convince himself to use her.

Peter reopened his laptop, opening her file. No one had deactivated her credentials when she was pulled from the program all those years ago. All he had to do was give them to her, and she would be one of them. Christy and Josh were right. It would be much easier to date Alyx if she were a Generation member. And she would probably be more than happy to help find Adison and Nathan, even spying on her dad to help them stay ahead of him. But she had homework, and translations, and if he distracted her from that, he would never forgive himself. He also had to think about the fact that the Generation was under attack, and anyone who was part

of the Generation had a target painted on them. Not to mention the fact that she already was a target.

At one point in time, Peter had been unbreakable. But he
wasn't so unbreakable now

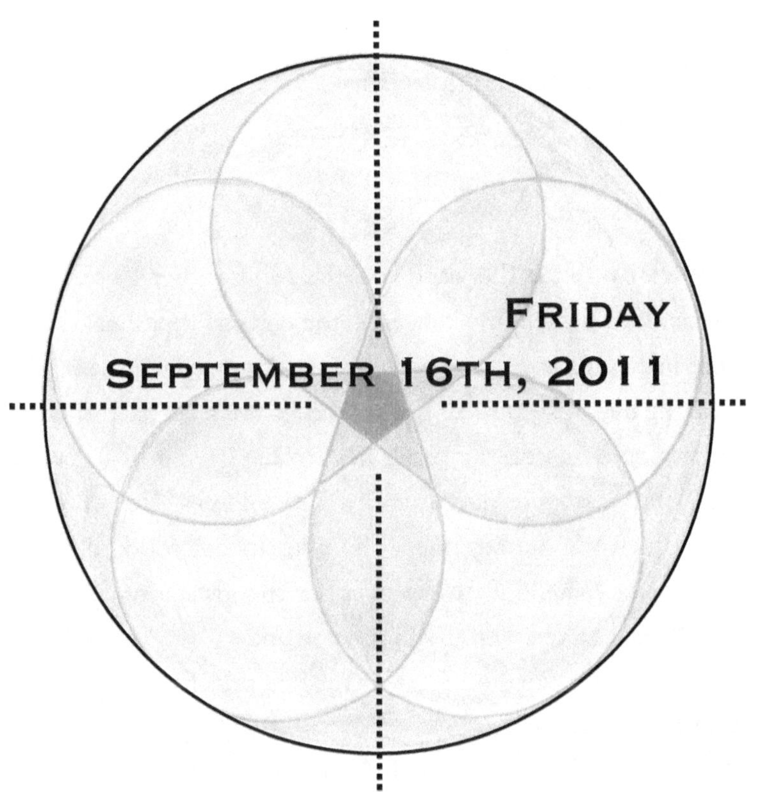

Friday
September 16th, 2011

11:50 PDT

Tracy, California

John C. Kimball High School

ALYX MOUTHED the words on the page of her Psychology textbook to herself, the words of the conversation her friends were having disappearing before she acknowledged them. She brought her nose out of her textbook for a second to write something down on the paper next to her, trying to complete the notes that were due in thirty-four minutes. Her eyes left her homework, finding their way over to her food, allowing her to take a bite, only to discover her friends staring at her.

"What?" She asked the four of them.

"Have you not heard a word we've said for the past ten minutes?" Savannah asked.

"We haven't been at lunch for ten minutes. We barely got out of class eight minutes ago." Alyx snarked.

Savannah rolled her eyes. "Yep, we lost her again. She hasn't heard a word."

Alyx shrugged. "What? I'm doing homework."

"Maybe you should do it at *home*, like the rest of us do."

192

Kaden mumbled.

Carlie rolled her eyes. "We're talking about going to the football game tonight."

"I have translating to do." Alyx lied. The reason she'd given Peter had worked well with her friends this week too, getting her out of most everything she didn't want to do. And while she would have loved to go to the football game and see Peter play, there were still two missing young men, and she didn't know why her uncle had taken them yet.

"Tough." Savannah told Alyx. "You've been working on it all week. You deserve a break. And apparently Chelsi told Thane that a certain cute football player parked next to you the other day. We began plotting."

Alyx glared at Thane. "And here I thought we were *friends.*"

Thane put his arms up in surrender. "Don't blame me." He let his concern and pretend terror morph into a smile. "You're the one who told me I should pay more attention to my sister."

"I'm going to remember this." Alyx threatened with a smile. "I can meddle too."

"Come on Alyx," Kaden sighed, "I think I speak for all of us when I say we're tired of watching you pine away and do nothing about it."

"I'm not doing *nothing.*" Alyx argued.

"Then it wouldn't be weird if you came with us to the football game." Savannah suggested.

"I walked right into that one." Alyx commented.

"Yes. You did." Carlie giggled.

Alyx rolled her eyes. "Fine. I'll make sure it's ok with my parents. But only if you guys let me finish my homework."

Savannah shrugged, the other three looking at her in silent agreement. Alyx turned her head back down toward her textbook and the notes that were due just after lunch, but glanced over a few tables at Peter in his orange polo.

Now she just had to let him know she was going to be coming to his game. Unfortunately it wouldn't be alone.

PETER SMILED as he walked out to see Alyx leaning against her car, her duffle and tennis racket bag hooked on her shoulder.

"Hi."

"Hey." She replied.

He could hear her lack of enthusiasm in her voice. His mind raced to Monday morning, and the way she had been overly enthusiastic to hide how *un*-enthusiastic she was feeling. His heart started pounding. She never told him what was wrong that morning, but he wondered if maybe it had something to do with the files she had to translate. If she had to cancel their date, it would crush him. It took all his power to act like he wasn't analyzing everything she did and said. He threw his backpack over the passenger seat into the backseat before closing the door and leaning against it, directly across from her. "What's up?" He asked.

Alyx forced a smile. "I have some good news and bad

news."

The forced smile paired with that statement never bode well for anyone.

She took a deep breath. "Good news: I'm coming to your game." Her smile brightened, if just a bit, but whatever the bad news that she was about to deliver dulled it. "Bad news: I won't be alone."

Peter took a deep breath. She wasn't canceling. But her words were still devastating just the same. "Who's coming with you?"

"Thane, Carlie, Savannah, Kaden." Alyx listed her friends names off in a rush. "Those are just the ones I know will be there. Chelsi will probably come too."

"That's ok." Peter replied. "I will just have to pretend that every time I look up and see you in the stands, I don't want to play a little better."

Alyx controlled a blush at his comment. Her eyes brightened for a second, before the light left again. "I'm sorry. My friends are meddling, and you're the one suffering because of it."

Peter smirked. He stood up so he wasn't leaning against his car, taking a step closer to Alyx. "You're not suffering?" He issued the question like a challenge. He could see that she was just as devastated as he was.

Alyx shrugged. "My friends may be insufferable, but they know I like you so I don't have to keep my feelings from showing. I'd cause more suspicion if I did."

196

Empathy. That was what drove her to learn languages. It was a characteristic that she may not have even been able to identify herself, but she had it. She didn't have to hide her feelings from her friends. He did. She cared enough about him that she was empathizing with him. *She hurt because he hurt.*

"Ah." Peter replied, a playful smile formed on his lips. "So you like me?" He teased.

"Well, when I agreed to be your girlfriend, I'm pretty sure I said as much." She replied.

Peter stepped in a little closer, pulling Alyx' hands into his, letting them hang between them. He angled his face down towards hers. "You said maybe." He said. "But it's nice to hear."

Alyx smiled. "I like you Peter Carlyle."

Peter shrugged. "You know, I don't have to hide anything on that field. My helmet will hide the smile I'll get every time I see you in the stands and hear those words echo."

"And when you leave the field?" Alyx asked quietly, her doubt returning.

Peter looked at their hands joined between them. "That will be harder." He looked back up into Alyx' eyes. "But if we make it through tonight, we get to go on a date tomorrow. No hiding necessary." He replied.

Alyx smiled. "I can't wait." She bit her lip. "But right now, I have to go to tennis."

Peter leaned forward, gently pressing his lips to her forehead. "I'll see you tonight." Peter said, taking a step back and dropping her hands.

Alyx turned, walking towards the tennis courts unable to wipe the smile off her face. The spot on her forehead where Peter had kissed her burned. She bit her lip, looking back at Peter as he started his car, catching the orange polo clad senior with a smile just as big as hers.

NATHAN SIGHED as the speakers that had been blasting AC/DC's 1980 album *Back in Black* on repeat finally shut off. He'd lost count of how many times the album had played. Worse, he hadn't even been able to count the number of times the album's title track had played, despite it usually being identifiable. After too long, all of the songs started blending together, creating an endless string of unidentifiable noise he wanted to stop.

He was sure of one thing: he wouldn't be listening to AC/DC when he finally got out of this room. Which was unfortunate, because until this, he'd actually liked their music.

Nathan looked up as the door opened and the infamous Dylan Hall stepped into the room. "I should have known it was you." Nathan commented dully. He had been one of the leaders of the program until his position was revoked by the CIA and handed over to the training division. Hall hadn't been happy with the CIA for taking control of the program he had helped create, although Nathan suspected that Hall was upset because he lost access to a great deal of files that the Generation had—files that only Peter had access to.

It made sense that he was the one targeting them, not only because was he one of only a few people who knew the program existed, but because he was the only person besides Peter who knew *exactly* what their files held.

"Good. You're talking." Hall said. He sat down across the table from Nathan. "That will make this much easier."

Nathan closed his eyes, showing Hall he was disinterested in their conversation. "Just because I'm in a talking mood doesn't mean I'm going to tell you what you want to know." Nathan opened his eyes, leaning across the table to show Hall that his tactics wouldn't work on him. "You knew that. That's why you've waited, how many days has it been? Six?"

Hall smiled. "Nice try. I'm not telling you how long I've had you. It would defeat my efforts to disrupt your circadian rhythm."

"Textbook interrogation methods," Nathan commented "Too bad I've been trained to withstand them. Nathan leaned back. "I've been taught counter-interrogation techniques."

Hall smiled. "You didn't pay much attention, did you? The best counter-interrogation tactic is to remain silent?"

Nathan shrugged. "Maybe." He pointed at Hall. "But see, I'd rather turn this back around to you." Nathan leaned forward. "Tell me Hall, how did you figure out where Adison would be? Did you use your textbook interrogation methods against Chelsi first? Which methods did you use to convince Thane to betray the rest of us?"

Hall clenched his jaw. He should have expected Nathan to use his kids against him. He was smart, and resourceful. Since he'd been backed into the corner, he was going to use everything he could to get out. "How long do you think you'll last?" Hall replied. Fortunately, he had a few more cards he could play. "I've been making bets with Adison. He seems to think you'll never break." Hall leaned forward lowering his voice. "How long do you think Adison would last? Do you think I could break him?"

Nathan took a deep breath, doing his best not to let Hall see that his threat was getting to him. Nathan had suspected that Adison was here. He had even guessed that his captors were keeping them apart to use Adison as a threat agains Nathan. But Hall's confirmation was much worse than guesses. It made the threat against his brother real.

"I'll let you think about that." Hall said. He got up, walking toward the door, his eyes darkening to tell Nathan he wasn't one to be played with. "I can play the family card too, only I think mine might trump yours." Hall knocked on the door, having the guard on the other side let him out, leaving Nathan in the room.

A couple more days and he'd get the information he needed out of one of them. If he couldn't break Nathan, Adison would give him another name to protect his brother. Hopefully whoever it was would be more willing to share.

ADISON SAT wringing his hands in his lap in front of a TV playing the surveillance video of his brother.

Video, no sound. Whatever was being said, Hall didn't want Adison to know. He just wanted him to watch, see what he had caused. He had to watch Nathan suffer because Adison got tired.

Adison turned to look back at the guard standing by the door. One guard wasn't much considering his training, but he knew better than to try to escape. There may have been one guard here, but he had seen at least ten more faces, and any combination of them could be between him and freedom. So he sat here, watching his brother be interrogated.

As he watched Hall get up and walk out on the video feed, Adison glanced at the guard once more, hoping to see some indication whether or not Nathan had given anything away. Unfortunately, the guard either didn't know, or he had a very good poker face. What Adison knew for sure, watching

Nathan's head fall after Hall left the room, was if he hadn't broken, he would soon.

Hall walked into the room where Adison was watching his brother, giving a content sigh. "Look at him. Head bowed shoulders slumped. He'll be begging for the opportunity to give me the Promising Generation files when I'm done with him. He's already so close, and it hasn't taken that long." Hall bragged.

"But he doesn't have them." Adison whispered.

Hall laughed. "He's the director of your pathetic program. If he doesn't have them, who does?"

Adison stayed silent, picturing Peter going through what Nathan was. Would Peter survive as long as Nathan had? Peter may have been trusted with the files because he didn't have the familial connections the rest of them had, and he had grown up training to be unbreakable, but Nathan had trained at the farm; he had been trained to withstand the very techniques being used against him. Peter hadn't.

Hall sighed. "Well, I can only stop once I get what I'm looking for, so I guess I'll just keep going until he tells me something useful."

Adison closed his eyes, trying to stop imagining where that would lead. He couldn't decide what would be worse, watching Nathan suffer or giving up Peter. If Peter broke and Hall gained access to all of the Generation's files, what would Hall do next?

"I don't know who has them," Adison lied, "but my guess

is someone who has graduated from high school and trained at the farm, like Nathan." Adison finally replied, his decision made. Peter hadn't graduated—*yet*. He hoped he could mitigate his brother's suffering without jeopardizing the files.

"Like who? For example." Hall prodded.

Adison took a deep breath, preparing himself for betraying one of the members. He stalled, trying to decide who he was going to suggest to Hall. If he wasn't certain Peter had the files, his guess would have been Ashley. She was only a few months younger than Nathan, but hadn't gone to training until after he returned, which might have suggested that she had to be in Tracy to lead the Generation while their leader was away. Plus, she spent more time with Nathan than anyone else in the Generation.

But Nathan would never forgive him if he told Hall to kidnap Ashley to save Nathan. She was, after all, his girlfriend—Hall wouldn't have to break Nathan, because Adison would have already done it for him.

"Cameron McKay is the next oldest." Adison said. "My guess would be him."

Hall smiled, leaving Adison alone with the guard and the footage of his brother.

ALYX SLIPPED into the garage man door as the door in front of her car slowly came to a stop on the concrete. Kimball had won their first game of the season, and she had gotten to watch Peter play, so it had been a pretty good night. Knowing that every time he looked up towards the stands—which he had somehow managed to do a lot—he was smiling as he looked at her, made the night even better.

She walked back into the heart of the house, expecting to see her parents snuggled on the couch watching a movie, like they usually did when she wasn't home. Instead, she found her mom, still in her scrubs, fast asleep on the couch with a pillow under her head, and a blanket pulled over her. It was something her dad did often when she fell asleep watching something, but instead of going straight to bed, he wanted to head into his office to work.

"Hey mom," Alyx whispered.

Her mom stirred, turning so she could see her daughter

over the back of the couch. "What's up?"

"I just wanted to let you know I was home." Alyx replied.

"Thank you." Her mom slurred tiredly, her eyes already reclosed. "Do me a favor and let your dad know too."

"Ok." Alyx smiled.

She turned around and walked back towards the stairs, slowly climbing them. She dropped her purse in her bedroom door, continuing down the upstairs hallway until she arrived in another, larger family room upstairs. Shelves lined every wall, floor to ceiling. It was a custom job, as evidenced by the way the shelves fit perfectly around the windows. Alyx suspected it was the reason her parents had chosen the house. They had books on most of the shelves, movies on another portion, and games on the rest. There was a table centered between the north and south walls on the west side of the room. But she didn't pay any attention to the bookshelves or the game room table. Instead, she turned left, heading to the west wall where the door to her dad's office was. The shelf over her dad's door was slightly ajar, as it usually was when her dad was in there working.

Alyx knocked lightly as she opened the door all the way to see her dad sitting at his desk. "I'm home." She announced.

Neil looked up from the open file on his desk. He smiled. "Thanks for letting me know," he said, before looking back down at his papers.

Alyx slipped farther into the room, looking at the papers strewn across his desk. He had a map on his wall with a mark about where Kimball was, and another in Oakhurst. Alyx guessed that must have been where Nathan was kidnapped. She couldn't help but notice how much her dad's office liked like her closet at Feilds Palace before the ball where Lynn was kidnapped, and the safehouse in Evereux. Both times, she had strewn papers across every available surface, trying to gather enough information to save Lynn. Anyone else would have seen the state of Neil's office as chaos, but Alyx saw things the way her father did. She saw the connections he was trying to make. She understood the need to spread out so as to compare things side by side. It was exactly how she solved problems.

"Are you making any progress on the case?" She asked her dad, closely inspecting the map hanging on the wall.

He sighed, looking at his daughter standing close to the wall with the map. "No, and staring at his file isn't going to help me solve any more of this case tonight." He set a paper down. "Do you want to watch a movie with me?"

"Um, it's almost midnight, and mom is still asleep on the couch where you left her." Alyx replied. "And I don't think she's going to be waking up to move anytime soon."

Her dad walked toward the door. "Well, if that's the case, I guess I'll just have to carry her to bed," he joked.

"Dad, why are you keeping me away from this case?" Alyx asked. "You didn't even tell me you had a case. I had to find out with everyone else watching the news last Saturday."

Neil turned, looking at his daughter. She looked hurt that

he wasn't involving her. Over the years, she'd helped him figure out how the clues fit together. She had a natural talent for it, and he'd had more than one of his coworkers at the bureau tell him as much, even expressing their opinions that she should consider a career at the FBI. Neil wasn't sure he wanted his daughter at the FBI, since he was only there to keep her safe. He'd given up his dream job with the CIA. To protect her. But now he was putting her back into the path of danger. He'd been selfish, letting them work on his cases together so he could spend time with her despite his crazy schedule.

"I'm afraid, Alyx. You ran off last summer, and when you came back, Stephan informed your uncle that you decide to jump out of a helicopter and take out *all* of the guards your-self. We could have lost you." Neil explained.

"But you didn't." Alyx argued.

"This time. What about the next time you go running into danger?" Neil asked rhetorically. "What happens next time when you don't come home? What happens when you get hurt? Last summer you came closer to that inevitability than I'd prefer."

"What does that have to do with me helping with your case?" Alyx asked her dad.

Neil took a deep breath. "Truth? This case is too close to home, which means it's too close to you. You have a conn-ection to the victims, and when you can find a connection... You barely knew Lynn, but you chased her and her captor across Europe, and threw yourself into danger once you found her. What happens when you decide you need to save Adison because he's a freshman at your school? You are innately protective, and I can't have that temptation dangled in front of you."

Alyx shook her head. "But I know who he is. Everyone does by now. And I literally go to school with his sisters, and all of his friends. But you don't want to use me to see if I can get information from them that your interviews will never give you?"

"And what if you asking those questions puts you in the crosshairs?" Neil asked. "It's not just that they're withholding. They are evasive and hostile."

"Of course they are." Alyx snarked. "They're spies. They're literally trained to use evasive techniques when they're interrogated. And I would know, because I've watched enough of Michael's press conferences to recognize it."

"*Spies.*" Neil repeated. "How would you know enough about this case to be able to infer that it involves spies?" Neil asked.

Alyx pursed her lips. She held up her pointer finger. "News." She put up a second. "Google." He rolled her eyes up and to the right. "Yeah, I think that's everything."

"You need to stop." Her dad said forcibly. "Because it would kill your mother if she lost you too. It would kill *me* if I lost you. You're all we have le—" Neil stopped, swallowing hard. "You're all we have."

Alyx nodded. "Okay. I'll stop." She promised. She left his office, turning right out of the family room into the hall.

Neil waited until he heard Alyx' bedroom door close before retreating to his office. He closed the door all the way, making sure it was locked. As he sat back down at his desk, he pulled out the top drawer, lifting up the false bottom to pull out a framed picture of their family almost twelve years before. He stroked their smiling faces, then set it up in front of him, letting the six of them remind him why he had to tell Alyx she couldn't help.

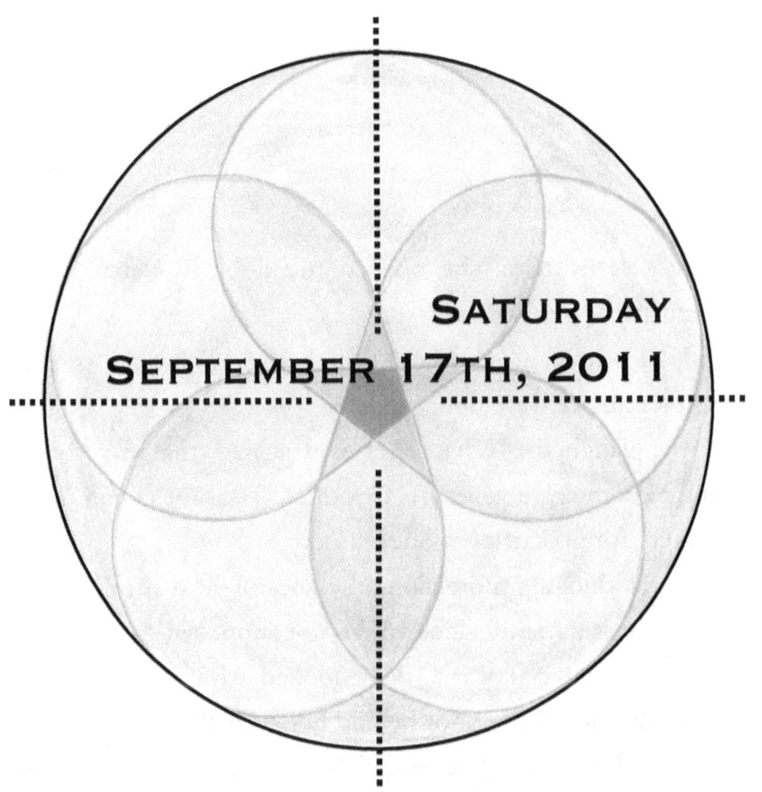

Saturday
September 17th, 2011

10:30 PDT
Tracy, California
McLean Home

ALYX SMIRKED as she opened the door to Peter. "Your punctuality is perfection."

Peter peaked around her in the house. "What did you tell your parents we were doing today?"

Alyx laughed. "What? Are you scared that my dad is going to come give you a BF Goodrich facial for taking me to Boomers for go carting?" She teased.

"I was thinking more along the lines of he'd shoot me for being your boyfriend, since you're not supposed to have one, but yeah, what if I was?" Peter looked Alyx straight in the eyes as she closed the door behind her. "Aren't you?"

Alyx shrugged. "You would be amazed what I get away with." She admitted sheepishly as she locked the door with her key. "Although, I'm sure it helps that neither of my parents are home, so I'm free to do whatever I want."

Peter took her hand, walking her to his car. "It's Saturday. Where are your parents?"

"My mom is working in the Trauma Center, and my dad has a lead on his case he needed to follow up on." Alyx answered.

"Convenient." Peter kept his response short to hide the panic he was feeling. What had the FBI found that he hadn't?

"Oh, it was entirely intentional on my part." Alyx smiled at Peter as he turned to her in surprise.

"How was it intentional?" Peter asked.

"My dad hadn't even told me about his case. I had to find out that my dad had a case when I saw his press conference. So last night I shared some theories. He's been gone since first thing this morning." Alyx explained.

Peter opened the passenger side door of his Mirage for Alyx. "That was a very smart move." Peter replied. "I'll have to remember to come to you when I need strategy."

Alyx shrugged, sliding into his car. Peter closed the door behind her, walking around the back of his car. He glanced back toward the front of the car, using the mirrors to make sure that Alyx wasn't watching him as he pulled out his phone and texted Christy Levy.

Peter shoved the phone back in his pocket, locking it as he did, then opened his door. He slid into his seat, smiling at Alyx as he did.

"What are you smiling at?" She asked.

Peter shook his head. "Just thinking. Have we ever been completely alone before?" He commented as he turned on the car.

"If you are considering this as being completely alone, then yes." Alyx replied. "But I'm not sure I would." She teased.

Peter made sure that the road was clear, backing out into the street, turning so he was pointed out of the neighborhood. "Already with the technicalities? Really?"

Alyx shrugged. "I gotta see if you scare off easily. I can't date someone that will scare off."

Peter started slowing to stop at the stop sign just a few hundred feet in front of them. "I met your dad the first night I came over to study. Lest I forget his conscious effort to not reach for the gun he was still wearing, there is your aunt's threat to think about." He glanced at Alyx just long enough to reach across the car and tap the tip of her nose the way a parent might tap a child's—the way he'd seen her parents tap hers. Peter tried not to think about his parents never showing enough affection to do something so small, as his hand returned to the gear shift as he downshifted to first and finished his thought. "If they didn't scare me off, I don't think you being pedantic will."

Alyx smiled. "You never cease to surprise me Peter Carlyle."

"So you know what pedantic means?" Peter guessed as he rolled away from the stop sign.

"I've spent every summer in London." Alyx said. She switched from her native accent to one that came almost as naturally. "You might say I have quite the proper British vocabulary."

Peter turned his head toward Alyx in response to the British accent she'd just used as he stopped at another stop sign, turning his right indicator on. "So now you do accents. That's cool."

"Between the three months a year I spend in London every summer, and the *I don't know how many moves*, I am actually what you might call accent neutral. It actually takes effort to keep myself from slipping into a British accent sometimes." Alyx admitted. "Especially at the beginning of the school year."

Peter was silent for a minute. He may not have had a good relationship with his parents, but at least he didn't move so often he didn't have a home. "Look at us learning all these new things about each other." Peter finally commented. "We should have gone on a date months ago."

"I agree." Alyx replied. "Especially since my respect for you has already increased."

Peter crept out past the last stop sign in the neighborhood, looking left to find an opening in the southbound traffic on Corral Hollow. "Your respect for me? From just using one moderately advanced word?"

Alyx rolled her eyes. "No. Because your car has a manual transmission."

Peter smiled. "Yeah? Does that mean you'll stop calling Mira a beater?"

"Let me think about that..." Alyx mused. "The fact that it has a manual transmission—"

"She." Peter corrected.

"What?" Alyx asked confused.

"You called Mira an it. You should have said she. Cars are girls." Peter explained. "You may continue."

Alyx smacked Peter's arm. "And you call me pedantic." She sighed. "I was going to say that the fact that *she* has a manual transmission is quite a redeeming feature. That puts her well above my dad's Civic, so perhaps her appearance doesn't matter quite as much."

"Wait until you see what she can do on the freeway." Peter commented. He blipped the throttle as he drove north on Corral Hollow, teasing Alyx with the car's potential.

Alyx threw her hands up. "Fine, I was wrong about Mira." Alyx confessed. "I guess I'll just have to make up for it by being right about being able to completely destroy you at Go-karts."

Peter laughed. "You can try."

Alyx rolled her eyes. "Trust me, I will." She paused, looking out the window. "Wait a second. Did you say we should have gone on a date months ago?" Alyx asked.

"I did." Peter admitted.

Alyx squinted at Peter. "We've been studying French for a couple weeks. Not months."

"Also correct." Peter observed.

"So we haven't known each other for months. How could we have gone on a date months ago?" Alyx asked.

"Algebra II." Peter replied. "I've wanted to ask you out since then. I just never had the nerve. French was the perfect excuse."

Alyx blushed, turning to look out the window.

"You aren't as invisible as you think. Not to me." Peter admitted. "I just didn't think you noticed me."

Alyx turned back to watch Peter as he drove his beat-up car towards the freeway. "I noticed." She whispered.

Her heart jumped across the car, a magnetism pulling her to touch him. His hand, his face. Or even to run her fingers through his hair. But she folded her hand tightly, placing them in her lap. Her worst fear was coming true. She was falling for Peter Carlyle. She didn't know what would be worse: knowing that it would hurt when she left to Oxford, or knowing that she would hurt him, leaving him just like his parents. She kept her eyes on the road, because if she looked at him, she would reach out, and once she admitted she cared, they would have an expiration date.

12:56 PDT
Tracy, California
Hall Base of Operations

HALL SAT watching the video feed of Nathan from his computer at home. He could tell Nathan was getting closer to cracking. In the last few hours, he'd become desperate enough to start pulling at the cuffs that held his wrists to the table. He'd been cuffed to that table for six days, yet he'd shown remarkable control and hadn't pulled at them once until this moment. He was losing control and composure telling Hall he was minutes away from breaking. And once he did, Hall would know if Adison was telling the truth.

Hall minimized the window playing the video as he heard a knock on his office door. He turned toward the door as his wife poked her head in. "Neil is here to see you," she said.

Hall got up, crossing the room to kiss his wife on the cheek. "You're my wife, not my assistant or secretary." He told her. "He knows where my office is."

Addy shrugged. "Maybe I just wanted to see my husband. It's not very often I get to see you here at home."

"We knew this promotion would mean some changes." Hall commented. "We just didn't consider they could be so positive."

"Be nice to Neil." Addy smiled, leaving the office. She was replaced by Neil, who did not look pleased to be seeing his brother-in-law.

Hall waited for Neil to come in before closing the door.

"We're going to have a problem." Neil started. "Alyx knows about my case, and she suspects it involves spies."

Hall shook his head. "That's more than a problem." He stated. "How did she even..."

"According to her, she figured it out using the news and google." Neil told Hall. "So basically how she seems to keep cracking my cases."

Hall sat down with a laugh. "We know she's talented. Has to be with you and Sarah as her parents."

"I'm glad you think this is funny. You know she's going to be hunting you." Neil told Hall. "And after last summer, she has this heightened sense of invincibility, and a lasting hatred for the agent Lynn trusted to keep her safe, but let her be kidnapped by a psychopath instead."

"Even Lynn doesn't have me for that." Hall protested. "Is it really fair to hate the agent trying to protect you?"

Neil shrugged. "She doesn't know." Neil cracked a smile. "It is fair that she hates someone who kidnapped his own niece."

"Lynn came willingly." Hall argued.

"Yes, but could she have left if she wanted to."

"I get it." Hall complained. "But I don't have Sarah's manufactured reputation that lets me *act* like a maniac and let the reputation do the work for me."

Neil smirked. "If it makes you feel better, people aren't as afraid of Sarah and I as they used to be. Sarah asked Emily to threaten the boy Alyx has been studying French with."

Hall shook his head with a smirk. "Things must be pretty bad if you have to call on our baby sister."

Neil shrugged. "Well, Emily bonded with Alyx. Sometimes it's the only way to manage her. Which brings me back to the problem. With Alyx working the case, you're going to need to hurry."

Hall nodded. He reopened the video, showing Neil the surveillance of Nathan. "He's ready to break."

Neil nodded. "I'll keep working his sisters. See where they lead." Neil returned. He turned and opened the door to leave the office. "Oh, and Dylan."

"Yeah?" Hall asked.

"Tell my dad I still don't like that he pulled me from actual cases for this. I'm not one of his agents anymore."

With that, Neil left. Dylan sighed looking at the computer screen. He didn't like this mission any more than his brother-in-law, but he knew why, which was more than Neil could say. Sarah had already lost so much. Sure, both Neil and Sarah had lost two children. But then in the same year, she lost her twin sister and her dream job. When Neil had quit, he'd stayed in the field, trading in his job at the CIA for one at the FBI. But Sarah had walked away from the life entirely, going into nursing instead. All to keep Alyx safe.

If Alyx ended up compromised after all these years, after all the sacrifices his sister had made to keep her daughter safe, he would never forgive himself. He'd made enough mistakes already. He didn't need this to be another one.

18:46 PDT
Livermore, California
Boomers Amusement Park

PETER SHOOK his head as he looked over at the sly smile on Alyx' face. "You must have been in a carting league when you were younger." Peter insisted.

"If I had grown up racing in a carting league, trust me, I would be off racing open wheel cars on the European circuit, not trying to get into Oxford. Alyx snickered. "Formula One wouldn't know what hit 'em."

Peter turned around, walking backwards so he could look at Alyx full on. "So you admit there was some thought about being a race car driver."

Alyx reached for Peter's hand, intertwining her fingers with his, then using her other hand to latch onto his elbow and pull him back her her side. "Turn around before you walk into something." She laughed.

Both of them were silent for a second, looking at how close the two of them were. Not only were the two of them still holding hands, but Alyx' left arm stretched across her body, gripping tightly onto Peter's left forearm. The gesture not only brought them closer together, but it felt to Peter like it was a very protective gesture on Alyx' part.

Alyx awkwardly dropped the hand holding onto Peter's arm. "I will admit that I have occasionally entertained the idea that it would be fun to be a race car driver in Formula One. I mean who wouldn't want to be able to drive as fast as your car will let you, and test its limits?"

Peter laughed again. "I can tell you right now that we were sharing the track with quite a few of them." He replied.

"Americans..." Alyx sighed.

"Your sense of British superiority is slipping out." He joked.

Alyx shrugged. "Compared to Europeans, American drivers just can't compare. I mean there's the Autobahn in Germany, which might be why the best Formula One Driver of all time is German..."

"I'm starting to understand why you bought a Volkswagen." Peter commented.

"The Germans make good cars." Alyx justified. "But back to my point. While some of the F1 greats like Phil Hill, who raced for Ferrari, and Mario Andretti were American, the last American that even made it into the sport was Scott Speed in 2007, and despite his name, he was not fast. He really was no match for the rest of the European drivers. Americans have just gotten lazy. And slow."

"I hope you realize I have no clue what you're talking

about." Peter admitted.

Alyx smirked at Peter. "Most Americans don't. You're just helping me prove my point."

"Just remind me not to take you go-karting again. It's kind of humiliating." Peter conceded. He used his right hand to pull his car key out of his pocket as they walked up to the passenger side door of his car. He turned to face Alyx, not letting go of her hand. "So what do you suggest we do next?" He asked.

Alyx looked at her watch on her left wrist. "Unfortunately, head back to Tracy. My mom's shift is ending soon, so she'll be heading home. And you promised me we would be going to a church dance."

"I wouldn't miss an opportunity to dance with you." Peter told her.

Alyx shook her head with a smile. "There you go again with the flirting."

"I can't help it." Peter admitted. "So what exactly do I have to wear for this church dance?"

"Dress slacks with a button up dress shirt and tie." Alyx said.

"And what if I don't have that?" Peter asked.

Alyx shook her head. "You don't have a dress shirt?"

"I haven't needed one." He smirked. "But if you come with me to buy one..."

Alyx shook her head. "I can't believe you're blackmailing me."

"Is that a yes?" Peter asked.

"Yes." Alyx conceded.

Peter stuck the key into the lock, unlocking the door for Alyx. He opened it, letting Alyx climb back into his passenger seat before walking around the front and getting in his door. He noticed Alyx was typing up a text.

Alyx looked at Peter. "I figured I better let my dad know that we got bored of our study session at the park, and I dragged you to the mall." Alyx told him. "Just in case."

"Study date at the park, huh?" Peter commented as he started the car "You know, I like the sound of that. I mean it would mitigate the worry of eavesdropping parents."

"I thought you said studying wasn't a date."

Peter looked behind them as he backed out of the parking spot. "Yeah, well, again, anything that means I can be alone with you is a date."

Alyx just smirked in the passenger seat as Peter left the parking lot.

19:43 PDT
Tracy, California
McLean Home

SARAH WALKED through the garage door, looking back at her 2006 Audi TT Coupe compared to her daughter's 2011 Jetta GLI. She had to smile, knowing her choice of cars had no doubt shaped her daughter's decision to buy the car she did. She glanced at the garage bay closest to the door of the house, where Neil's car should have been, not surprised to find it empty. This case had been really stressful on him. Any case with children was hard on him. Then again, they'd had a son and daughter who had gone out then disappeared, their bodies never to be found.

While no parent wants to bury a child, there is nothing worse than burying an empty casket that represents that child.

"Hey Alyx. I'm home!" She called, but the only reply that came was the shrill beep of the alarm indicating it needed to be turned off. Despite Sarah's attempts to convince Alyx that she needed to set the alarm anytime she was home, especially alone, she always forgot. The only time she remembered was when she left, so the alarm was enough to tell Sarah her daughter wasn't home. She pulled her phone out of her pocket, unlocked it, then selected Alyx from her list of favorite contacts, a list that only included her husband, daughter, best friend (who was also her sister-in-law), and her mother.

Sarah punched the code to the alarm into the panel, holding her phone up to her ear with her shoulder as it rang. "Come on Alyx, pick up," she urged, the way people do, despite knowing the other person can't actually hear them. She always hated listening to the ominous ringing, waiting to see if the person on the other side would pick up, could pick up. It made her consider the plethora of things that could be preventing her daughter from answering. She didn't usually consider herself a pessimist, but when it came to her daughter, she *always* panicked. Maybe that was just what mothers did, or maybe, that was what having Alyx as a daughter did to her.

Sarah's breath hitched in her throat as the ringing stopped mid ring, the moment of silence that followed feeling like hours. "Hey mom, what's up?" Alyx answered.

At the sound of her daughter's voice, Sarah let the breath she was holding out. "Where are you?"

Alyx looked across to the dressing rooms, where Peter was trying on a dress shirt. "Peter and I had plans to study today, but dad left to work on his case, so he told me he didn't mind if I went to the park to study."

"And you didn't think to let me know?" Sarah scolded as

her concern turned into anger. "I don't think you know the panic I felt getting home and finding you weren't here."

"I'm sorry—"

"No, I don't think you get it. You *have* to let me know where you're going. Your a dad and I decided you were responsible enough to buy your own car, to have that freedom, but that doesn't mean that you can just go and do whatever whenever you want. We explicitly told you that you still need to get our permission before you just leave." Sarah chastised.

"I asked dad." Alyx argued. "He said it was fine."

"And how am I supposed to know where you are? What if something had happened? How would I know where to start looking for you? You have two parents."

Alyx sighed. "I'm fine. Nothing happened to me. And dad knows. That was the rule. One of you has to know. You were at the hospital. I have a hard time getting ahold of you on a good day, and it's *Saturday*."

Peter came out of the dressing room, concern crossing his face when he saw Alyx quietly arguing on the phone. *Are you in trouble,* he mouthed. Alyx shook her head.

"I don't get it. Dad's keeping me away from his case, and you're freaking out over the smallest things. You guys used to trust me." Alyx retorted.

"We still do." Sarah sighed. "But we're just concerned after last summer."

Alyx rolled her eyes. "Yeah, that makes sense. I proved I

can take care of myself, so now you're freaking out."

Sarah let out an exasperated sigh. Alyx wouldn't understand why last summer changed everything. Sarah hoped she wouldn't ever understand. She hoped that her fears would be wrong. But she'd seen the look her brother had when he had mentioned what had happened over the summer. Dylan was keeping something from her. Alyx wasn't safe anymore.

"What time will you be home?" Sarah asked.

"I'll be home soon. But then I'm going to the dance tonight, if that's allowed."

Sarah closed her eyes. "That's fine. Be safe."

"I will." Alyx promised, then hung up.

Sarah looked at her phone as the line went dead. All she wanted was for her daughter to have a chance grow old. She didn't want to bury another casket for one of her children.

21:20 PDT
Manteca, California
Church of Jesus Christ of Latter-day Saints

THE CULTURAL hall vibrated to the beat of the music being played. Groups of kids were gathered in circles, jumping up and down to the music while singing, rather loudly, along.

"Swing swing from the tangles oof... My heart is crushed by a former love"

Peter shook his head that a song from 2002 was still such a popular song at a church dance almost a decade later. Then again, there was a lot about this dance that wasn't like the school dances he'd been to. One of those things had been the fact that before he could go into the dance, he'd had to meet with Bishop Jones to get a dance card. That was an adventure he hadn't agreed to when Alyx invited him. Then again, Alyx agreeing to date him would involve all sorts of adventures she hadn't agreed to.

Alyx had been very good at explaining things for Peter, which had been nice. Things like *Bishop* was a title, and not Bishop Jone's first name. Peter had joked about that, and while it elicited a laugh from her, Alyx explained it all the same. She had also explained that as a Mormon, they tried to live a certain set of standards, and as part of that, tried to listen to uplifting and appropriate music that was free of vulgar language. (She had also explained that Mormon was a nickname, and technically it should have been *as a member of the Church of Jesus Christ of Latter-day Saints*). He smiled to himself listening to the song being played. They had to go back pretty far to find *uplifting and appropriate* music, but he couldn't find Alyx to tease her about that.

He checked the cultural hall again, trying to find Alyx in the mess of bodies. He hadn't been able to stop himself from noticing how well she thrived in this atmosphere. She seamlessly flitted in and out of the crowds, blending in when she wanted to, standing out if the situation called for it, then becoming invisible as she slipped through the crowd on whatever mission she'd set for herself.

He smiled when she reappeared next to him, eclair in hand, shamelessly singing along to the song. He shook his head. "I guess you wouldn't agree that this song is a bit old to be played still," he teased.

Alyx rolled her eyes. "Wait a few minutes. They'll play something older."

"Aren't there any new songs you guys listen to?" Peter teased.

Alyx smirked. "Only Taylor Swift."

Peter shook his head. "Seriously?"

"She's a popular artist at these dances." Alyx admitted. "If you wait long enough, they might play some One Direction."

Peter sighed. "Really?"

Alyx smirked as the song faded and the opening notes of the new song answered his question. Peter deflated as the overplayed lyrics of "What makes you beautiful" filled the hall.

Peter pointed at the eclair that Alyx was holding. "Where'd you get that? I will go anywhere for food if it means I get away from this music."

Alyx shrugged. "If you can keep up with me, I'll show you."

Peter grabbed Alyx' free hand, following her as she began slipping through the cracks between groups of dancing teenagers with an ease that made it obvious she'd had quite a bit of practice doing it. Even dragging Peter, she didn't seem to slow down.

Alyx led Peter out of the cultural hall to a crowded hallway. They eventually got up to a window with a countertop that was off of what looked like a full kitchen complete with ovens, microwaves, and a refrigerator. To his surprise, the countertop was covered in serving trays. There were the eclairs that Alyx had been eating, cups of trail mix, and nachos.

Peter glared at Alyx. "You've been holding out on me. You didn't tell me there was food."

"You didn't ask." She challenged.

Peter grabbed a thing of nachos, as well as an eclair. "Consider this my lifetime question as to whether or not there is food."

Alyx smirked. "Only if you ask in French."

Peter brought the eclair he'd been about to shove in his mouth down. "You've got to be kidding me. Not French again."

"What?" Alyx asked, feigning innocence. "I like French."

Peter smiled, concession imminent. He had a massive weakness for Alyx McLean, but he couldn't admit to her how big of a weakness it was.

"Est-ce que tu sais comment le dit?" She asked.

He shook his head. "You are one stubborn girl."

"Merci." She replied.

"Est-ce qu'il vais être des nourrissants?" Peter asked, giving in. Alyx smiled content, turning to return to the dance. "Hey, would you mind if we sit out here a second?"

Alyx shook her head, leading him up the hall a ways. Someone had cracked open a door, letting the cool air inside. Peter hadn't even realized how warm the building had gotten with the number of people inside dancing, until he felt the almost frigid air. A group of kids came back in through the door, their break in the cold over. Alyx led Peter out the door, jumping up so she was sitting on the railing that lined the handicap ramp outside.

"My feet were killing me." She admitted.

Peter couldn't help but notice how regal she looked, even sitting on a railing. She had crossed her ankles, keeping her legs together so her knee length skirt didn't open to reveal anything. She was poised, and made the balance seem effortless.

"I'm glad you came tonight." Alyx told him. "You made the dance bearable even though Thane and Carlie aren't here."

"Of course." Peter replied between bites of his nachos. "So who were you fighting with on the phone earlier?"

Alyx rolled her eyes. "My mom. Since I got back from London, both of my parents have been acting weird. They're being *hyper* protective, and it's getting annoying."

"Can you blame them?" Peter asked. He hurriedly finished chewing as he realized what he'd said. "I mean, aren't you keeping secrets from them." He pointed between him and Alyx.

Alyx shrugged. "I hope you realize their behavior will mean it's going to be a lot harder to sneak out on dates with you."

Peter was silent, eating his nachos. Alyx watched him carefully. She got the feeling that he knew more than he should have. The way he had sided with her parents made it seem like he *knew* what she had done in London. It made it seem like he *knew* she had saved Lynn. But how could he?

Peter finished his nachos. "The song should be over. Should we go back inside?"

Alyx nodded, sliding off the railing with a grace similar to the one that had placed her on the railing in the first place. She landed perfectly, despite the spike heels strapped to her feet. Even with the added noise of her heels, she was almost silent as she led Peter back into the cultural hall. With a slow song playing, Peter did the only thing he could think of: he put his hand out to Alyx, inviting her to dance.

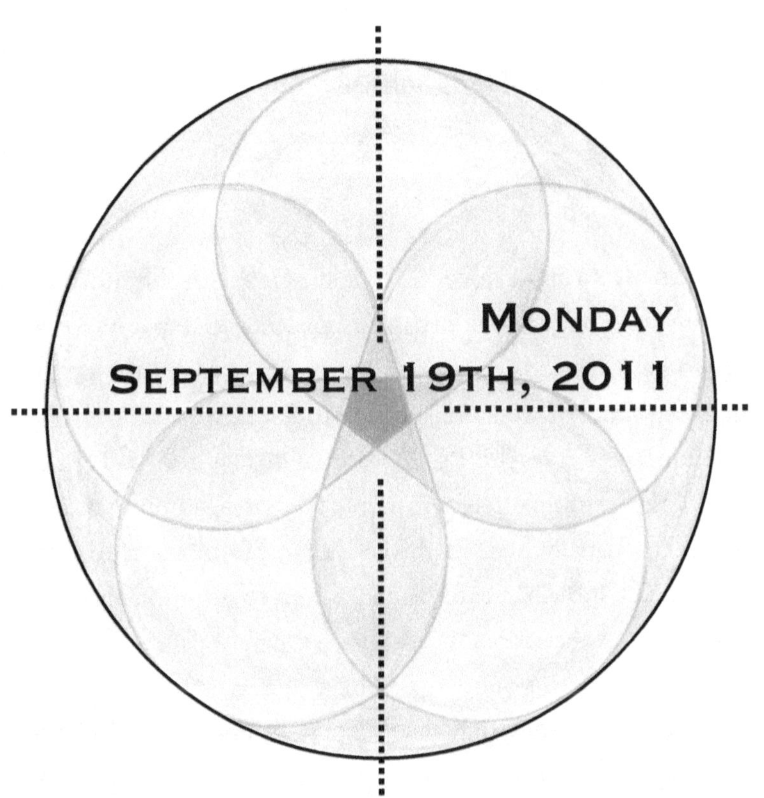

MONDAY
SEPTEMBER 19TH, 2011

5:25 PDT
Tracy, California
John C. Kimball High School

CAMERON MCKAY loved Mountain House in the mornings, before everyone was in a rush to start their day, parents rushing to get their kids to one of the K-8 schools in the community on time, professionals trying to get down to the freeway hoping traffic into the Bay Area wouldn't be too bad. In the morning, he didn't feel the urgency that a commuter town like theirs usually had. In the morning, Mountain House was just a quiet suburb, a safe place for him to go on his morning run.

McKay's feet pounded on the concrete sidewalk in front of the town homes that lined the Wicklund side of Central Parkway. The cords of his Apple earbuds hung down from his ears before sweeping back up and connecting to the phone that was snuggly fit into a case on his armband, but there wasn't any music coming through the tiny speakers housed in the white shell in his ear. He'd learned early on the importance of being aware of one's surroundings, even if his quiet suburb gave him the sense of security.

Training had taught him that a spy would never truly be safe, even if they were at home, and not abroad on a mission.

No, his headphones served another purpose. Two of them, actually. It helped him blend in, look like just another runner out for a morning run in the beautifully crisp air that only a Californian town like Tracy and its suburb Mountain House could have. It also let him easily take, or make, phone calls. Usually McKay didn't use them for that purpose, but The Generation was in crisis. He had to be ready at a moment's notice.

McKay ran through the crosswalk at the intersection where Heritage Drive crossed Central Parkway. As he ran across the street, he noticed another runner leaving the neighborhood, and begin pacing just a few yards behind him.

Nothing made him more uneasy than another runner running just behind him.

He casually checked the street, to see if it was clear for him to cross, catching another runner pacing with him on the other side of the street in his peripheral vision. He swore under his breath. His suspicions about the runner behind him increased, seeing there was another one of them preventing him from crossing the street to get away. He kicked up his pace just a little bit, hoping they would fall back because they weren't really following him, but the distance between himself and the other runners stayed the same.

The next intersection felt like it came slower than it had

before, despite his increased pace. He needed more options, more streets to turn onto, more bushes to run through, all the things that would help him get away, but that he was currently lacking.

He breathed a sigh of relief when he saw Legacy Drive approaching at last. He leaned to the right, guiding his legs with his upper body so he could go around the corner without losing any speed. He didn't see the car and the men standing next to it until he'd already swung around the corner, The runner that had been on the other side of the street was crossing Central, falling into step with the runner that was behind him.

He'd been boxed in. If there was anything a spy hated, it was being boxed in.

McKay took the first exit he saw, and hung another right down the alley that allowed access to the garages of the homes whose front doors faced Central. He held down the button on his head phones, proceeding to tell Siri to call Peter —his last phone call.

ALYX TURNED to look at her dad as he ran past her down the stairs. He had his suit jacket over his arm, so she could see his holster clearly, with service weapon in place. He looked up from his phone for a moment, pausing to kiss her on the head. She could see his badge on his belt, prominently displayed. Her dad was never up and dressed before her in the morning. Usually, he was meandering downstairs about the time was she leaving for seminary. But she could tell where he was headed. His nose was buried in his phone. Someone else had been kidnapped. He had a crime scene to get to.

Usually, Alyx would be able to ask her dad for details, but he wasn't sharing anything with her. Not recently. As he hit the bottom of the stairs, his phone started ringing, which he quickly answered.

"McLean." He answered. After a pause he continued talking, addressing a question the person on the other side asked.

"Yeah, I was just going over the file. Do me a favor. I want to see if we can get his phone records. We know the connection between the other two, so we need to find a connection between him and the others."

Just like that, Alyx knew she was right.

She desperately wanted a chance to glance at the file her dad had been reading on his phone. She followed her dad down the hall to the kitchen, walking past him as she headed to the fridge to grab a yogurt. Her dad set his phone down on the table as he slipped his computer into his brief case. The opportunity she was looking for.

"You heading out?" She asked him.

Neil nodded. "Got called in."

Alyx crossed the kitchen, setting her yogurt down on the table as she wrapped her arms around her dad, giving her an opportunity to glance at his phone as she did. "Have a good day." She said, before grabbing her yogurt.

Neil kissed her forehead again. "Be safe kiddo." He told her. He grabbed his bag and car keys, before picking his phone up. "I love you sweetheart."

"I love you too." She replied as he left the kitchen. She stuck a spoonful of yogurt in her mouth, getting a smile as she did.

Cameron McKay was the newest victim. Now she just had to figure out who he was, and how he was connected to Adison and Nathan.

ALYX TAPPED on her steering wheel as the phone rang, waiting to connect on the other end. It was only 3:30pm in London, so Stephan had little excuse not to pick-up. It wasn't meal time, and if he was asleep, he was sleeping on the job.

"It's about time." Alyx snapped when the line finally connected. She paused as she heard his heavy breathing on the other side. "What are you doing, Cross?" She asked. "Training for a marathon?"

"Now's not really a good time." Stephan complained. "I just had to chase yet another paparazzo off the premises."

"Didn't you get a promotion out of my work last summer? Head of security or some cushy job like that? What are *you* doing chasing the paparazzi away from Feilds' Palace?"

"I happen to be on holiday." Stephan corrected. "Part of the perks of the promotion."

Alyx smiled. "Your holiday wouldn't happen to be in Moscow would it?"

Stephan sighed, almost returned to normal breathing. "Should I even ask how you know?"

"Well, I'm guessing you wouldn't be chasing a paparazzo off the premises of a hotel if you were on holiday by yourself. But if you were visiting Lyshiria, who told me you two are dating, you probably would."

"What do you want?" Stephan demanded, not even acknowledging that Alyx was correct.

"Who says I want something?" Alyx snarked. "Maybe I just wanted to call and annoy you."

"Alyx." Stephan scolded. "What do you want?"

Alyx sighed. "Can you by chance get me the phone records for someone? His name is Cameron McKay, born 5 March 1992, and he lives in Mountain House, California."

"No." Stephan said. "Absolutely not."

"You owe me." Alyx argued.

"How do you figure that?"

"Cushy new job, time off to see your girlfriend. You got credit for my genius." Alyx listed.

"Are you going to tell me why you need his phone records?" Stephan asked.

Alyx was quiet for a second, contemplating what she would tell him. "He was kidnapped this morning. He's the third one kidnapped here in Tracy, and I have reason to believe Hall is involved. I'm still peeved he got away last summer. If I find the boys, I find Hall, and I can have a conversation with him."

Stephen huffed. "I don't think going after the man that kidnapped Lynn is very wise."

"Technically, I'm going after the man that convinced Lynn to come with him, and let Jackson kidnap Lynn from him." Alyx reasoned. "Besides, he's my uncle. And clearly I'm better than he is. Otherwise we wouldn't have been able to find Lynn."

Stephan sighed. "If I do this one favor, we're even. I didn't try to take the credit. Your uncle gave it to me to try and keep your anonymity." Stephan bargained.

"That sounds fair." Alyx conceded. She smiled out her window as she saw Peter pulling into the parking spot next to her. "If you could just send them to me when you get them, I'll pretend I never left Feilds Palace."

"What am I going to do with you when you move to London to go to school?" Stephan complained.

"I don't know." Alyx teased. "You might have to quit. I gotta go, but if you would send it to me as soon as you can, I might not make your life unbearable when I come back next summer."

She hung up before Stephan could protest. While Oxford had a course she thought would be very interesting for her to study, she would be lying if she didn't consider it a major plus that studying at Oxford would give her more time to annoy Stephan Cross, the one man who was as close to a brother to her as she had ever known. As a responsible younger sister, it was her job to annoy him more than anyone else could.

Alyx smiled at Peter as she climbed out of her car. "Good morning."

"Good morning." Peter replied. "Who were you calling?"

"A friend from London." Alyx told him. "The best time to call is usually in the morning."

Peter nodded. "And when is the best time to call me?" He teased.

"Let me think about that..." Alyx said, tapping her chin. "Why would I call, when it is much more fun to talk to you in person."

Peter beamed at Alyx, his eyes twinkling. "I like that response." He admitted. "Dare I say it was a very *diplomatic* reply. Just like your grandmother."

Alyx smiled. "No one has compared me to her in a long time." She found herself stepping in closer to him. "You know, she is my name sake. At least one of them."

"I did. Emily told me, remember?"

"She did, didn't she. Alyxandrie Madelyn McLean after Alyxandrie Devreaux Hall. My middle name comes from my paternal grandmother." Alyx told him. She let out a deep breath. "I've never told anyone my full name before. Everyone just knows me as Alyx."

Peter grabbed Alyx' hand. "I feel honored you're telling me." He looked down. He too was named after someone. His parents had decided he deserved not just one, but both of their last names. The difference between him and Alyx was that she was named after someone she revered and looked up to. Peter wished he didn't have the name he did, because he had to share it with the two people he least wanted to be like. "My parents decided I deserved to be their legacy, so they gave me both of their last names." He told Alyx. He looked up into her eyes. "Peter Stevens Carlyle."

Alyx bit her lip. "You don't talk about your parents much." She observed. "I'm sorry."

Peter smiled. Despite only telling her about his parents once, she somehow knew that he felt his name was a curse. For the first time, he felt his name really didn't matter. It didn't matter that his parents only viewed him as their legacy. Alyx saw him as something more. She liked him for who he was, not who his parents were. She saw his worth beyond his heritage.

Peter took a deep breath. The school had faded away. All he could see was the girl standing in front of him, apologizing for something she had no control over because she felt his pain.

"I love you." He said before he even realized he thought it.

Alyx smiled, her heart melting as Peter said those three simple words. He loved her. "Je t'aime aussi." She whispered.

Peter smiled. It wasn't the first time she'd said *je t'aime*, but it was the first time that he knew she meant it as *I love you* not *I like you*. It was amazing how big of a difference one small word made. *Aussi. Too.* She loved him *too*.

Peter let go of her hand, running his thumb down her

cheek. He leaned down searching her eyes as he got closer, hoping he would see her reciprocate. Alyx stood on her toes, meeting Peter halfway, their lips meeting softly, their eyes closed. For just that brief second, neither of them cared what any of their classmates saw.

Alyx slowly returned to her heels, biting her lip as she did, a smile on her lips that broke through anyway. "I better head inside."

"Yeah." Peter replied. "I kind of stole your entire Saturday. You probably have homework."

Alyx shook her head. "I made myself do it before our date." She told him. "You're a good influence on me."

Peter smiled. "And here I could have sworn you told me I was a bad influence."

"I lied." She admitted. She took a deep breath, pulling herself away from Peter and his magnetism, pulling her backpack from her car. "I'll see you tonight at 7:30?" She asked.

Peter nodded. "Of course."

Alyx smiled, walking away. He couldn't help but watch as she did, a part him wanting to chase after her and give her another kiss. When she turned and looked back at him, he could only guess she was thinking the same thing.

If Peter had one thing, though, it was control. *Espions*. He mouthed. She smiled, turning back around.

THANE LOOKED up as Alyx sat down at the table in the middle of the cafeteria that their friends typically sat at before school. He glanced at his watch. Alyx had left Seminary before he had, and somehow he had beat her to school by more than twenty minutes. He glanced towards the doors as they opened, and suddenly it made sense. Peter walked towards his group of friends with a sly smile on his face. He'd heard at church the day before that Alyx had brought a date to the dance on Saturday. He wouldn't have guessed it would be Peter.

"Traffic must have been horrible." He commented as Alyx sat down.

"Nope. I was just sitting in my car doing homework." Alyx replied. "I knew as soon as I came in here, you guys would do everything you could to distract me."

Savannah shrugged. "If you don't want me to tell you that a certain football player just walked in, and he looks…"

Savannah turned to Carlie. "I just can't. How would you describe how he looks today?"

Alyx bit the inside of her lip, turning red as she looked over at Peter and his group of friends. He looked amazing.

Thane rolled his eyes as Carlie and Savannah continued to debate how they would describe Peter's appearance. "So how was your weekend?" He asked Alyx. "Meet anyone fun at the dance?"

Alyx nodded. "There was this guy there. Kinda cute." She smirked at Thane. "There were lots of cute girls there too. Then again, none of them were Savannah."

She might not have realized it, but she had certainly had the training of a spy, especially with her ability to turn things back around onto others, like the way she'd effortlessly turned his attempt to figure out if Peter was the guy from the dance into a dig at him.

"Hey, you and Chelsi should come over after the two of us girls get done at tennis." Alyx told Thane. Chelsi looked up from the book she was reading at the mention of her name.

"Oh no, he's leaving." Savannah complained, the subject of their still ongoing debate frantically grabbing his backpack and giving his apologies to his friends as he left the cafeteria. "What are we going to do to distract Alyx now?"

"You guys weren't really doing much to distract me before." Alyx snarked. Thane got up from the table, grabbing his stuff. "Where are *you* going?" Alyx asked.

Thane pointed towards the door. "I just remembered that

Ms. Christensen told us to bring a book to read in class today because she was going to give us some time to read. I need to go to the library to find one."

Carlie rolled her eyes. "Seriously? I even texted you this morning and you said you had one."

Thane shrugged. "I left it on my bed."

Carlie shook her head, but Thane walked out the door all the same. "What are we supposed to do with him?" Carlie asked Alyx, but she was too distracted watching Thane push his way out the door after Peter. She stared out the door as she tried to come up with a reason why Thane might know Peter. They could have had a class together.

But then she had to come up with a good reason why he hadn't told any of them. For that, there was only one good answer: Peter was a spy. Thane wouldn't tell any of his friends that he knew the boy that made his way into almost all of their conversations if he was part of the same training group Thane and Chelsi were part of.

8:22 PDT
Tracy, California
John C. Kimball High School

PETER WAS buried in his phone as Thane walked up. "Hey Peter, can I talk to you for a second?"

"Now's not really a good time." He replied distracted. "Cameron was kidnapped this morning on his run, and I missed his phone call because I was too busy sleeping."

Thane took a deep breath. "I think you'll want to take a second to listen to what I have to say then."

Peter looked up from his phone. "What's your lead?"

Thane shook his head. "Not mine," he admitted. "Chelsi's. She believes our dad is the one who kidnapped Adison and Nathan, so reason states he probably was the one that kidnapped Cameron too."

Peter stared at Thane for a second. "She's sure?"

Thane nodded. "I mean it makes sense. He's never been in town this long. It's not a vacation. He must be working." Thane paused. He needed to add something else to make sure Peter believed him. "She remembers showing my dad how to find people on Twitter. Did Adison post anything on there that might have compromised him?" Thane replied.

"That'd be a good thing to check." Peter admitted. "Thank you for letting me know. I'll look into it."

"If Chelsi is right, there is only one thing my dad would want by going after the Generation." Thane added.

The bell rang, but Peter didn't move toward his class. He glanced around as the bell awakened the rest of the students, causing them to scatter like a hive of ants when their hill was disturbed. "The files." Peter guessed. "What's in them he might want?"

"The name of the organization after Alyx. I'm pretty sure they identified a few of them before they closed the file and hid it on our servers." Thane told him. "After last summer, he's trying to get as much information together as he can to make sure he's prepared for when they come after her." Thane started walking off, heading towards his class.

Peter couldn't focus on anything as he walked to class. Thane had told him before that Alyx was a target. He suspected the BOLO was proof of that. But the new information Thane had dumped on him, added to the guilt of not answering Cameron's call, and the feelings his conversation with Alyx had revealed was almost too much. Cameron didn't have access to the Generation files. Neither did Nathan. Or Adison. Peter did. And giving Hall access to the files he needed might protect Alyx.

LYSHIRIA SLID her arms over Stephan's shoulders, looking over him to see what he had up on his laptop. Stephan moved his head, looking at Lyshiria as she read the phone records he had pulled up. He kissed her cheek, eliciting a smile from her.

"What are you working on?" She asked. "I thought you had handed everything over to Harris while you away."

Stephan sighed. "Alyx called. This is for her."

Lyshiria smirked. "You know, if you hadn't told me about your past, I might be concerned."

"I know. That's why you know everything. And that's why you're the only one." Stephan admitted.

Lyshiria sat down next to him. "Do you want help?"

Stephan smiled. "I would love your help. All she asked me for were these records, but I want to make sure there's nothing there that might endanger her if I give them to her."

Lyshiria pulled her laptop down the table from where she usually left it, opening it. "If you give me some phone numbers to run down, I'll find out who owns them."

Stephan moved his computer over so it was in between he and Lyshiria. He couldn't help but watch as she began working, looking up the American numbers she'd copied. She may have been an heiress, but she was also the daughter of a Russian spy, and she took after her mom just as much as she took after her father. Maybe he hadn't trusted her when she, Alyx, and himself were searching Europe for Lynn, but Alyx had. It had taken him a little to see what Alyx had seen, but now that he did, he trusted her with his life. But even more than that, he trusted her with Alyx' life.

Stephan pulled his computer back to him, starting to search the numbers Lyshiria hadn't taken. He decided to start with Cameron's last phone call.

As soon as he hit search, and he got the name of the owner of the phone, he froze, a flashback to when he was ten taking over. He took deep breaths. An explosion rocked the house. Flames licked the walls of the basement bunker he was in protecting it from the explosion that leveled the house. He banged on the door, desperate to get out. His sisters were with him. When the door opened, he didn't expect to recognize the face of the enemy. But he did. A woman opened the door: Elisabeth Stevens—Peter Carlyle's mother.

While she had saved him that day, carrying him out of that prison as he passed out from smoke inhalation, he knew that she was Circle of Fifths. There was no other explanation for how she knew where to find him. He knew she was likely forced to participate, with the way she had shown compassion towards a child, but that didn't mean her son wasn't the pawn that kept her loyal. The only way that pawn would still work, was if as he entered adulthood, he too was Circle of Fifths.

When he woke up, he discovered he had lost his sisters. He couldn't save them. That was when he joined the MI:6 orphans. He couldn't lose anyone else to the Circle of Fifths. Especially not Alyx.

Stephan pulled out his phone, calling Lynn, hoping beyond hope that Peter Carlyle wasn't the young man that she had sent the information on Alyx to. If she had, they had literally given the Circle of Fifths what they wanted: information to recruit Alyx.

ALYX ALMOST couldn't wait until her sixth period let out. The second she stepped out of AP US History, she had her phone out, checking her email for the phone records Stephan was supposed to get for her. When she didn't see it, she called him. Sure, it was after ten his time, but she needed those records.

"I was about to send them to you." Stephan answered. "I knew you were at school, and I wanted to make sure you weren't getting in deeper than you could handle."

"What did you find?" Alyx asked.

"He didn't call Hall." Stephan told her.

"Well since Hall kidnapped him, I would hope not. I was hoping I might find a connection between him and the other boys kidnapped." Alyx paused. "Did any of his calls go to someone with the last name Levy?"

"No." Stephan told her. "But his last phone call did."

"You pulled the records for his last phone call?" Alyx

asked. "And why would you have done that?"

"Lynn sent him information about last summer. He's part of a training group. The CIA put a BOLO out for you, and he wanted proof." Stephan admitted.

"And you didn't tell me? Really?" Alyx asked.

Stephan sighed exasperated. "Yeah, because that was totally a conversation I wanted to have with you."

"Who was it?" Alyx asked.

"Some guy named Peter Carlyle."

Alyx stopped walking, frozen as the school moved toward the parking lot. "You're sure."

"Positive." Stephan told her. "Why? Do you know him?"

"I thought I did. Can you email them to me?" Alyx asked.

"Yeah." Stephan told her. "And Alyx,"

"Be careful, I know."

"No. I'm sorry." Stephan said.

Alyx took a deep breath. "Thank you." Her voice was quiet, almost quiet enough Stephan didn't hear her. But he did, and it made him hate Peter Carlyle all that much more.

Alyx hung up the phone, checking her email, despite knowing what it would say. Sure enough, Peter's number was the last one Cameron had called. And when she opened Peter's records, besides her number popping up from time to time in his texts, it was full of nothing but phone calls. Cameron made quite a few appearances, as well as Thane, and Chelsi. His phone activity increased dramatically since Adison had been kidnapped. Whatever was happening, Peter was

258

right in the middle of it.

It shouldn't have surprised her that he was a spy. She'd made up a story in her head about it. And he never had told her he wasn't when she'd let that slip. He'd only asked who had told her. But it was outlandish, and she thought there was no way it was possible.

Then again, she was right about almost everyone else, so she shouldn't have second guessed herself.

There was also the fact that he had suggested that they be spies together.

Even searching for ways that he had lied led her to realize that about most things, he had been surprisingly candid. About everything but the fact that he had asked her cousin for the MI:6 file on what she'd done the summer before. He hadn't told her that the CIA was looking for, and she couldn't help but wonder if that was the real reason he'd suggested they be spies together. If she stayed under the radar, the other spies couldn't exactly turn her in.

And still, she felt betrayed. Maybe it was just a reason to push him away before she left for Oxford, and they both got hurt. But it did hurt, knowing he hadn't told her everything. It hurt her to know that she should push him away.

It hurt to think that maybe he had been lying when he said he loved her. He was a spy, trying to recruit her. Or maybe turn her in. How could he love her?

10:57 PDT
Tracy, California
John C. Kimball High School

NEIL POURED over the phone records that he'd had his agents pull. He may have known who was kidnapping the Generation members, but his bosses had told him to investigate as if he didn't. That meant trying to find connections and identifying the next target to surveil them and catch the guilty party. He had to give it to his brother-in-law. He sure knew how to cover his tracks. That was why identifying the next target was all he had left. None of the crime scenes had given him anything useful to identify the kidnappers.

Plus, if he could connect the Generation members, so could Hall, and that meant they didn't do a very good job of isolating themselves from each other, so if one of them were compromised, they all were.

When he had been to Oakhurst Lodge, where Nathan had last been seen, he'd found a burner phone on the bed with one outgoing phone call. He hadn't expected that the same phone number would appear in Cameron's outgoing calls. He definitely didn't expect it to be the last phone call both of them made. But it was. If he found that number, and this was a regular case, he would wonder if the people kidnapped were into something, and he would bring in the owner of that phone number to ask them what.

He already knew why they were being kidnapped, so his want to find the owner of that phone number meant he could predict either who was next, or who Hall would *eventually* kidnap.

Neil looked up who the number belonged to, not quite believing what he saw. *Peter Carlyle.* All he could do is hope that Carlyle wasn't the same Peter his daughter was studying French with. If it was, he had significantly more problems than his daughter liking a cute boy.

But he had a way to check. He knew that Alyx had been texting Peter, so he signed into their cell phone provider, pulling up the usage for Alyx' phone number, searching her texts for the same number that he'd seen on the other two phone records. Sure enough, it was there.

His daughter was spending time with a spy, and one that when he'd left the agency, they weren't sure if they could trust.

19:28 PDT
Tracy, California
McLean Home

PETER WALKED up the driveway of the McLean's house to-wards the front door, his backpack slung over one shoulder, with his hands shoved in his front pockets. He'd been a little disappointed when he'd left practice and Alyx hadn't been waiting for him. He knew it wasn't a promise between the two of them, and it was probably because she was giving Chelsi a ride home again, but the disappointment was still there.

Then there was the little voice in the back of his mind telling him Alyx had left because he'd freaked her out this morning when he said *I love you*. It had freaked himself out a bit when those words left his mouth, but now that he'd said it, he knew it was true. He knocked on the front door, anxiously waiting for it to open, hoping it would.

He'd gone soft. He realized. *That was one way to piss his parents off.*

Peter smiled as the door opened, and he came face to face with Special Agent McLean.

"Hey Peter! Is Alyx expecting you?" He asked.

Peter shrugged his backpack a little higher onto his shoulder, drawing attention to it. "I hope so. She said I could come over and study tonight. Is she not home?"

Neil turned as Alyx came running down the stairs in a pair of sweatpants and a semi-fitted short sleeve shirt, with her French book tucked under her arm to protect it from her still dripping hair. As she turned to bounce down the last few stairs, Peter could clearly make out the boastful *Oxford* on the front.

"I guess she snuck in." Neil commented.

"You know, it's not hard with how loud you have the TV. I could hear the news upstairs in the shower." She teased her dad.

Neil stuck his tongue out at his daughter. "That's fine. Make fun. I'll just remember that when you need help with something. No hug or kiss when you got home, *and* you made fun of me."

Alyx stood on her toes, gaining the extra couple of inches needed to giver her dad a quick peck on the cheek. She turned to Peter. "I was thinking we could study out back tonight. That way the updates on the Primaries don't distract us."

Peter smiled. "Sounds great."

Neil stepped out of the way, letting Peter in the door. "Actually, I was hoping I could steal Peter for a moment."

Alyx nodded, disappearing down the hallway. As soon as

she saw Peter's number on the phone records, she knew her dad would want to talk to Peter. And she was mad enough at both of them that she figured she'd let them.

Peter followed Neil back into the house, thankful that he was taking him back into the living quarters he'd been in before, and not the home office that Alyx mentioned her dad kept. He couldn't help but notice that despite being home for a while, Neil still had on his badge and gun. He was still on duty. That meant he was about the be questioned, not about his intentions with Alyx, but his involvement with the kidnappings.

When they walked down the hallway between the couch and the kitchen island, Neil picked up the TV remote, muting the TV. He gestured for Peter to sit down at the kitchen table. Peter gingerly sat down in the chair closest to the hallway. Neil remained standing, leaning on the chair at the head of the table.

"As I'm sure you know by now, I am the FBI agent assigned to find the missing teenagers from here in Tracy." Neil started.

"You want to know why Cameron called me this morning." Peter guessed.

Neil nodded.

"I'm afraid I don't know." Peter admitted, "I missed his phone call."

"How do you know Cameron?" Neil asked.

Peter paused. He may have been in the McLean's kitchen,

instead of an interrogation room, but Peter knew this was an interrogation nonetheless. Special Agent McLean was being very gentle because Peter was a friend of his daughter, but he wouldn't fall victim to thinking that if he didn't adequately answer McLean's questions, he wouldn't drag him into an interrogation room.

"Cameron and I were on the football team together at West High my freshman year." Peter answered.

He suspected that wouldn't be enough to satisfy McLean, but he had to carefully transverse the truth in such a way that would give McLean a satisfying answer, but omitted any mention of espionage, the CIA, or the Promising Generation. That was going to be in itself pretty hard, as the different members of their group were, of necessity, pretty disconnected socially. Sure, he played football with Jacob, and had played football with Cameron, but trying to explain how he knew Thane, or Nathan, or any of the other members was just about impossible without mentioning the Generation. Then again, he could use their cover—Pacific Gold Tutoring.

"We got pretty close when we both started tutoring with Pacific Gold Tutoring."

McLean placed a phone on the table. "I found this phone in the last location Nathan Levy was seen. It made one phone call: you."

"Nathan directs the tutors. He was going out of town and wanted me to make sure the tutors knew what they doing while he was gone." Peter lied. He hoped that it sounded like he was telling the truth, not that he had lies ready, as if he knew what McLean was going to ask him.

"Was Adison one of the tutors?" McLean asked.

"Yes."

McLean nodded. "So the connection between all of the kidnapped young men is that they are all tutors at Pacific Gold. Do you have a list of all the tutors? I would like to make sure no one else gets kidnapped."

Peter shook his head. "Nathan was the only one with that list."

"Thank you for your help." McLean said, walking toward the living room.

"Of course, sir." Peter replied.

"Oh Peter, before you go study with Alyx I have one more question." McLean commented. "What subjects are you a tutor for?"

Peter held his breath. He knew what McLean was doing. Even if this was an interview more than an interrogation, he was proving just how skilled he was at this. If Peter was lying about being a tutor, he wouldn't have an answer ready for what he tutored. The difference was Peter was a spy in training. Pacific Gold Tutoring was a cover, so naturally, Peter had an answer prepared. He had to, for situations just like this. "Math. I tutor most of my clients in the Algebras, both One and Two, but a couple of them I tutor in Pre Calculus, and even Calculus." Peter told him.

"So you're good at math." McLean commented.

Peter smiled. "Not as good as your daughter. She made me work hard to beat her in Algebra II." He admitted.

McLean nodded. "She has that affect on people." He turned the volume on the TV back on.

Peter slid out the back door, letting out a sigh of relief. Special Agent McLean seemed to buy his story. He smiled as he looked around the back yard, finding Alyx sitting on a picnic blanket spread out under the tree in the Northwest corner of the yard. He walked over, setting his backpack on the corner of the blanket. "When I didn't see you after practice, I was concerned I'd done something wrong." He admitted.

"Français." Alyx replied.

"Come on." Peter complained. "I thought we were past that."

"Je t'ai entendu dire à mon père que tu étais venu ici pour étudier, alors je te demande que nous parlons français." Alyx replied, turning her attention to her textbook.

Peter's countenance fell. "So you are mad at me." He sighed when she responded with silence. "If this is about this morning, and your concerns about Oxford... Just because you're leaving to school doesn't mean we can't try long distance." He paused. "Who knows. Maybe I'll apply to Oxford. It's not like I know where I want to go yet."

Alyx looked up at Peter. Her eyes still carried the anger they'd had moments before, but they seemed to hold surprise as well. She looked away. "Why was my dad interrogating you?"

Peter sighed. Maybe it wasn't what he wanted to be talking to Alyx about, but at least she was talking to him. "I work with two of the young men who have been kidnapped."

"You never did tell me where you worked." Alyx commented.

Peter watched Alyx as she seemingly read out of the textbook. She almost sounded like her dad, except a lot less blunt. She was looking for information without seeming like she was—she sounded like he had when they'd first started studying together. He wondered how much she knew. He knew she was smart. She was certain to have figured out at least something about the case. She had even guessed at one point that he was a spy, even if she had corrected herself, and pretended like she hadn't.

"Pacific Gold Tutoring." Peter answered.

"Cool." She said quietly. She almost sounded disappointed. With her eyes locked on the textbook, Peter decided to just join her in studying. If she didn't feel like having an actual conversation with him, maybe he could coax a conversation out of her in French in the name of studying.

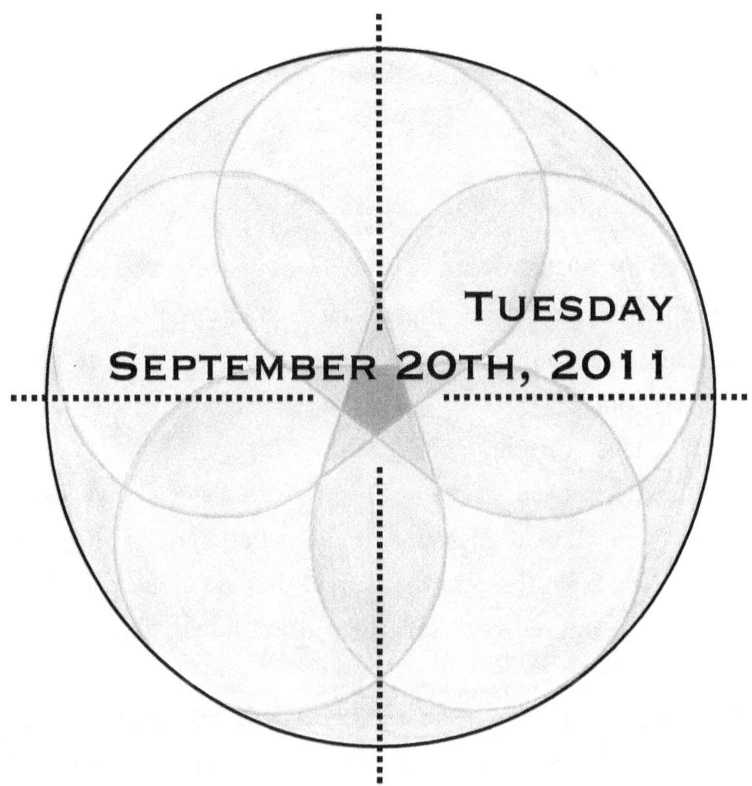

TUESDAY
SEPTEMBER 20TH, 2011

3:08 PDT
McLean, Virginia
William and Madelyn McLean House

DIRECTOR MCLEAN rolled away from his wife, checking the caller ID on the ringing phone. He bolted upright, any remnant of sleep clinging to his eyes suddenly gone as he answered the phone.

"Neil? Is everything ok? Is Alyx—"

"Alyx has been studying French with Peter Carlyle. The same Peter Carlyle that was under investigation when we pulled Alyx from the program, afraid that the Generation had been compromised, and now he's in my house, flirting with my daughter."

Director McLean took a deep breath. "So Alyx is fine? You didn't call me after three in the morning to tell me they'd gotten her."

"Yes dad, your granddaughter is alive. For now. But she's gotten awfully close to Carlyle, who is part of the Promising Generation, and you authorized a CIA training mission where Hall kidnaps members of the Promising Generation. Thank you for pulling me from actual cases by the way. It's already been hell trying to keep her away from this case, but guaranteed, if Hall kidnaps Carlyle, she's going to charge straight into danger. Which brings me back to why you didn't tell me Carlyle had been cleared."

Director McLean sighed. "I'm the director of the CIA. I do lots of things that I don't tell you about. I do lots of things that are classified, that I *can't* tell you about. You gave up the right to be read in on agency secrets when you traded your clearance for a badge at the FBI."

"Dad, that's not fair and you know it." Neil argued. "You're the one that advised me to take Alyx and hide her. You're the one who told me to walk away from the CIA to protect my daughter. You promised me that you would advise me of anything pertinent to my daughter's safety."

"How was I supposed to know that Carlyle's status with the Generation was pertinent to Alyx? It wasn't like you kept me advised of where you were living, or who she was dating. Besides, the Generation has been there for ten years, and it's only now become a problem, so obviously it wasn't pertinent until now. Maybe you shouldn't have let your guard down. You could have told him to get away from your daughter. Why didn't you?"

"Because I didn't know that the young man studying French with my daughter at my dinner table had the last name of Carlyle. I didn't think it was a possibility because the Generation was supposed to be attending Feilds' Prep in Chino

Hills." Neil replied.

"You don't do backgrounds on all the boys Alyx brings home?" The director criticized. "You've definitely let your guard down."

"Dad—"

"You and Sarah need to come in." The Director said quickly. He waited silently as he heard his son exhale on the other side of the phone. "Neil…"

"Dad, we don't work for you anymore. We can't just clear our schedules and fly to DC at a moment's notice. You especially can't call us in just because you don't like the way I'm vetting my daughters friends."

"I know." The director spoke softly, his tone telling his son that what he was saying was serious. "I kept yours and Sarah's credentials active in case things got bad enough I needed to recall you." McLean paused to let what he was saying sink in for a second. "The only reason I haven't done it sooner is that McLean stubbornness." He chuckled, trying to lighten the mood, but his heart wasn't in it. "I'm recalling you now."

Neil let another shaky breath out. "That's why your first thought was that something had happened to Alyx."

"You called me at three in the morning. What other possible reason would you have to call me so early? Besides, apparently to yell at me for doing my job."

"How bad is it?" Neil asked quietly.

"Dylan is working on a Hail Mary, but they've been

looking for her since her birthday. If I'm being honest, they might find her any day now."

"If that's the case, Sarah and I can't exactly leave her so we can come in." Neil countered.

"How secure is your house?" McLean asked.

"Not as secure as any of the safe houses, but the Halls know how to secure a house." Neil replied.

"If Alyx stays in the house she should be safe." Director McLean said it more as a statement than a question. He had worked with the Halls for years, and if you needed to hide an asset, you threw a bag over their head and gave them to a Hall. Their safe houses were impossible to find, and impenetrable once you finally got there. If his daughter-in-law had used even a fraction of the security mechanisms that her family used for their safe houses, it wasn't a question; Alyx would be safe inside that house.

Neil laughed. "Dad, Alyx is definitely her mother's daughter. It's like someone combined Ally and Sarah into one person, then thought it would be a good idea to add my curiosity, drive, and the McLean stubbornness." He took a deep breath. "There is no way she's staying in the house unless we physically restrain her, and while that option is tempting, it's also frowned upon. Plus there's the fact that I couldn't even guarantee that option would work." Neil explained. "She is, after all, her mother's daughter."

Director McLean laughed. "Sounds like you're starting to understand why I was always so frustrated with you three."

"She hasn't even had training, and she's causing me more trouble than we ever gave you." Neil sighed.

"Believe it or not, I actually believe that training made you guys better behaved, not worse." McLean suggested. "If we were to train Alyx it might improve her behavior, and make it so she's prepared for the coming attacks."

Neil sighed. Years of hiding his daughter, years of hiding *his life* from her, and now his father was suggesting they'd hurt her by hiding her. Unfortunately, he agreed. "Yes, but how would we even train her at this point? We can't send her to the farm. They would find her before she has a chance to learn anything."

"I sent Dylan after the Generation. As far as I can tell, he's succeeding at his mission. As soon as he gets the files from them, I will have adequate reason to take the Generation away from the Training Division and give it back to Dylan, an agent directly under me." McLean explained.

"Who has access to the files?" Neil asked.

"Peter Carlyle."

Neil released a breath he hadn't realized he'd been holding. "So Dylan's not quite there yet, and he's going to be going head to head with my daughter and her boyfriend"

"But he understands the urgency better than most." McLean stated, then paused for a second. "Wait did you say boyfriend?"

"I don't know if that word is entirely accurate, but I've seen the way she looks at him. It's the same way Sarah looks at me. She thinks she's hiding it, but our cameras caught her sneaking out to go on a date with him while Sarah and I were at work. You can try and fault me for plenty of things when it comes to her, but Sarah and I keep a close eye on our daughter, especially after last summer."

McLean laughed. "You really are starting to understand what it was like trying to raise you." He took a deep breath, letting the laughter go so he could convey the seriousness of his next request. "Neil, do what you can to convince Alyx to stay in that house, but then I need you to come in with your wife. ASAP."

"Understood." Neil replied. "I love you dad."

"I love you too." Director McLean replied. "Be careful." The line went dead as the director ended the call on his end.

Neil looked at his phone as he locked it. He shoved it in his back pocket, and walked out of his office, making sure to lock the door as he left, then walked out of the upstairs family room, and straight down the hallway into the bedroom he shared with Sarah. As he walked into the room, Sarah set the book she was reading down.

"What did your dad say?" She asked.

Neil was quiet as he plugged his phone in. "He called us in." Neil replied.

Sarah crinkled her forehead. "But we quit twelve years ago."

"He kept our credentials active in case things got bad enough… the threat against Alyx is worse than we thought.

He called us in to read us in on it." Neil explained.

"When?" Sarah asked gravely.

"As soon as possible."

"Can you even get away? You're working a serial kidnapping."

"About that." Neil coughed. "All of victims have been members of the Promising Generation, and your brother is the one that has been doing the kidnapping. My dad called my bosses to have me work it as part of a training mission."

Sarah sighed. "Ok, so I guess I just need to find some time off." She sometimes missed being read in on some things. But she'd given up that right when she quit the CIA to protect her daughter, and she definitely loved her daughter more than she loved spying—most days.

"Or..." Neil said with a conspiratorial smile, "I could call my dad back and tell him he needs to come to us. Our daughter is, after all, in grave danger, so the last thing we want to do is leave her here alone."

"You know just as well as anyone that there are some things that shouldn't leave your father's office. He brings the intel he has on our daughter to us, and it both opens him up for the possibility of attack, and it reveals her location to the people looking for her." Sarah replied. "It's a day. How much trouble can she really get into."

Neil grimaced. "You know you just jinxed it, don't you? Alyx would take that as a challenge."

"You mean like her father used to?" Sarah asked, a playful

smile playing at the corner of her lips. "And I never said we had to tell her we were leaving. We could go and be back without her knowing."

Neil smiled. "I've missed that devious mind of yours."

5:35 PDT
Tracy, California
McLean Home

SARAH CHECKED the clock on the microwave again. If Neil didn't hurry, they were going to be late to the airport. She looked down to make sure she had everything she needed in her purse. She would yell at him, encouraging him to hurry, but that would wake Alyx up, and if they were trying to sneak out without her knowing, that was the last thing she wanted to do. She looked up as someone came around the countertop, hoping it was her husband, but finding her daughter instead.

"Where are you off to?" Alyx asked. "The calendar says you don't work, and you're not wearing your scrubs." Alyx set her backpack on one of the chairs at the table.

Sarah looked at her daughter, realizing there was a flaw in her thinking they could leave without Alyx noticing. She hadn't thought up an excuse to cover for where she and Neil were going, convinced that if she and Neil could get out of the house before Alyx left for seminary at six o'clock, they'd be fine. But Neil was running late, as usual, already fielding work calls despite the early hour, and Alyx was up early.

"Emily and Brian are heading to Washington for a few days. They asked your father and I to join." Sarah lied.

She could tell right away that Alyx didn't believe her, and the hurt look on her face just proved it. Sarah and Neil had achieved a very open relationship with their daughter by convincing her they wouldn't lie to her if she didn't lie to them. "Emily hasn't been back to D.C. since she graduated from high school, and she refuses to leave California." She argued.

"My mom is going to be stateside for once, and Emily wants her to meet Brian. I think he's really close to proposing." Sarah took a deep breath, watching to see if Alyx believed her, and she seemed like she might. Then again, everything she had said was true, meaning it was perfect for hiding the true reason for their visit. Sarah smiled, thinking of something else to add. "And while we're there, we're going to visit your dad's parents, and make sure we intimidate Brian, I need to make sure he'll take great care of my baby sister."

Alyx rolled her eyes. "Remind me never to take my boyfriend to D.C. with you psychos."

"Boyfriend, huh?" Sarah asked, honing in on the detail Alyx had let slip.

Alyx controlled her breathing so she didn't show her mom the panic she felt, knowing she'd let that detail leave her mouth, nor the heartbreak she felt, realizing that she was pretty sure it was all fake. "Yeah. Boyfriend. You don't think

I'm going to be single forever, do you? Eventually I will find someone, and we will date, and I will be able to imagine a life with him, and he will be able to imagine a life with me, and… that is *so* not the point. The point is you and dad have issues, and try to chase away every guy Emily and I are interested, and Emily is a full grown adult, with an adult job and everything."

"Emily does a great job of chasing off guys on her own." Sarah muttered under her breath. "Besides, it's my job to worry, as your mother, and as Emily's older sister." Sarah argued. "Which reminds me, you have a tennis match today right?"

Alyx nodded.

Sarah watched for her daughter's nod, going back to making sure she was packed. "After the match tonight, I want you to come straight home. Lock the doors, and please, please, don't forget to set the alarm. Try not to go anywhere, and call me if you need anything."

"I will." Alyx replied.

"It's just, with the kidnappings, I want you to be extra cautious."

"I know." Alyx said.

"Oh, and no *friends* coming over to study." Sarah added, giving Alyx a knowing look.

Alyx smirked. "So you're telling me that you're concerned about me getting kidnapped, but the number one deterrent for kidnappings is numbers, and you're telling me you want me to sit in this big, empty house alone?"

"Chelsi and Carlie are just fine." Sarah amended. "But you need to tell Peter he can't come study. I don't want you alone with a boy."

"So if Chelsi and Carlie come over to study, then Peter can join us?" Alyx said sweetly. Sarah glared at her daughter. "What? You said you didn't want me *alone* with a boy. If Chelsi and Carlie are here, then I'm not alone, am I?"

"You know what I mean." Sarah scolded.

Alyx laughed as she nodded. "And trust me, I wasn't planning on it."

Sarah gave Alyx an accusatory look.

"Stop worrying about me. I know how to be responsible. You send me to London by myself every summer, and I handle myself very well without supervision. I think I can handle a few days alone at home. Go enjoy torturing your sister's boyfriend." Alyx patronized.

Sarah gave her daughter a scolding look. "London isn't the perfect example of your responsibility. If I remember right, last summer, I got a call from my brother-in-law telling me you ran away to look for your cousin."

"And you had no clue that the cousin I was searching for existed until then, right?" Alyx challenged. "Because you are perfect, with no secrets, and definitely no lies."

Sarah and Alyx stared at each other, Alyx challenging her mother, and daring her to tell her she was wrong.

Neil walked into the kitchen, observing the situation and

the obvious confrontation that was happening. "Are you ready?" He asked, daring to interrupt.

Alyx gave her dad a questioning look. "Don't you have a case?"

Both of her parents were oddly quiet, until her father finally answered. "I'm headed to D.C. to follow up on some leads. I suspect we found the next target, and we have a team watching him. To be safe, there will be a team here too."

"Peter." Alyx guessed.

Neither of her parents answered. Instead, her mom turned to her dad, "Let's take my car." She grabbed her bags, and started toward the door. She turned back to Alyx as she walked past. "Remember—"

"I'll come straight home. I won't go anywhere. I'll set the alarm. I won't have anyone over." Alyx promised.

Sarah nodded with a sigh, turning back around and heading out the garage door to her car.

Neil watched his wife before turning back to his daughter. "She's just concerned about you." He said. "We both are."

Alyx didn't say anything, staring off into space behind her dad, noticing his suitcase, and the open outer pocket with the distinctive shape of his keys.

Neil opened his arms, inviting his daughter in for a hug. She walked over to him, allowing herself to be drawn into a hug. "Just be careful this weekend." Her dad urged.

Alyx nodded in his shoulder, hoping the movement would distract him from the movement of her left hand off his back and towards his suitcase.

Neil kissed the top of her head. "I'll see you Tuesday."

Alyx stood in the kitchen, watching as her father left. As she heard the garage door close, she opened her hand, looking at his keys in her palm.

She had a weekend with the house to herself, the key to get into her dad's office, and questions she desperately needed answered.

5:51 PDT
Tracy, California
McLean Home

ALYX WALKED over to the panel, holding down the 9 key, watching as the panel went from saying ready to secure, to a dark, blank screen. Maybe it was evil of her, having found that their Scofield 2009 security system had a bug that let her reboot it, not to tell her parents, or send an email to Scofield Security Service letting them know that their security systems were flawed. Then again, she never knew when she might need to break into her own house... or her dad's office.

Alyx didn't think there were any cameras in the house, but she didn't want to take the chance. Her dad had ensured that his office, if nothing else, was extremely secure, with a lock that you couldn't pick, because he knew Alyx did pick locks. So with the security system rebooting, and the chipped key to her dad's office in hand, she crept up the stairs, past her bedroom, and into the giant family room. Alyx didn't waste time pretending to be there for any legitimate reason, heading straight for the hidden door of her dad's office. She pulled the key out of her pocket, and stuck it into the well disguised lock for the door. She watched, waiting for the LED hiding in the spine of a fake book to switch from red to green before turning the key, hearing the satisfying click as the door swung toward her just slightly.

With the security that her dad had installed in his office, she should have guessed they might have secrets, like an uncle… who was a spy. Her dad's office had always been locked, and while they may have argued that the secure office was to keep people who might break in from accessing his office, the upgrade to an RFID enabled lock and key came after her dad had caught her picking locks. That was no coincidence. They didn't want her in here.

Alyx glanced around the office as she pulled the door most of the way shut. Her parents had something in this room they didn't want her to know, and it was something they were willing to pay extra money for special locks just to keep her out. It seemed more important than case files.

She just had to figure it out.

With a mental picture of where everything sat in the room, she glanced at the countdown she'd started on her watch. Just because she didn't see any cameras didn't mean there weren't any. Scofield had gotten good at developing affordable cameras that could be hidden in spaces like this. She had until the security system finished the reboot to search the office. That left her just under 18 minutes left.

17:36 If she was was going to find her parent's secrets in the time she had, she was going to have to think like them. She was fortunate as far as the fact that her dad had the same approach to solving problems, which meant his current case could be found on the various boards around the room, with the file close to him so he could access it easily. She didn't know what the FBI had that she didn't but she'd already figured out the same thing her dad had: Peter was most likely next.

The fact that her mom and dad both felt it was important enough to go to D.C. while her dad was working a case, and they had tried to hide it from her, told her this was bigger than just her dad's current case. While she knew the secrets her dad kept closest were going to be in the same desk drawer as her dad's current case (she guessed), anything that didn't require frequent access would be filed away someplace that didn't impede the wall space and whiteboards her dad used while working cases.

She checked the closet first.

17:30 As she slid the closet door open, she was grateful that even if her parents might be keeping secrets from her, she knew how they thought, since opening the closet revealed two filing cabinets with four drawers each; two small safes, one that she knew was a gun safe as a matching one sat in her parents room for her father's service weapon, the other she could only guess; and three duffle bags big enough for a week-long camping trip. While she knew the answers she was looking for most likely lived in the filing cabinets, her curiosity drew her to the clearly full duffle bags, and the safe she didn't recognize. She pulled the duffle bag closest to her out of the closet and unzipped it, revealing an assortment of clothing, with make-up pallets unlike any she or her mom had ever used—which wasn't hard, since they rarely wore make-up—as well as a couple different wigs with different colors and styles. She pulled the other two out to find similar contents. One was clearly for her dad, and one that, after looking carefully at the clothes, she decided was for her mom, the first she'd opened being for her. She'd read enough books and watched enough movies about spies to recognize the duffles as go bags.

15:45 She didn't know the combination for the safe, so despite her raging curiosity, and a feeling that told her that she could figure it out, she decided to move onto the filing cabinets to see what she could find.

15:40 As she opened the drawers from the first filing cabinet, she found the neat, all caps lettering of her father labeling most of the files, the names of which related to the various cases he'd worked over the years. She opened and closed the drawers, finding as she descended the filing cabinet, she was unfamiliar with more and more of the case names, until she got to the bottom drawer, and found they were all completely foreign to her. She didn't think anything of it, as they were filed in reverse chronological order, meaning the files at the bottom were from the years of 1990–2000. She hadn't been alive for some of those.

15:10 As she began going through the files in the second filing cabinet, she found her mother's flowing, almost-cursive script intermingled with her father's labels. The first drawer she opened had what she guessed were medical records, as various labs, and prescriptions were present in the few files she looked at. It made sense that, of all people, her mother had labeled and filed them, since her profession as a nurse taught her the importance of having a complete medical history.

14:50 Feeling the pressure of the clock, she closed the drawer without heading all the way to the back, and the earliest medical records. If there was something significant in their medical histories, her parents wouldn't have lied about that. As she opened the second drawer, she saw the files once again in chronological order, this time with her father's handwriting, with her mother's interspersed, mostly featuring their income tax returns. However, in the front, without a year on it, was a file labeled *Maintenance.* She pulled out the thick green folder, looking at the titles of the Manila folders inside, with various names on them like *Waterfall, Rainpail,* and *Somerset.* As she scanned through each of the folders, she discovered that most of them had maintenance dates from long before her parents were even married.

While her parents had neglected to put addresses on the files, she figured they were houses. All she had to go on were dates and what she guessed were code names, to figure out where they were but otherwise they were quite thorough.

With the listed dates of uses, she figured out that *Sagebrush* referred to the house she'd lived in during their stay in Vegas, *Emerald*, the house in Seattle, *Skypark* the house in the Bountiful Hills, and *Waterlogs* was the house in Mountain House.

Her parents had told her they were simply renting each of those houses, but this proved other wise.

Her parents had lied.

10:50 With the unwavering knowledge that time was ticking away, she closed the drawer. If her parents lied about something that was as insignificant as owning a house, what else did they lie about? She felt a sense of urgency, knowing that this office held answers about her parents lies.

10:48 Alyx opened the third filing cabinet drawer, and for the first time, the labels on the files didn't make sense to her. The drawer had two metal dividers, creating three sections, each with green folders with various names on them. She pulled one out at random from the front section, pulling one of the manila folders out to read what was inside. Her dad's label on the folder read "legend" and the paper inside was a typed list of a bunch of background information. She opened the next folder and found paper documents, like a birth certificate for the person whose name was on the file, a Social Security Card, a drivers license with her dad's photo on it, and a passport.

9:53 Alyx shoved the folder back in the drawer where she'd gotten it, quickly pulling out another file from the section behind it, this time finding the same thing with a woman's name, and her mother's face on the photo ID's.

9:06 She grabbed a file from the back section. Evelyn Qui was what the file said. Opening the document folder revealed the same papers that she'd found for her parents, this time with her face on the Driver's License and Passport. She grabbed the two photo ID's and shoved them in her pocket. She didn't know why her parents needed go-bags and aliases for all three of them, but given that they'd lied to her, and she had her own secrets piling up, she didn't see the harm in having an alternate identity at her disposal.

8:22 She closed the drawer, moving onto the last drawer of the filing cabinets, finding another three sections in the bottom drawer, with the files for the aliases substantially smaller than they had been in the first drawer. She pulled out one of the files from the middle section, her attention drawn to the fact that the alias had the same last name as the ID she had shoved in her pocket. Since she had seen one of that last name for all of the sections in the first drawer, she knew that it wasn't for her mom. She decided to look in the document folder first, finding everything but a drivers license. As she opened the passport, she found the smiling face of a seven-year-old girl she recognized from her dreams, with a birthday two and a half years before her own, and an expiration date two years past due, meaning it had been issued in 2000.

6:51 Without putting the file back, she rifled through the other files in the drawer, trying to see if the others were the same. As she pulled one after another out, she found that they all belonged to three young children, and none of them had been updated since 2000. She saw photo after photo belonging to a ten-year-old boy, a seven-year-old girl, and a baby.

5:43 Alyx looked off across the room. She felt like the year 2000 held some importance for her and her family, more than just the fact that it was the start of a new millennium, and the year she knew her earliest memories fell in. She'd turned five in 2000, and she faintly remembered starting school. They were living near the nation's capital, because she'd gone to some private school in McLean, Virginia with her aunt Emily, who had been a senior that year. She remembered that it was McLean because it was the same as her last name. She remembered sharing a room with Emily at Grandma and Grandpa McLean's house. She didn't remember her parents much that year. Had that been the year her mom finished Nursing School at John Hopkins? If it was, her dad was training at Quantico.

5:27 She grabbed the folder for Eliana Qui and closed the filing cabinet. With time ticking away, she decided to leave figuring out the importance of 2000 until later, and check the desk, just to make sure she'd been as thorough as she could. She ran across the room, looking at her dad's desk from his perspective. It was too clean, like he'd intentionally cleared it before he left. She could still see outlines of dust from where everything had been, and based on the amount of dust, until recently, they hadn't been moved in months. There were a couple of rectangular shapes left that were the correct size and shape as file folders, but there was also a thin dust shadow that almost looked like a picture frame had been removed.

Why would he hide a picture? Especially one important enough to be framed?

4:58 Alyx used the small key on her dad's key chain to unlock the drawers of the desk. She found the files, searching them to try and find Peter's address. She had to thumb through most of the folders, but she found it. Her dad noted in his file that he was most likely a target, if not the next one, then one in the future. He also noted something about a security detail, and Peter declining it. Alyx took her phone out, taking a picture of the page. If Peter was going to be kidnapped in the near future, she wanted his address to search his house and find out why.

4:01 Despite looking through all of the drawers of the desk, she didn't find the frame that had left the hole in the dust on her dad's desk. Frustrated, and running out of time, she almost missed the fact that the top drawer was shallower than the ones below it, despite it being the same size. With the files removed from her search, she knocked on the bottom, hearing a hollow sound in return. She pulled the Evelyn Qui ID from her pocket, using it to slide between the sides of the drawer and the bottom, using it to pry the bottom up. Fortunately it wasn't that stuck, and the bottom lifted away easily to reveal the picture frame. She pulled it, examining the picture in it. She recognized her five-year-old self, as the picture of her taken in the same studio was hanging downstairs above the mantle. She had always wondered why they didn't have any family portraits from the same time period, and looking at the picture her dad had hidden finally explained why.

She wasn't an only child.

3:38 Alyx used the camera on her phone to take a picture of the one her dad had hidden, quickly putting it back. As she replaced her father's files, she felt the monotonous drone of her internal clock fighting with her curiosity for more answers. The clock won out, causing her to close the drawer and take a step back.

3:07 She looked back at the room one more time before leaving, checking to make sure everything was as she had found it. From a cursory glance, everything appeared as it should, which was what she wanted. Only a deep search would betray the missing passport and ID for Evelyn Qui, or the missing files with all of Eliana's documents. If she didn't give her parents any reason to be suspicious that she had been in here, they probably wouldn't find her thievery.

2:24 She closed the door to the office, returning everything in the house to how it had been before she'd rebooted the security system. She hurried into her room, stashing the things she'd stolen from her dad's office before grabbing her tennis rackets off her bed and running downstairs.

1:30 Alyx grabbed a microwaveable breakfast sandwich

from the freezer, throwing it in the microwave, before sitting down at the table with a mug of hot chocolate, opening the book they were reading in English.

0:00 By the time the system came back up, she was perched on the chair, nose in a book, taking sips of hot chocolate from time to time. There was no indication that she'd done anything other than get her tennis rackets from her room, then come in to get some homework done while she ate breakfast.

PETER WATCHED as Alyx' car pulled into the parking lot. It was much earlier than he would have liked, but he knew Alyx got to school early, and he had a feeling she wouldn't wait for him. He hadn't gotten through to her the night before as they studied French, and he hadn't heard much from her since. He was worried about her, so if waiting for her before school was his only option, he would.

As she pulled into the spot next to him, she didn't so much as look at him. Peter's heart fell. She must have been pretty mad at him, and he had no clue what he'd done. He slid off his car, walking over to the driver's side of her car so she had no excuse not to talk to him.

"Hey," he said as she climbed out.

"I'm not in the mood." She snapped.

Peter sighed. "If I did something, just tell me." Peter pleaded.

Alyx glared at Peter. "Were you serious last night about

applying to Oxford?" She asked.

Peter nodded.

"What do you need to submit to apply?" Alyx asked.

"I don't know." Peter admitted.

"And you want to be an engineer." Alyx prodded.

"I'm not sure, but I've thought about it." Peter told her.

"And your parents are professors. Not spies." She added.

Peter froze. *How did she know?*

"See, because I started investigating after Adison was kidnapped, and I found evidence that Nathan was a spy who had trained at Camp Peary. And then Chelsi told me Dylan Hall was involved. I *know* Dylan Hall is a spy, and after meeting him last summer, I figured out that not only is he my uncle, but he is Thane and Chelsi's dad. Then Cameron was kidnapped, suggesting he's somehow connected to Nathan, and a spy. And you were his last phone call. In fact, you have connections to all of the people kidnapped. And you never denied being a spy. You asked who told me. But then that begs the question of what you were doing talking to me. Stephan was kind enough to tell me that Lynn sent you the files from last summer, since you are part of training program, and were told to *Be On the Look-Out* for me."

"Alyx—"

"Here's the thing. I discovered this morning that my parents are lying to me too, and they're in D.C. for a few days, so you can't come over to study. So um I hope you don't get kidnapped, but you're the one who declined the FBI protection detail, which I have no way to get out of, because my dad ordered them to follow me, and they're more afraid of my dad than me, so good luck. Maybe I'll see you next week. Maybe I won't." Alyx stormed off, throwing her backpack over her shoulder.

Peter wanted nothing more than to take Alyx' pain away, but he couldn't. He'd caused some of that pain. He didn't know if she was more mad at him, or her parents, but finding out about their collective lies was apparently more than she could handle. As he walked onto campus, his mind replayed everything she said, a heartbreaking realization hitting him: she thought him dating her was related to the BOLO.

She thought he lied about loving her.

7:48 PDT
Tracy, California
John C. Kimball High School

CARLIE WALKED up next to Alyx, a knowing smile on her lips. Alyx was distracted, looking at her own reflection in the doors of the not yet opened Cafeteria thinking about the picture she had found in her dad's office, and the number of times she had thought she was going crazy. Alyx pulled her sleeves down over her hands, folding her arms. It wasn't very cold, but it just starting to be chilly enough in the mornings that Alyx needed a sweatshirt, especially when it was a day she had a match and wore her uniform to school. It would be off in a couple of hours, but she needed it now. Without thinking, she'd grabbed the hoodie that Peter had given her the night after he'd asked her out. For her, it reminded her of the emotions she'd felt that night, not the anger she felt now, and it was comforting contrasted to the turmoil her brain was currently in, trying to figure out what was real, and what was a lie.

"So what did Peter Carlyle talk to you about?" Carlie

asked, as she interrupted Alyx' spiral into her dark thoughts.

"What are you talking about?" Alyx asked.

"Peter was waiting for you to talk to you this morning." Carlie told her. She grabbed Alyx' hands, pulling them away from the sweatshirt. "And since when have you had a seniors hoodie…that drowns you?"

Alyx looked down at the sweatshirt, frustratedly pulling it off. Carlie wasn't a spy, as far as Alyx knew, but she was definitely more observant than Alyx liked. As Alyx stored the sweatshirt in her backpack, she weighed the pros and cons of wearing it. She definitely regretted taking it off as the cool morning breeze licked her arms, making her hair stand up. She felt bare. Usually she wore some sort of jacket with the dress that acted as her tennis uniform, so having her shoulders uncovered made her extra cold. She looked back up at Carlie. She wasn't going to drop this. Especially not anytime soon.

"Peter asked me to be his girlfriend." She admitted.

Carlie's smile grew. Alyx could see her excitement building, like she was about to explode. Alyx couldn't help it. Seeing Carlie's reaction made her smile, despite everything else making her not want to.

"Calm down. I don't even know how long it's going to last. We agreed to keep it secret, so you can't tell anyone."

Carlie took a deep breath, drawing her pointer and thumb across her lips, promising to keep the secret. Her calm only lasted a second, though, then she was bouncing again. "I have to know all the details."

Alyx shrugged. "He's been coming over to study for the AP French test. He was flirting with me so much I had to enact a French only rule, then he asked me out. We went go-karting then to the dance." Alyx couldn't help but smile, but it didn't last long. "I don't know how long it will last though. I mean, there's Oxford, and I don't know if he really likes me, or if I am just another one of the girls Peter Carlyle has kissed at this school."

Carlie shook her head. "And here I thought you told me everything."

"Not even close." Alyx sighed. As the words left her mouth, she realized she was just as guilty at lying as everyone else. "But then again, I don't want some of our other friends knowing as much as I've even told you... so maybe we will need to start doing things just the two of us."

"I'd like that." Carlie admitted.

The janitor came by, unlocking the cafeteria. Alyx shiver-ed. "Thank goodness. I was about to freeze."

Carlie rolled her eyes. "Didn't you used to live in Utah?"

"Yes. And I froze. Like all the time." Alyx complained.

PETER OPENED his door, inviting Thane into the house. "What did you need me for?" Thane asked.

Peter closed the door behind Thane. "I have a question about what you said about your dad's motivations."

"OK." Thane said.

"How do you know what his motivation is? How do you know exactly what he's looking for? Unless, of course, he told you." Peter postulated.

Thane opened his mouth to argue, but Peter just shook his head.

"I'm not accusing. I wasn't trained by Wraith. I'm not stupid." He sighed. "Look, I think your dad gaining control of the Generation is a great idea. We need help training the members. But I also know you told me Deputy Director Hall needs the files to protect Alyx for a reason. I want to help protect her. Help me show up on your dad's radar. Help me get kidnapped next."

Thane took a deep breath, contemplating his options. "I might be able to do that." He folded his arms. "This won't look good for you or your training."

Peter rolled his eyes. "Oh no! You mean I might lose the mission Wraith has been planing for me?" He sighed, looking at Thane. "Alyx is more important than Wraith's mission, or even my image with the CIA."

Thane shook his head with a smirk. "Let me see what I can do."

THANE SLIPPED into the safehouse where his dad was keeping Adison, Nathan, and Cameron, letting himself into the control room, where he saw Stevens and Banthup watching the security feed of Cameron.

"Has he broken yet?" Thane asked.

Banthup shook his head. "No. We've made fun of your program, but they're only breaking because Hall knows what he's doing."

"Yes, but anyone who knows what they're doing could break them. That's the problem." Thane commented.

"We're running his phone records." Stevens commented. "He made a phone call right before we grabbed him, and Hall thinks it might be someone important from the program."

Thane nodded. "What have you found so far?" He asked.

Stevens gestured toward the phone. "All we have is the phone number. Getting access to phone records is kind of a government thing, which we're not allowed to use."

Thane picked up the phone. "Have you tried calling the number?"

"No." Stevens admitted.

Banthup pulled out his phone. "All we need is his name, correct?" He asked, reading the number from the phone Thane was holding, then typing it into his own.

"If we have a name, Stevens can do the research, and Hall can ask Nathan. He's still rather fragile." Thane commented, pointing to the screen playing the surveillance of Nathan.

Banthup put his phone on speaker, letting the other three listen as the phone rang. As Thane listened to the phone ring and ring, he wondered whether or not Peter would answer. He suspected he would, since Peter had literally just asked for Thane's help getting kidnapped, but he couldn't help but wonder if it was a ploy to get Thane to admit guilt.

But then the phone picked up. "Pacific Gold Tutoring," a male voice answered.

Stevens opened an internet window using the computer he was sitting at, typing *Pacific Gold Tutoring* into the search bar.

"Uh yeah, um I'm a student at Kimball High, and I need some help with math." Banthup said, hoping to keep whoever it was on the phone. They really needed the name of the guy on the phone, assuming it was the same guy Cameron had called.

"Unfortunately, none of our math tutors are currently accepting new clients, as their schedules are full. If it's urgent,

I can suggest you visit out website, pgtutoring.org. We have lots of videos that our tutors have uploaded to help as many students as possible." The voice replied.

"Thanks for the suggestion." Banthup replied. "Hey can I get your name, so if I need to call back with another question, I can ask for you?"

"I'm glad I could help." The voice replied. "Thank you for calling Pacific Gold tutoring, and have a great day." The room went silent as the call was terminated from the other end.

Banthup set his phone down, leaning over Stevens to watch what he was doing on the computer. "Please tell me you found something."

"I have an address." Stevens replied. "And a very detailed cover website. He wasn't kidding about the tutoring videos."

Thane smiled. "You better take that address to Hall. My bet is he can get a name out of Nathan."

Stevens nodded, writing the address down on a piece of paper before handing it to Banthup, knowing that Hall would assign Banthup to watch the address as soon as they gave it to him. That would give them the opportunity to watch the member who lived there, and form an extraction plan, so as soon as Nathan gave up a name, they would be ready to go. Time was of the essence.

21:01 PDT
Tracy, California
Hall Base of Operations

HALL SAT across the table from Nathan, closely watching him, waiting for an answer to his question. "Come on Levy, don't make me bring Adison in here, again."

Nathan scoffed. "Yeah, because that has worked *so* well for you before. Adison doesn't know anything, and neither do I. Why don't you ask Cameron, and just let Adison and I go?"

"Nice try." Hall answered. "Try again. Promising Generation Mission Reports."

"I was not privileged with that information." Nathan shrugged. "I told you. Ask Cameron McKay."

Hall shook his head. "That is the one thing I still wonder about. How did you and Adison both give me the name of a member that doesn't have the files any more than Adison does?" Hall leaned across the table, getting closer to Nathan. "Who are you protecting? Clearly it's not your brother."

Nathan sat quiet across from Hall, staring him down. Hall watched Nathan, he knew he'd hit a soft spot, but it was a spot Hall had hit so many times, Nathan had grown accustomed to it. He had accepted that he'd failed his brother, and that failure was strengthening him against failing whoever had the files.

"Maybe it's one of your sisters." Hall commented. "I'll bring Christy in first. And if she doesn't break, I'm sure bringing Stephanie will break her." Hall kept his joy from showing on his face, seeing his threat cause a reaction. Nathan's loyalty to the Generation was either deep enough that Nathan had withstood every interrogation technique Hall had used on him without giving up the files he needed, or Nathan was telling the truth about not having them, and his loyalty to the person who did far outweighed anything Hall had threatened. Hall wanted to see what happened when he upped the stakes.

Nathan shook his head. "My sisters don't have what you are looking for."

Hall leaned back. "If you don't have the files, you are clearly protecting someone else who is more important to you than Adison. Logic states your sisters. Then again, maybe it's your girlfriend. Ashley spends a lot of time with your family. Maybe I should bring her in."

"They don't have those files. I can promise you that." Nathan argued.

Hall folded his arms, making himself look as comfortable as possible. He could sit here for as long as it took to break Nathan, and the more he settled in, the more Nathan would see that. Nathan had his breaking point. He'd seen that when he'd given up Cameron McKay. Unfortunately, he just hadn't been broken enough to give up the truth. "Please forgive me if I'm not inclined to believe you." Hall yawned. "You did, after all, tell me that Cameron has them, and he clearly doesn't." Hall sat back up, unfolding his arms. "See, when my team apprehended him, he called someone. He wouldn't do that if he was in charge, because he wouldn't have anyone *to* call. You wouldn't have run if there wasn't someone else to turn the operation of your program over to, and my guess is that you turned it over to whoever has the files."

Nathan took a deep breath. He'd called someone too, right before he was captured. Did they have his burner phone? He fidgeted with the cuffs holding his arms, which made Hall smile. He was nervous.

"I will give you one last chance to tell me who has access to the files." Hall offered. "Just tell me who lives on Golden Leaf Court."

Nathan shook his head. "It could be anyone in the Generation. We use the house on Golden Leaf for our meetings." Nathan let out a quiet breath he'd been holding. He didn't know who Cameron had called, only where the call had come from.

Hall knew as much about the house. He'd gotten the address from Stevens, who had identified it as location for Pacific Gold Tutoring, which was registered as an LLC. He'd asked Stevens to dig into the records of the company while

Banthup watched the house. It was a shell company owned by the CIA, which he'd suspected, but having that confirmation made his interrogation easier.

"Just because the CIA owns the house, and it's used for Generation meetings, doesn't mean that no one lives there. More than likely, the same person tasked with protecting the files lives there to protect the servers that the files are kept on. And they have to be there, because for a residence, which you just told me is used only for meetings, it draws a lot of power from the grid, which supplements solar panels." Hall reasoned. "Who. Lives. There?"

Nathan stared at Hall in silence, contempt emanating from his clenched jaw and steel eyes. He knew they were caught. Why did Cameron call Peter before he was captured? How could Peter have been so naive to have let his phone call be traced to the house?

Hall returned the stare, taking note of the moisture gathering in the inside tear duct of Nathan's left eye. All he needed was One. More. Little. Push. All he needed was one more reminder of what was at stake.

"Ok, that's fine." Hall turned and knocked on the door, signaling the guard waiting on the other side to open the door. The guard peeked in the door, looking at Hall for his order. "Stevens, please activate the extraction order on the team following Ms. Levy."

"Which one?" Stevens asked.

"The one in college. I believe she should be in her art

class right about now. Photography Principles and Techniques." Hall answered, looking back over his shoulder at Nathan as he casually dropped the name of one of the classes his oldest sister was taking. He knew that he had sufficiently deprived Nathan of any ability to keep track of time, so it didn't matter what class he mentioned. Just knowing what classes Christy took showed quite a bit of knowledge on Hall's part. "That class is in the building on Sutter Street, correct?" He asked Nathan for confirmation, despite not needing it.

"FINE!" Nathan yelled. He took a deep breath as Hall turned the rest of his body back around to look at him. "Peter Carlyle."

Hall nodded to Stevens. The guard hesitated slightly as he closed the door, leaving Hall alone with Nathan again.

Nathan shook his head. "But if you thought I was hard to get information out of, good luck." Nathan let out a strangled laugh. "Carlyle is unbreakable."

Hall shrugged. "Everybody has their weakness. I found yours, I'll find his." Hall got up, knocking on the door again. Another guard opened the door. "My niece's life depends on it." He mumbled to himself as he left.

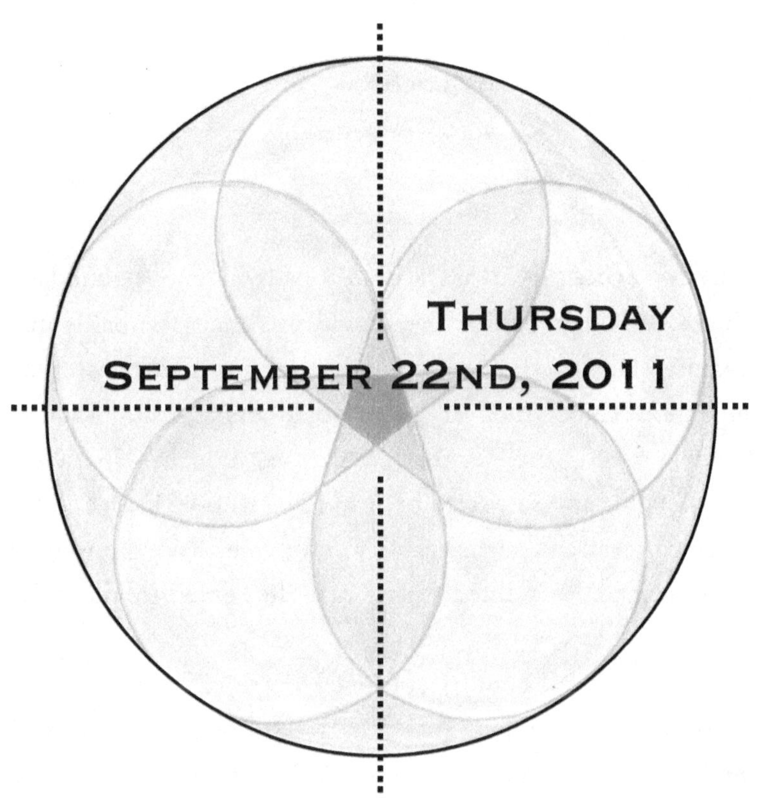

Thursday
September 22nd, 2011

8:10 PDT
Tracy, California
John C. Kimball High School

PETER ZONED out as Jacob droned on about mundane things. Whether or not they could win their football game against Manteca High School didn't seem to matter as much any more. Not when all Peter could think about was his missing friends, the files they didn't have, and Alyx. Somehow his thoughts always circled back to Alyx, who he hadn't talked to since yesterday morning. He wanted to explain. He wanted to apologize. He wanted to kiss her. He wanted to know she was ok.

The minute he and Jacob entered the cafeteria, his eyes swept the space looking for Alyx. If she wouldn't talk to him, he had to at least know she was ok. He needed to know she was alive.

His breath caught in his throat when he caught sight of Alyx at the table with the rest of her friends. Her eyes were locked on the textbook in front of her when her friends caught sight of him, one of the girls elbowing Alyx to get her attention, while Carlie's face held a knowing smile. Alyx looked up to see why they were getting her attention, and locked eyes with Peter. He watched as she mumbled some excuse to her friends, closing the textbook and shoving it into her backpack. He stopped walking as she made her way through the cafeteria, hoping it was to come talk to him. He was in her way, but as she bumped into him, her head shot up with a mumbled apology that died on her lips as soon as she saw it was him.

"Alyx" he whispered. "I'm—" He started, but she kept just walking.

Jacob slugged Peter in the arm, and Peter's attention suddenly shot back to the friend he was walking with.

Peter looked at Jacob. "I messed up." He admitted.

8:17 PDT
Tracy, California
John C. Kimball High School

PETER FIDGETED with a piece of paper that he needed to pass off to Alyx. How was he supposed to apologize if she wouldn't talk to him? How was he supposed to make sure that she was going to be safe?

Doing his job was so much easier before he loved her.

Scarlett grabbed the folded piece of paper from him. "What do you have here?" She asked.

Peter snatched the paper back. "Nothing." He lied. "Just something the girl dropped earlier when she bumped into me." He stared at the paper knowing that what it really contained was an apology and a plea that Alyx go spend some time in London, away from where she was in danger. "I'm trying to figure out how to get it back to her, you know, in case it is important."

"That's something I've always loved about you." She said with a smile. "You are always thinking about someone else and their needs." She rubbed his arm. "That's hard to find in anyone today, never mind a friend."

Peter involuntarily moved away from her touch. It felt weird, knowing that he was dating Alyx. Then again, Scarlett didn't know that. She was a friend. They'd been to a lot of the same parties the last couple years. He'd even made out with her at a few of the parties the year before. He had a reputation for never dating the same girl for very long. He'd never found anyone he could see himself being with long term, and he was always thinking about the girl that sat in front of him in Algebra II, the girl who was now his girlfriend, if she ever talked to him again.

She had to talk to him.

"Hey Peter, are you okay?" Trevor asked.

"Fine." Peter lied. His girlfriend was pissed at him, and he was currently waiting to be kidnapped to protect her.

"Really? Because you haven't been to any of our parties this year, and you seem to be spending more time sneaking off than usual. I thought maybe there was a girl." Trevor said.

"No girl." He lied again… Maybe it wasn't a lie anymore.

Jacob rolled his eyes, recently read in on why Peter's mood was so sour, which meant it was up to him to come up with Peter's excuses, since Peter was suddenly incapable of doing it himself.

"He's just taking Cam's disappearance hard." Jacob remarked. Peter looked up at Jacob, gratitude in his eyes, noticing the chorus of nods around the table. Most of their friends were seniors, and that meant they started at West before Kimball had opened two years before. Half of them had been on the West High JV football team, so they too knew Cameron, and even those that didn't play on the same team knew of him. Teammates had a habit of getting close to each other. Teams felt like a family.

Peter looked at Trevor, realizing something he'd forgotten until just a moment before. "Hey, the girl on the track team that you were always complaining was the coach's favorite—you have a class with her, right?"

Trevor took a second before replying. "You mean Miss Track Star McLean. Yeah. She's a TA for Calculus. I think she took the class last year."

"What period do you have Calc?" Peter asked.

"Third." Trevor answered.

Scarlett smiled. "I could give it to her. She's in my first period Stats class." She told him. "And I won't even read it, which is something Trevor can't say."

"Thank you." Peter said, handing the note to her.

"I might slip her your phone number, though." Scarlett admitted as she slipped the paper into her binder. "She's really nice. I think you'd like her."

ALYX LOOKED up as a folded piece of paper appeared on her desk, on top of her Statistics homework. "Hey Scarlett," she greeted. "What's this?"

"You dropped it in the Cafeteria this morning. The guy who picked it up asked me to return it." Scarlett said. "I figured I'd slip you his phone number too."

"I'm dating someone, but who is it?" Alyx asked. "I can still thank him for getting this back to me."

Scarlett handed her another piece of paper with a number that she recognized before Scarlett told her the name. "Peter Carlyle. He's on the football team, and I for one, am very sorry to hear you can't go out with him."

Alyx smiled sadly. "Thanks."

Scarlett found her way back to her desk, sitting down just before the bell rang. Alyx looked at the folded piece of paper, shoving it in the pocket with all of her pens and pencils.

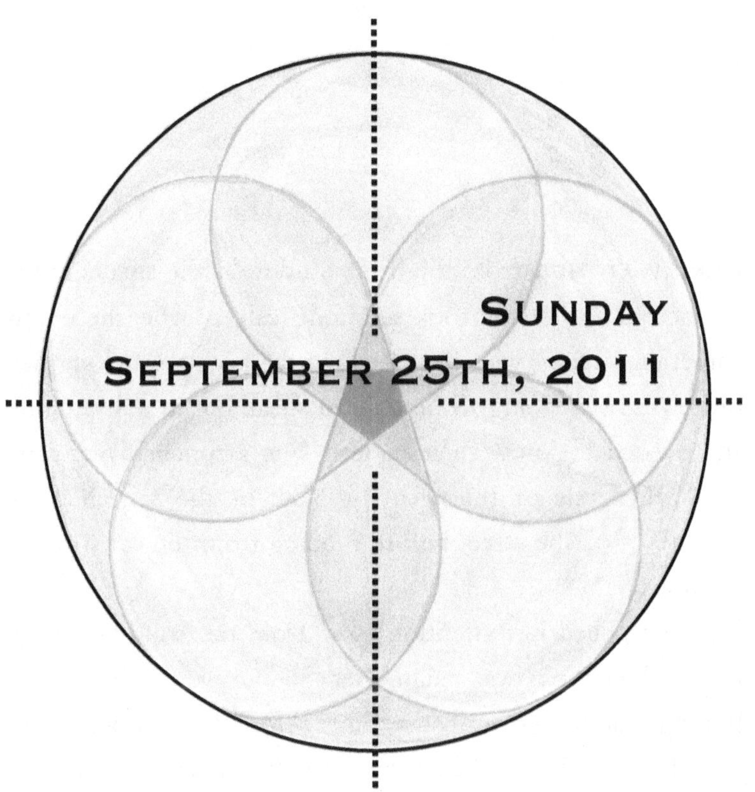
SUNDAY
SEPTEMBER 25TH, 2011

16:16 PDT
Tracy, California
McLean Home

ALYX WATCHED from the front window as the agents in the car across the street took a phone call. Maybe there was something wrong with her watching the agents watching her, but if she was going to be able to sneak out at some point, she needed to know their pattern. She scrunched her forehead when one of the agents got out of the car, checking both sides of the street before running from the car towards the house.

Alyx pulled her attention away from the window to her phone. Her mom was calling her. She answered the phone, putting it up to her ear just seconds before the doorbell rang.

"That will be the FBI agent." Sarah said as she heard the doorbell through the phone. Let the agent in the house."

Alyx sighed, walking down the stairs. "Are you going to tell me what's going on?" She asked her mom.

She heard nothing but silence on the other end. Her mom was probably having one of her silent conversations with her dad. Usually she wouldn't mind, but she'd just discovered that her parents had been lying to her about more things than she could have ever imagined. Then again, her parents phone numbers themselves were evidence of some lies. Her earliest memories occurred in Virginia, and her parents tried to tell her that was where she was born. She had believed them. Why would they lie? But she wasn't so sure anymore. The 909 area code of their phone numbers came from Southern California, and her parents had always kept the same phone numbers, saying it was easier for friends to get ahold of them, despite their frequent moves. But she didn't remember living in Southern California. She'd never been to California at all until they'd moved here when she was 13.

She remembered countless other places, but never California.

"Why is the FBI watching me? I'm sure dad told them it was because he was concerned about me with the case he's working, but I know quite a bit about this case, and that's not a real concern. I'm not part of whatever training program all of the victims have been. Unless this is about last summer." Alyx heard another short pause.

"Let the agent in." Her dad insisted. Clearly he'd been listening. "Peter's car was just reported as abandoned on Steven Bridges Court. The proximity to our house, and his connection to you is more than enough reason to assign an FBI detail."

"If you insist on those agents being in the house, I *will*

find a way to sneak out." Alyx promised.

"Let them in before they break the door down." Neil sighed exasperated, hanging up the phone. Apparently her dad figured it was easier to not answer questions if she never asked them.

Alyx disarmed the alarm, walking to the door to let the agent into the house. If she was honest, she did feel a pit growing in her stomach. Finding out Peter was a spy didn't change her feelings for him. She loved him.

ALYX CHECKED the hallway outside her bathroom before closing it. She turned a faucet on, so if the agent sitting downstairs came up, she would just think Alyx was getting ready for bed. Alyx then walked through the second door into the room with the toilet and shower. She lowered the seat on the toilet, sitting on the lid as she selected Thane's contact from her phone.

She didn't even wait for Thane to say *hi* when the line picked up. "What does Peter have access to? He's part of the training program, and everyone seems to report to him, including you. So what does your dad want from him?"

"It's too dangerous." Thane replied. "You should stay out of it." The line went dead as he hung up.

There were two things that Alyx didn't do. She didn't give up, and she definitely didn't walk away because something was *too dangerous.* So Alyx decided to call Chelsi.

"What might your dad achieve by kidnapping Peter?" She

asked as soon as Chelsi answered.

Chelsi was silent for a second while she thought. "Well, he would gain access to the Promising Generation database."

"The what?"

Alyx could hear the deafening silence coming from the phone. No doubt, Chelsi was biting her lip, realizing she'd probably said more than she should have.

"Listen. Peter's been kidnapped. I need to find a way to save him, but that involves identifying your dad's motivations."

Chelsi sighed, giving in. "Peter is the one with access to all of the training program's files."

"Can he sign on using any computer?" Alyx asked.

"No. It can only be accessed using his laptop."

Alyx nodded. "Thank you."

As she left the bathroom, she knew two things: she was sneaking out, and she was breaking into Peter's house to steal a laptop.

PETER SMILED as he watched Dylan Hall walk into the room he was being held in. "Took you long enough." He taunted.

Hall remained silent as he closed the door, and sat down in a chair across from Peter. It was unsettling to see Carlyle so pleased to be here. That made Hall feel like he was missing something, and when spies missed something, that typically meant their life was in danger. There wasn't a lot of room for mistakes in espionage, and Hall couldn't help but feel like he'd made one by kidnapping Peter.

"Do you know why you're here?" Hall asked.

Peter smiled. "If you ask your daughter, she'd say it's because you're a psychopath. Lynn, however, seems to give you the benefit of the doubt."

Hall couldn't help the sinking feeling in his stomach. Not only had Carlyle figured out who he was much quicker than Nathan had, but the first card he played involved not only his children, but his niece as well. He not only knew who he was, but the operation he'd been involved in months before. Either someone had given this young man files that he shouldn't have been, or he was an enemy.

"I've figured out enough that I know that I have what you want, and I want you to make me a deal. I will give you what you want, but I want more than just freedom for me and the friends you've kidnapped." Peter explained. "See, I know who you are, I know what your job title is, and I know your children. My guess is that you want control of the Generation back. Honestly, I would be glad to be rid of Wraith, and I think you would do us quite a bit of good.

"I'm assuming that in order to prove to the Training Division our training has failed, you need the files only I have access to. I'm willing to tell you where they are. If I do, however, I need your report to the Training Division to paint me and the other members who've kidnapped in good light. Since I figured out what you wanted, and let you kidnap me, I think that should be easy. I give you the files, and you give your daughter the credit for finding you and sending me here. You prove Wraith's training is flawed, and that yours is significantly better with one little report."

Hall stared at Carlyle after letting him talk. His proposal, while tempting, also sounded like a trick. Carlyle wanted Hall to believe that they wanted the same thing, but he wasn't sure that was true. "My daughter found me?" Hall questioned. "And what might a highly trained spy do that gave away my covert activities to a spy in training?"

Peter smiled. "Chelsi remembered a conversation with you about Twitter, then suddenly her friend who had posted things on twitter with the ironic hashtag of *spylife* ended up kidnapped. Exactly how dire is the situation with your beautiful niece, by the way?"

Hall got up, knocking on the door to be let out.

"Wait." Peter pleaded. He was *desperate*. It was the first time he had used anything other than a calm, calculated tone, and it was that, aside from the actual word that made Hall pause and think maybe he wasn't being played. "I'll tell you where my computer is. It's the only way to access the server. I want to help. That's why I'm here."

Hall looked at Carlyle, trying to figure out what could have caused him to be so desperate to give him the files. Then again, Hall was desperate himself, so he wasn't going to turn down an opportunity to get what he needed. "I'm listening."

"The alarm code is 2599. The computer is sitting on the dining room table charging. When you bring it back, I can give you the password, and help you find whatever you are looking for." Peter rambled.

The door opened and Hall left, not answering Carlyle's intel to make sure he left him in a state of unknowing. He knew too much already.

Hall looked at the young man he had hired to gather his intelligence to break the trainees he kidnapped. "I want you to find out why he willingly gave me what I wanted. He's scared of something, or protecting someone. I want to know what, and who."

Derek Stevens looked at the door, but nodded, walking off.

Hall turned to Banthup. "I want you to keep eyes on the house. I'm taking a team to grab the laptop tomorrow. I want to make sure it's still there when I do."

He might just have a chance of protecting his niece after all.

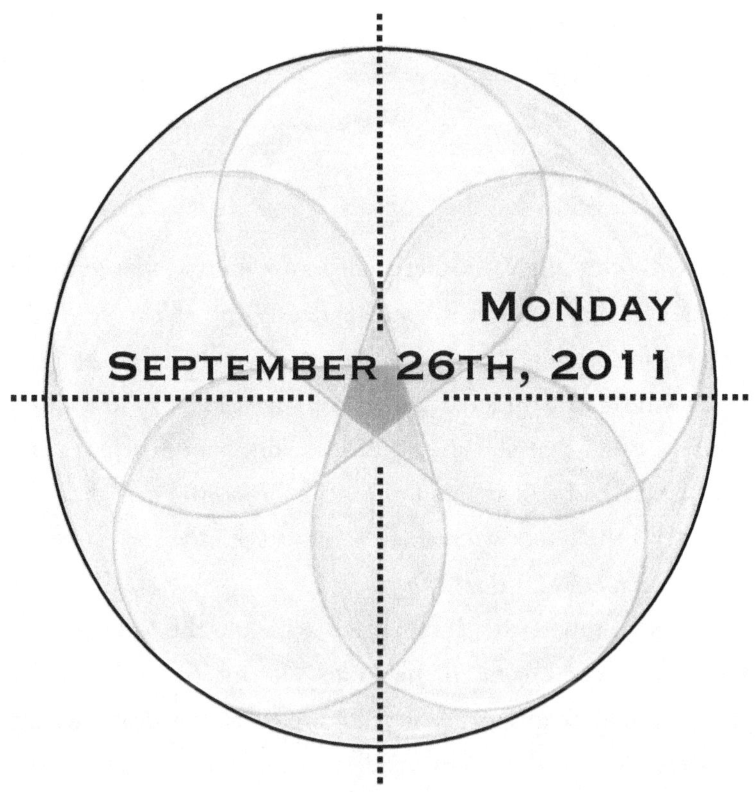
MONDAY
SEPTEMBER 26TH, 2011

ALYX CAREFULLY slid her bedroom window open enough for her to slip through it. Before setting the alarm the night before, she'd opened it a crack, like she usually did, telling the agent who had wondered why the alarm told her there was a window open that she slept with the window open just a bit. The agent had called her father, but he confirmed that she slept with the window cracked. It was a second story window. What harm could it do?

Alyx grabbed the small black tabs on the side of the window screen, using them to pry it out of the window frame, rather than kicking it out to let it clatter down to the ground, alerting the agent inside to what she was doing. She set it carefully on the roof just outside her window, propping it up on the outside wall to the right of her window, where her dad's office sat. She followed the screen out the window, closing the window back down to the crack it had been open before, then replaced the screen as best she could, while ensuring she could remove it to get back in.

With her out of the window, the easy part of sneaking out was behind her. The hardest part was right in front of her. She had to get off the roof, and across the backyard, without the agent inside seeing her. From her spot on the roof, she could see that the blinds of the family room were closed, but the lights on inside made the window glow, and she could see the shadow of the TV. Even if the blinds prevented people from seeing in or out, it didn't prevent people seeing shadows created by someone walking between the light and the window. In order to succeed, she somehow had to drop down off the roof without letting her shadow alert the agent inside to her movement.

Alyx decided that her best bet was climbing down the tree just feet from the roof she was currently squatting on. While she knew that was the worst option for getting away without notice if the window was open, as the time it would take for her to climb the tree was much longer than just jumping and rolling from the roof, she knew that right now, she needed something without sudden movement, which would draw attention to the window.

Alyx looked at the distance between the edge of the roof and the tree, trying to decide how best to reach the tree.

On second thought, it was *much* easier to drop off the roof.

The section of roof she was sitting on slopped down towards the tree she had originally been planning on using to jump down, meaning that by the time she reached the edge of the roof, she was standing on a surface lower than the floor of her room, and if she held onto the edge of the roof and lowered herself down, she would only have to drop maybe three feet, and since she jumped hurdles about that height for Track all the time, she figured that was much more doable then trying to jump to the tree.

She got as close to the edge as she could, turning around and squatting down, then found a good place to grip the roof so she could kick her feet off. Finding as good of a handhold as she could, she dropped her feet off the roof, letting the swinging that resulted push her toward the wall under the overhang created by the roof, where she planted her feet. She lowered herself as far as she could, dropping her feet back off the wall, and waited for the swinging to stop, then let go of the roof. She landed softly on her feet, her knees bending to absorb some of the fall, but also help her drop below where the bottom of the window was so she could run across the side yard without being seen from the windows in the family room. As she reached the corner of the house, she went straight, running across the concrete sidewalk that led to the fence, and into the grass at the back of the yard, straight to the back fence next to the oleander tree in the north-east corner of the yard. As she ran across the yard, she pulled her body up into a sprinting position, and didn't slow as she approached the fence. Instead, she planted her right foot on the fence, launching herself up, where she grabbed the top of the fence and pulled herself over into the yard of one of the neighbors behind her, where she ran around the pool to their gate, which was fortunately unlocked. She slipped out and onto the court where the house was located, running to the main street it was off of, then east to the corner of that street and her own.

As she ran across her street, she couldn't help but smile, as her shortcut through the neighbor's yard had taken her far enough away from her house that she wasn't visible to the FBI agent in the car. In her black running leggings and hoodie, with her hood pulled up, it didn't matter much any-way, because she almost just looked like a runner that got up at an insane time to get their morning run in. She knew that the street she was on had a park a short way down it, and that across from the park there was a court that backed itself onto the court Peter lived on. All she had to do was jump one more fence. She turned when she saw the court, running toward the last house on the east side where there was a small section of exposed fence. On the other side of that fence was the mailbox for Golden Leaf Court.

BANTHUP SAT watching the house two in from the corner, at the outer edge of the cul-de-sac, annoyed that once again, he was the one staking out a potential lead for Hall, but not helping with the actual interrogation happening. He may have been one of the few people on Hall's team with CIA training, but amateurs like Derek Stevens were the ones helping Hall with the interrogations, while Banthup's training was wasted by sitting in a car, watching an empty house.

Banthup sighed, checking his watch. He tried not to look up startled as he heard a knocking on his passenger side window, finding none other than Kalen Mckenzie standing at his window. Banthup unlocked the door, letting the teenage nephew of his *real* boss in the car. At least Jackson appreciated him enough to use his talents to their full potential, and sent him undercover into enemy territory. Kalen handed Banthup a Redbull, as he climbed into the passenger seat, looking across to the house Banthup was watching. "I thought you might need something to keep you awake."

Banthup eyed Kalen suspiciously. "And why might you care?"

"McLean and I have unfinished business. If helping you gets me to that sooner than leaving you to suffer on your own, I'm going to help." Kalen answered.

"And what exactly has some cheerleader done that has pissed you off so much?" Banthup prodded. "Did she turn you down for the dance?"

"She knocked me out and left me for dead in the middle of the Austrian Alps." Kalen replied. "She's not just some teenaged girl. She is a well trained enemy operative."

"Then why is it that none of these teenage spies have had any contact with her?" Banthup questioned. "I have been assigned to follow every single one of the spies that Stevens has discovered, and not a single one of them has led me to McLean. And just in case you had forgotten, Hall may have only kidnapped four of them, but this teen makes number eight. Eight spies in this tiny town, and McLean hasn't so much as *passed* a single one on the street."

"Because she knows you're watching." Kalen suggested.

"Eight well trained spies had no clue I was watching them, but she does." Banthup scoffed. "It sounds like you are trying to justify failure the last time you faced her. I'm not even convinced that she's in this stupid town."

"Trust me, she's here." Kalen answered.

"So what exactly are in these files that both Hall and

Jackson want them so bad?" Banthup asked.

"The name of every agent who knows we exist, and have at least at one point in time gone after us." Kalen answered. He smiled. "We're getting close."

"No, McKenzie. Hall is getting close to what he wants, and we are no where near to being close to what Jackson wants, which is Hall's niece in his employ. Banthup retorted. "In fact, I believe Jackson's orders were to make sure Hall got the files, so he didn't start to suspect me."

"Then why is McLean picking the lock on your target's front door at four in the morning?" Kalen asked.

"You can't possibly tell that's her." Banthup criticized.

"I have watched the video of her fighting my uncle's men so many times over the past few months, that I know how she moves better than she knows herself." Kalen claimed. "Trust me, it's her."

"How did she get there?" Banthup asked. "She didn't come past us."

Kalen chose his uncle's contact from his favorites list holding the phone up to his ear as it started to ring. "She came from the cul-de-sac."

"Like she lives here?" Banthup asked.

Kalen shrugged getting ready to reply, but Jackson picked up, so his reply was postponed. "We found her. She's at Carlyle's house."

Banthup watched the smile fade from Kalen's face as his uncle gave him orders for McLean. Whatever they were, they weren't what Kalen was hoping to hear.

"Yes sir." Kalen said, hanging up.

"Don't tell me, your revenge will have to wait." Banthup teased.

Kalen clenched his jaw. "I may not have been given permission to shoot her tonight, but trust me, the day will come when I will, and she won't have any warning." With that, Kalen opened the door, and climbed out. "Now I have an elusive girl to follow home."

4:21 PDT
Tracy, California
Promising Generation Training Program HQ

ALYX KNEELED in front of Peter's front door, her lock picking set in her hand as she worked on opening the front door. Despite suspecting that the house would have a security system, she didn't see any cameras, and she wondered how much of that had to do with the fact that cameras would be evidence of who came and went, and spies were nervous of that sort of thing.

The door swung open as she got the lock, and turned the handle. No one could say she wasn't good at picking locks. Then again, she had been practicing on various locks her dad bought her, because he'd caught her practicing on their home door a few houses back, and he didn't want the neighbors calling the cops on her. She heard the warning from the alarm panel that the alarm needed to be disarmed. Fortunately, it didn't take her long to find where the panel was. When she saw it she smiled. Peter had a Scofield 2009, the same as her house. She walked up to it and held down the 9 key to reboot the panel, just like she had with her own panel a few days before. This time, however, nothing happened.

Leave it to Peter to fix a flaw in the security system.

She sighed. She had less than a minute before the alarm went off, and way too many permutations of the four-digit code to try in that minute. She could try his birthday, even though that was unlikely the combination, but she didn't know it. She thought about it for a second, then pulled a compact of blush from one of the make-up kits she had stolen from the kits in her father's office and one of the brushes. She twirled the brush in the powder of the blush, then brushed it on the keys of the panel, finding the 2, 5, and 9 keys with fingerprints on them. With only three keys showing use, one of them being the one that she herself had used to try to reboot the system. Since the 2 and the 5 keys had the same amount of blush on them, she was guessing they saw similar use, she tried 2525, 5252, 2255, 5522, 2552, and 5225 but none of them worked. The 9 must have been used too, and it had substantially more blush on it, meaning it saw more use than the other two keys. She tried 2599. It worked.

When she found Peter, she would have to talk to him about the simplicity of the code. In order for a code to be hard to crack, it really shouldn't have numbers repeated, and they shouldn't be in numeric order.

With the alarm disarmed, Alyx was free to roam the house and find what she was looking for. Fortunately, it didn't take long, because Peter had left his laptop on the kitchen table.

If Peter wasn't going to make sure Hall didn't get the files he wanted, Alyx would.

Alyx slid the computer into the black backpack she'd brought with her hidden under her hoodie, then checked her watch. She knew that the FBI team assigned to watch her would switch out soon, with the team arriving in about five minutes. They would discuss the previous watch, and any pertinent details, before checking the house. That gave her about ten minutes before she had to leave Peter's house.

She couldn't help but feel a pang of sorrow as she walked through what should have been Peter's home, but was nothing more than his residence. The house was obviously used for official Promising Generation business, if the name Chelsi had let slip was correct. His story about his absent parents had clearly not been a lie.

Alyx slipped into the garage, curious as to what a spy might keep there. Surprisingly, she found it empty aside from a black 2012 BMW 335i convertible, complete with a big red bow on top. She walked over, curious about the car given the grief Peter had given her about her car, and all the parents at Kimball that bought their 16-year-old a brand new car for their birthday. She found a card, dated in August.

Happy 16th Birthday

-love mom

She may not have known when Peter's birthday was, but she knew he hadn't just turned 16. He was definitely 17. His mom had bought him a car for a birthday that was a year before. His parents would never win the title of *Parent of the Year*, but looking at the car Alyx had an idea. She took the bow off the top, setting it on the ground behind her. Peter could get mad at her later. She opened the door of the car, smiling as she saw that the keys were inside. Peter must not have so much as touched the car once he'd received it. Sure, it was a little flashy, but if she played her cards right, it would be perfect for saving Peter.

She checked the time again. There was no way she could take the car, and sneak back into her house before the FBI agents checked her room. She'd have to come back for the car. She grabbed the keys. With a smile, she slid the backpack off, hiding it in the trunk. She hit the lock button on the key fob once, before hiding the key in her sports bra.

4:28 PDT
Tracy, California
Madison Park Housing Development

KALEN WATCHED as McLean came running back down the cul-de-sac from his hiding spot in the yard of the house at the end of the court on the west side. He was hoping to see what house she lived in, so he could start watching it until Jackson decided what he wanted to do to get her to join him. As McLean ran past him, however, and jumped the fence, he realized his guess that she lived on the court was wrong.

He hated this girl. She couldn't make anything easy.

Kalen was up and running for the fence seconds after McLean's hands left the top of the fence. He needed to see which way she was running if he was going to follow her home, and he was unfamiliar with this neighborhood and what stood on the other side of that fence. As he reached the fence, he used the upper body strength Jackson had insisted he develop to do a pull up, bringing his chin above the top of the fence so he could watch where McLean went, quickly dropping back to the ground after he'd taken note of the direction she was running. After waiting for a decent amount of time, long enough that McLean was unlikely to notice him following, but not so long that he would lose her, he jumped the fence, sprinting to gain ground and regain visual. He got close enough that had she not been distracted planning how to get back over to Peter's house to steal his car, she would have noticed him before ducking into some bushes where he could watch to see where she ran.

He watched as she turned up another cul-de-sac, and, creeping closer to the entrance of the street, he watched as she ran at the house in the middle, slipping through the un-locked gate. As the gate closed completely behind her, he began sprinting straight down the middle of the street. Side-walks were not the most direct route, and he wanted to see where she entered the house, if this was her house. He quietly slipped through the gate, using the house as cover as he searched the yard and the many windows of the house for where she might be. As he came to the corner of the house, he finally saw her, behind the trees in the corner of the yard behind the pool, climbing the fence.

He waited behind the house until she had completely disappeared, following her to the corner, but opting to climb one of the trees to watch where she went, rather than expose himself by following her over yet another fence.

The house whose yard McLean had climbed into had lights on downstairs, but she didn't seem all too worried about that, although she did seem to be a bit more cautious, waiting just on the other side of the fence from Kalen, her body aimed for the house rather than the fence this time.

"She's asleep up in her room." A female voice came from somewhere in front of the house Alyx was running towards. "It's the last room before the library upstairs, if you need to check on her."

"And the house is secure?" Another female voice asked.

With the second voice, McLean shot off across the yard, running towards the bit of roof lower than the rest on the side of the house with three fruit trees, directly across from where she had jumped over the fence.

As she ran past the two windows with light glowing behind them, seemingly unconcerned about being caught, Kalen heard the first female voice report about the alarm, and the hourly walks around the first floor, details that someone joining a security detail would care about, which McLean only answered by jumping to grab the lower roof, and pulling herself up onto it, where she pulled out the screen, slid the window open, and slipped inside, before returning the screen.

It would be so easy to follow her, and drag her out without anyone knowing. "I've got you McLean." Kalen whispered to himself.

He was getting ready to do exactly that when he watched as a woman, who was very clearly some form of agent with her pressed dress slacks and matching blazer with her hair slicked back into a tight knot on the back of her head, walked out the back door, doing a visual sweep of the yard.

So McLean had a protection detail. That made things difficult, but not impossible, as evidenced by McLean's ability to sneak out under the noses of the agents meant to be protecting her.

Kalen shifted his gaze from the house McLean had snuck into, and to the single story house next door that had a perfect line of sight to the room he guessed McLean slept in. He climbed down out of the tree he was perched in, shifting his position in the yard over to where he knew the other yard was, pulling himself up over the fence into the yard of the other house. He walked to the fence on the opposite side of the house from McLean's and jumped over to the front, fortunate to find the front door on the same side of the house as where he was, blocked from the view of the agents watching the McLean house. All it took was a quick brushing off, a walk down the sidewalk from the front door, and a wave to the agents who turned their attention to him. "Beautiful morning for a walk," Kalen said, "Don't you think?"

The agents nodded, and turned their attention back away from him, the apparent teenaged-son of the family that lived in the house next door. Two of the agents got in their car, leaving one agent to climb into his own and watch the house, while the other car drove off.

One agent watching the house, the other in the house watching the girl. Kalen smirked as he began walking down the street in the direction he hoped would lead him out of the neighborhood.

Getting McLean would be very easy indeed.

10:58 PDT

Tracy, California

John C. Kimball High School

ALYX THREW her backpack in a booth across from Carlie and Thane. Carlie rolled her eyes. "Are you still stressing about the note? Just talk to him. Forgive him already."

Alyx gave Carlie a dirty look. "You don't even know what he did."

"What note?" Thane asked.

Carlie turned to Thane, her turn to pass the dirty look onto Thane. "Have you not been listening to the conversation in every one of your classes today?"

Savannah slid into the booth next to Alyx. "Ooh. Are we talking about the ever mysterious *Peter Carlyle* who apparently sent one of his cheerleader friends to Alyx with a note Thursday? I've heard conflicting rumors today, one saying that it was accompanied with his phone number, another saying you two are secretly dating.

Carlie laughed, the sound disappearing into the deafening noise of the 1000 teenagers sitting in the lunchroom. "She'd

346

have to actually have the nerves to talk to him first." The laugh sputtered out from nerves. "Seriously, who started that one?" Carlie looked knowingly at Alyx. "It certainly *wasn't* me."

Savannah looked across at Carlie. "No one suggested you did." She flipped her hair over her shoulder. "Besides, even though *we* know she can't talk to him, it doesn't mean anyone else does. As far as they know, McLean is disinterested in dating. Did I hear correctly that you turned down three dates last week?"

"I started the rumors." Alyx admitted quietly, pulling out a textbook.

While Carlie and Thane just stared at Alyx, Savannah went on like Alyx hadn't said anything. "All I'm saying is that going on a couple of dates wouldn't hurt. It might improve your image, and stop a crazy rumor or two. This week you have a secret boyfriend. What if next week they are closer to the truth."

"I really am secretly dating Peter." Alyx insisted, but Savannah didn't seem to hear her, intent on delivering her lecture.

"What did the note even say, anyway? Did you get his phone number? Does he think you're cute?" Savannah interrogated.

Alyx pulled the note out of her back pocket and slid it over to Savannah. She unfolded it, reading it.

"*I'm sorry?* What is he *sorry* for? And why does he think

you need to go to London?" Savannah questioned.

Kaden came running up to the table, squeezing into the booth next to Savannah. "You guys will never believe who didn't show up to school today." Kaden huffed. Three sets of eyes settled on him. "None other than Mr. Peter Carlyle."

"And that's what he's sorry for." Alyx mumbled into her textbook.

Kaden gave Alyx a confused look, then continued. "Clearly I've missed something, but first, the news. According to the whispers from the teachers, authorities suspect his disappearance is related to the other missing boys. He was friends with Cameron McKay, the third boy kidnapped."

"When?" Thane asked. He may have been one of the only people at this table who knew *exactly* when, but he asked to keep up appearances, and to gauge how much Alyx knew.

"Sometime over the weekend. Neighbors found his car abandoned on Steven Bridges Court yesterday afternoon," she answered.

"Okay. What did I miss?" Kaden asked.

Alyx just bit her lip, not taking her eyes off her textbook, even though her focus was on everything but school.

"Alyx has been secretly dating Peter. It started with him coming over to study for the AP French test." Carlie said, staring at her friend, waiting for her to jump in and add the details only she knew, but Alyx maintained silence.

"The rumors are true?" Savannah verified. "Alyx, I'm so sorry."

"Was it pretty serious?" Kaden asked.

"They were exchanging *I love you*'s," Carlie scoffed, "And she decided not to tell us that she had not only had the courage to talk to her crush, but start dating him."

"Yes, I love him, and yes, I told him. He's charming, and funny, and he loves me. But…" Alyx trailed off, deciding to gesture around the at the note, and all the friends that brought news of the kidnapping. "We clearly have our problems."

"What can we do?" Carlie asked.

"Make sure the rumors that we're dating keep circulating. I have a plan to save him, but that rumor is the key."

Alyx turned her eyes back to the textbook, and for once, her friends let her.

11:27 PDT
Tracy, California
Promising Generation Training Program HQ

HALL WALKED through Peter's house, searching for the room where he was told Peter's laptop would be. He heard the beeping of the alarm stop as Neil finished punching in the alarm code, disarming the alarm. Hall didn't mind working with his brother-in-law again, and he definitely trusted Neil for this mission much more than he trusted any of the agents he had hired to help him with the Generation members, but he was unused to having someone with a badge working with him.

Then again, considering the importance of the mission, and what Neil had just been read in on while he was in D.C., he was lucky it was just Neil working with him, and that Sarah hadn't tried to take over the mission yet.

Hall entered what he guessed was the dining room, noting the long table that hosted Generation meetings, and a TV. Neil followed him. "Where did he say it was?" Neil asked again.

"You mean if the young woman that matches your daughter's description didn't steal it last night when she broke in?" Hall replied sarcastically. "Charging on the table, and it's not here."

Neil walked across the room, to the head of the table where he could see a charging cable resting. "Well, it *was* here." He picked up the cord, signaling the truth of Peter's statement.

Hall joined him at the head of the table, noticing the small sticky note in the center of the place where the computer should have been.

"I don't know where it is." Hall stated. "But I know who has it." He picked up the note, showing it to Neil.

"Your daughter took it." Hall told Neil.

Neil smirked. "You know, I really should be mad at her, but part of me is really proud." He admitted.

"The trick is figuring out how to convince her to give us those files. We need them if we're going to protect her." Hall pointed out.

Neil sighed. He had a feeling *that* was going to be impossible.

DEREK STEVENS anxiously watched the camera feed from the room Peter was being kept in. He had watched as Hall had interrogated and broken all three of the other boys who had been kidnapped, but watching Hall instigate a staring match with Peter made him nervous. After all, he hadn't known the first two young men, and he'd been friendly with Cameron, but Peter was his friend. He liked to think they'd been best friends.

Something seemed off about Peter. He'd seen the desperation in Hall's first interrogation, but it wasn't just because he knew Peter that he'd seen it, because Hall had seen it too, tasking him to figure out why. *Scared of something, or protecting someone?* Those had been the options that Hall had suggested was the cause of his desperation, but Stevens still hadn't figured out which one. The first one was unlikely. He knew Peter well enough to know that nothing scared him. Then again, who would Peter be protecting.

While Hall and Peter sat in silence, both of them just staring across the table at the other too stubborn to concede to the other, Stevens pulled out his phone, pulling up the contact for one of the few people he still remained in contact with from West High Football: Trevor Williams.

He watched the muscles twitch in Peter's jaw as he held the ringing phone up to his ear, hoping Trevor would pick up.

If anyone had any clues into Peter's current psyche, it would be Trevor, since he would have been one of the last people to see him before Hall activated the extraction team. Fortunately, he picked up.

"Hey Derek. Did you hear what happened to Peter?" Trevor answered.

"Yeah. That's why I'm calling." Stevens admitted. "I was wondering if you knew what happened."

"Not really. Dude, it's weird. He was fine last week, then Thursday he asked me to take a note to this girl on the track team with me. Scarlett ended up being the one to deliver it, but then today he's gone, and there are rumors that he's been dating the girl. He didn't tell anyone, and he's not really the boyfriend type, at least he hasn't been, but I'm inclined to believe it because I don't think Thursday was the first time they passed off notes. He was being super cagey about a note last month, plus she's totally his type. I just didn't know he knew her." Trevor explained. There was a moment of silence, and through it Stevens could hear Trevor's coach yelling at him to hang up the phone. "I gotta go."

"Who's the girl?" Stevens asked before Trevor could hang up. "Anyone I know?"

"Uh, I don't know. Some Junior. Her last name is McLean." Trevor rushed. "Call you later." He promised, then hung up.

So maybe he was protecting someone after all. Stevens turned to another computer, ignoring the video of Peter and Hall, and pulled up the Kimball High track records from the year before. Trevor had mentioned that she was on the Track team with him the year before, so he began searching all the Sophomore girls names for one that had the last name McLean. And he found one. Alyxandrie McLean.

15:05 PDT
Tracy, California
Hall Base of Operations

HALL STORMED into the room he'd set up as a surveillance room, heading straight to Stevens. "Tell me you got something."

Stevens nodded. "I talked to a football player at Kimball who is friends with Carlyle. He told me that Thursday, Carlyle asked him to give a girl from the track team a note. Today, there were rumors floating around that Carlyle is dating said girl, and the rumor seems to be substantiated, as this isn't the first note Carlyle has hidden this year. Evidence seems to suggest that he is dating her, and is very protective of the relationship, which might suggest he is protective of her as well."

"Is there a reason he needs to protect her?" Hall asked. "I'm looking for something that would justify giving up the government secrets he has sworn to protect."

"I haven't been able to find anything yet. She seems to be a ghost. Besides her name appearing on various websites that record Track times, and newspaper articles recounting her wins in Tennis, I haven't found anything on her yet." Stevens admitted. "But I did just get her name, so I will keep digging."

"What's the name?" Hall prodded.

"Alyxandrie McLean." Stevens reported.

Hall paled. "You're sure."

"Yes. All Williams had was her last name, but she was the only McLean on the roster for Kimball High's Track and Field team last year." Stevens confirmed.

"Good job, Stevens." Hall grunted, turning to leave the room. "I need to go back in and interrogate Carlyle some more."

Stevens shook his head. "But I don't know what he's protecting her from."

"I do." Hall commented, and left.

"What kind of name is Alyxandrie?" Banthup asked when he was sure Hall was a safe distance away, and couldn't hear him.

Stevens shrugged. "French, I think. It's an odd spelling, but it closely resembles the French form of Alexandra."

Stevens and Banthup returned to silence, watching as Hall reentered the room Peter was being held in, setting a piece of paper in front of him.

"We're going to talk about Alyx McLean, and why she left this note where you told me your computer would be." Hall commanded.

Stevens watched as the desperation returned to Peter's face, distracted by the monitors, making him oblivious to the shift in Banthup's demeanor as Hall said *Alyx McLean.*

15:35 PDT
Tracy, California
McLean Home

NEIL MCLEAN sat down at his desk in his office, the door closed tight against the frame. He'd made sure the room was soundproofed, so even though Alyx shared a wall with his office, there was no way she was going to be able to eavesdrop. He pulled out his phone, selecting the phone number that belonged to his brother-in-law.

Fortunately, Hall didn't take too long to answer. "Did you find anything?"

"No. I've searched everywhere. It's not in her room; it's not in the library. It's not anywhere in the house. I even went over to the school and convinced them to let me search her car. And her sports locker. I didn't find it there either. If she has it, she didn't hide it anywhere I've looked."

"Trust me, that note was her. She has it." Hall asserted.

Neil sighed. "I know. I recognize her handwriting. My point is she took it. That doesn't mean she still has it. She's a smart girl. She knows that you are her uncle. Guaranteed, she took precautions to make sure we can't find it without her wanting us to."

"Either that, or she has it with her." Hall suggested. He sighed. "We might have bigger problems than that. Carlyle *wanted* to be found. He knew I was the one behind the kidnappings, and he knew about the operation I participated in over the summer."

"How?" Neil asked, panicked. "I seem to remember that when we pulled Alyx from the program, he was under investigation. He was pretty close to McKenzie, who ended up killing his own parents for the Circle of Fifths."

"McKenzie disappeared, and never made contact with Carlyle." Hall admitted. "I don't know how he knows, but I don't think he's our enemy."

"You don't *think* he's our enemy. But you don't *know*." Neil almost yelled. He sighed, regaining composure. "I'm sorry. I don't mean to question your judgement, it's just I want to make sure she's safe, and that job alone has nearly taken over my life."

Hall laughed. "You two have more in common than you know." Hall took a deep breath, letting the laughter sputter out. "He turned himself in because of Alyx. I don't know how much he knows, but he's trying to protect her. Rumors at the school are that they are secretly dating. And I think that's our bigger problem. Until I talk to her, I won't get the files or answers we need out of either of them."

"You want to kidnap her." Neil guessed. "You realize, Sarah will kill you. That's if Alyx doesn't first."

"I just want to put an agent on her. Let them follow her. Maybe she will lead us to the laptop." Hall suggested.

Neil sighed. "If it doesn't work, we try my way first, before you decide to just kidnap my daughter. Understood?"

"Yes." Hall replied, ending the call.

This was not going to end well.

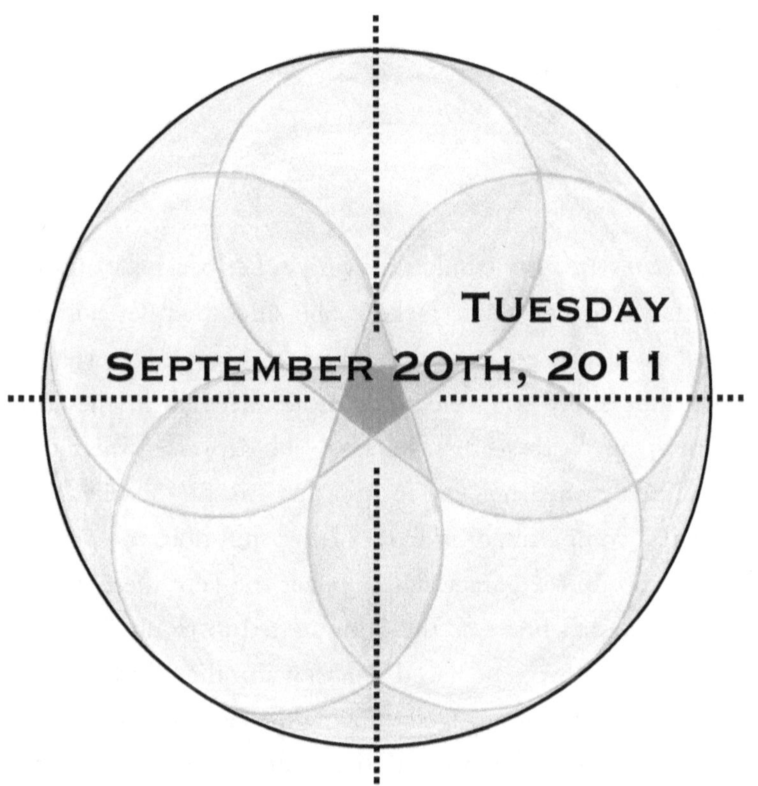

TUESDAY
SEPTEMBER 20TH, 2011

6:18 PDT
Tracy, California
McLean Home

ALYX OPENED her trunk, throwing in her backpack and the
bag that held her tennis rackets. She smoothed her uniform
down as she sat down in the driver's seat, zipping her jacket
up a little more to protect her from the chill in the early
morning air. With seatbelt buckled, she depressed the clutch
pedal, and turned her key to start her car. She reached into
the small compartment in front of her shift nob, and pressed
the button on the garage door opener she kept there, releasing the parking brake as the door started to climb. With the
garage door open, she eased her foot off the clutch, feeling
the clutch bite as it engaged, moving the car forward into the
driveway, where she pressed the clutch to the floor once
again, this time paired with the brake. With the car stopped in
the driveway, she hit the button again, watching as the door
returned to its home on the ground.

Out of habit, she took the car out of gear, moving the
shifter back and forth in the middle, before pushing it back in

first gear. She once again engaged the clutch by letting it off the floor, this time adding gas as she left the driveway, accelerating down the street, shifting as she reached 3000 RPM, not because she had to, but in an attempt to keep her speed under the low limit in the neighborhood. As she stopped at the stop sign where Robert Gabriel Drive crossed Carol Ann Drive, she caught the same black Ford behind her that had been watching Peter's house Monday morning when she'd snuck out. Her plan had worked. The rumors had made their way to Hall.

If Hall's agent thought he was going to be able to follow her, though, he was sadly mistaken. Sure, she'd let him think she didn't notice. She could let him follow her to Seminary, and to school. She would even let him follow her to the Tennis match. Once she had lured him into a false sense of ease, she would lose him.

She wondered for a second as she drove out of the neighborhood what Hall would do to the agent that let a teenage girl follow him back to where the Generation members were being held.

18:36 PDT
Tracy, California

CHELSI LOOKED at Alyx with incredulity. "You want me to drive your car? You realized I'm not even old enough to get a permit, right?"

Alyx shrugged. "And? Do you honestly expect me to believe that your training program doesn't teach you how to drive before you have a permit? If it were me, not only would you learn how to drive the second you could reach the pedals, but you would learn evasive driving techniques."

Chelsi sighed. "Well yeah, but this is your *baby*. I've seen the looks you've given Thane for even *asking* to drive your car. Plus what if I get pulled over?"

"Don't get pulled over." Alyx advised. "Look, I need you to just let this moron follow you home. I'm hoping the combination of seeing you, not me, get out of the drivers seat, and the fact you are getting out at his boss' house will make him drive back to where your dad is keeping the boys. If he thinks he's lost me, then I can follow him. Following the idiot that I pegged as following me two seconds into the day will be much easier than trying to follow your dad." Alyx explained.

Chelsi sighed. "Fine, but how are you going to follow him if I have your car?"

Alyx smirked. "I'll need you to drop me off at the school. I have an alternative transportation arrangement waiting there already."

"You're the one driving." Chelsi pointed out.

Alyx shrugged. "I won't be once we stop at the car wash."

18:48 PDT

Tracy, California

John C. Kimball High School

BANTHUP SIGHED, watching as the tennis player McLean had given a ride to climbed out of McLean's Grey Volkswagen Jetta. Following McLean had been boring. Mckenzie had led him to believe she was a talented spy, which suggested she would take various counter surveillance techniques, and following her would be difficult. It hadn't. She hadn't so much as taken a single turn she didn't need to. She'd taken the easiest and most direct routes to all of her destinations for the day. She also hadn't gone anywhere outside of normal, which meant he hadn't found the laptop, which was the entire reason he had been assigned by *both* of his bosses to follow her.

He was starting to question the praises everyone had been singing.

He eased into place behind the Volkswagen, following her North towards the traffic light. If she maintained her boring nature, she would turn right and head home. As the car reached 11th, however, she pulled into the left-hand turn lane, that would take her a short distance further down 11th, before placing her on the freeway.

Banthup smiled. She was finally being interesting. Why else would she head west when her house was east?

Banthup gave the Volkswagen some room, hanging back far enough that he could still see the car on the freeway, but not so close it was obvious he was following the car. They didn't go very far on the freeway, however, getting off at the next exit for Mountain House Parkway.

Perhaps this was where she had hidden the laptop.

Banthup almost missed seeing the Volkswagen turn left onto Mascot Boulevard as a Black BMW came blasting past him, cutting him off, distracting him, but they hadn't finished building out here, so the corner was free of buildings, allow-ing him to catch sight of the Volkswagen again, and follow it.

DYLAN AND Addy Hall drove up to their house, pulling into their driveway. "Someone is next door." Hall told his wife.

"Sarah didn't mention that either of them would be coming by." She said, looking back at the car parked in the bottom of the driveway. "And that doesn't look like one of their cars."

"It isn't," Hall agreed. "BMW is not in Sarah's taste. She has that Audi that she loves, and Neil drives that boring Honda."

"I'll call them and let them know." Addy said, pulling out her phone, as the two of them climbed out of the car. She paused as Alyx' Volkswagen pulled up out front. "Or maybe Alyx knows something we don't."

The two of them watched as a uniformed tennis player climbed out of the drivers seat, but it wasn't the tennis player that they expected to be driving. It was their daughter. Addy and Dylan stormed down the driveway. "Chelsi Elenor Hall.

What are you doing driving Alyx' car?" Addy asked.

Banthup pulled up to the stop sign down the street just in time to watch the wrong uniformed tennis player climb out of the Volkswagen, realizing that the one he was meant to follow had gotten out at the high school, and he had no idea where she had gone. He swore, flipping a u-turn on the narrow street, peeling out of the neighborhood.

Chelsi smiled as she watched him leave. Alyx' plan had worked. She pulled out of the driveway next door to the Hall's in a Black BMW right after Banthup left, heading out to follow him.

Hall just shook his head. He pointed at Chelsi. "You and I are going to have a conversation when I get back." He promised, then walked past his wife, back up to the car. Thane poked his head out the door, trying to figure out what was going on. "Get in." Hall told his son.

Thane looked from his sister standing next to Alyx' car with no Alyx in sight, and the rather pissed look on his father's face and put a rather loose idea of what must be happening. He climbed into the car with his father. "Alyx is onto us isn't she."

"If it was her in the BMW, she's following Banthup back to the safehouse as we speak." Hall told his son.

Thane pulled out his phone. Hall grabbed it.

"No. We let this play out. Alyx identifying Banthup as following her, and turning a tail into an opportunity to rescue the others is exactly the kind of note we need in the report of this training operation. It proves our training could be better." Hall backed out of the driveway. "Also, Neil told me I couldn't kidnap his daugh-ter. But if she shows up at my front door..."

Thane shook his head. "So you want her to beat you. Again."

"If you can't beat them, recruit them." Hall said.

ALYX GLANCED up at the house where she'd tailed the agent in the Ford to. If she was right, Hall was keeping her boyfriend here. She knew she shouldn't be surprised how close it was to the high school, but she was. It annoyed her that he had been so close, and she, nor anyone else had noticed.

She grabbed a box with a knife in it off the seat next to her, taking the knife out of the plastic wrapping and slipping it between her leg and the compression shorts she was wearing under her tennis dress, the clip on the knife holding itself in place. She was glad she had stashed it in the car when she'd snuck back over to Peter's house after the FBI detail switched over. She was fortunate she'd had just enough time to run to Peter's house, drive his car to the school, and run home through Redbridge community. It had been difficult, but doable, and totally worth it.

She looked at her phone sitting in the center console, trying to figure out what she wanted to do with it. If she succeeded, she might need it to call in some reinforcements before Hall showed up. Then again, if she, nor any of the young men Hall had kidnapped were able to get out to the car before Hall showed up, the point was rather moot, and she wouldn't be at school the following day. She opened Peter's glovebox, slipping her phone into it before closing it back up. She took a deep breath, her hand on the door handle.

She couldn't miss school. Her grades had suffered enough already because of this case.

Alyx opened the door, strutting across the street up to the front door. As she stood on the front porch, she couldn't help but think that she was either about to do something that was very brave, or very stupid. As much as she knew she was an intelligent person, she was pretty sure this was the latter. But if a psychopath kidnapping her cousin a couple months before necessitated she go after them, what should she do if her uncle kidnapped her boyfriend, even if she was mad at him for lying?

Her life would have been so much easier if the people she loved stopped being kidnapped.

Alyx raised her hand to knock on the door, only to have the door pull away from her hand, leaving her face to face with the man who had been in the car following her all day. She recognized the jacket from when he'd stormed into the house a couple minutes before. What she hadn't noticed before, was how *young* the man was. And at six feet tall, she was just taller than him, meaning he was probably taller than the average American man who was five foot nine inches. His straight back, and choice of shoes, however, told her his height was something he was self-conscious about.

Alyx smiled, a plan starting to take form. She stepped up onto the concrete of the raised threshold, showing the true height difference, albeit small, between the two of them. "Hello there Tiny Tim. Hall sent me to make sure you aren't failing at the job he gave you. Oh wait—" Alyx pointed at herself. "You are."

Alyx watched as the agent's jaw clenched, an indication that what she'd said was having its intended effect. When Banthup threw a punch, she was ready for it, dodging it, and throwing one of her own: a well placed punch to his solar plexus. With Banthup doubled over in pain, Alyx grabbed the back of his head, driving his nose to her knee.

Alyx inhaled sharply. "You know, I was really hoping I could drop you without drawing blood. Now it looks like I had to *try* to incapacitate you." Alyx taunted, stepping over his body on the floor, crumpled in pain, his hand not knowing whether it should be grabbing his stomach, or his now bloody nose. "You don't mind if I take a look around, do you?"

She ignored his moaning. It would be at least a few minutes before he was in any position to get up, let alone come after her, and she was hoping she could find the boys and get them out before that. She knew the smart thing to do was to knock him unconscious, but she was in a hurry. She looked around the empty living room, trying to figure out where the other guards would be, and where Hall would keep his prisoners.

"Hey, where is everybody?" She hollered back to the guard, who was still wriggling on the floor. His eyes opened, revealing a fire that may have helped him win if he'd shown it earlier. She knew that until she'd yelled she'd had the benefit of surprise on her side, and her question had just thrown it away. Surprise was how she'd saved Lynn back in July, but she didn't care. It was like something broke inside her. She was being reckless. She would do just about anything to save Peter, and she didn't care what would happen to her in the process.

Maybe it was a way to defy her parents. They'd used lies to protect her. Now, she was about to show them what their lies had actually done to harm her.

Alyx smiled as she heard footsteps exit the hallway she had seen off the living room. "Well, it was great talking to you, but it sounds like someone else would like to dance with me," she said to the agent she'd already dropped to the floor. She spun to the agent who's footsteps she'd heard. "Isn't that right?"

Alyx dropped the smile, charging yet another young looking agent, who was well built, like a Fullback. If someone didn't know Alyx' extensive martial arts training, and most people didn't, they would probably put their money on the agent, rather than Alyx, yet before she even threw her first punch, his hands went up in the air. She paused, close enough that should she need to, she could still throw any number of punches that would be effective in laying him out. She observed him suspiciously, used to be underestimated. She had intentionally stayed in her tennis uniform to maintain an aura of innocence. Then again, maybe seeing his friend in the doorway, bleeding, was enough of a testament to what she could do, and had shattered any illusion of her not knowing what she could do.

"Stevens." The agent still laying in the door hissed. "What are you doing."

Stevens pulled the keys off of his belt loop, carefully leaning forward to hand them to Alyx. "I've locked the one guard in the surveillance room, but he's probably called Hall by now. There are two other guards that you will have to deal with. One is upstairs outside your boyfriend's room. The other is in the bathroom, and I can't tell you when he might show up."

Alyx narrowed his eyes. "Why should I trust you?" She asked.

"Peter is my friend. We were on the football team together, and I can tell he really cares about you, so anything I can do to mitigate the harm that comes to you will really help me get back on his good side." Stevens explained.

"Where are the others? Cameron, Nathan, Adison?"

Stevens gestured with his head towards the hallway he had come from. "Nathan is down there. The other two are in the other two bedrooms upstairs."

Alyx pulled out her knife, flipping it open, still not quite trusting Stevens. She tossed him the keys back. "Show me."

As Alyx left, following Stevens to Nathan's room, Banthup couldn't help but curse all the times he underestimated the girl, despite being warned against it, and hating her for it. Stevens cast a cautious glance back at the girl with a knife as he reached the door where Hall had been holding Nathan.

As Stevens stuck the key into the lock, Alyx decided to prod for more information. "Is he restrained."

"Yes. I don't know where Hall got them, but he has all of them restrained with prison grade shackles." Stevens told her.

"Hall is CIA, and has convinced the FBI to play nice." Alyx reported. "Well, he convinced my dad to play nice at least, and he's FBI."

Stevens looked Alyx up and down. "Explains a few things."

"And the key to the shackles?" Alyx prodded.

Stevens held up one of the keys on the ring. "Right here."

Alyx smiled. "Good. Now why don't you go in there and re-lease him. I'll be right behind you." Stevens turned the doorknob in response, entering. As Alyx entered behind him, she watched as Nathan lifted his head off the table he'd been sleeping on.

"McLean." Nathan stated. "What are you doing here?"

Alyx smiled, crossing her arms. "Rescuing you."

Nathan rubbed his wrist as Stevens unlocked the shackles. "Took you long enough."

"Excuse me?" Alyx snarked. She looked at her watch. "It took me less than 50 hours to find Peter after he was kidnapped, and that is including the hours it took before I found out my boyfriend had been kidnapped, as well as the hours I spent at school, practice, a tennis match, and sleeping. Clearly your training program couldn't do any better."

Nathan cocked his head to the side. "Weren't you working with Peter to find us?" He asked.

"No." Alyx laughed. When she saw that Nathan wasn't laughing, she frowned. "Was I supposed to?"

Nathan stood as his last limb was unlocked. "He was supposed to ask you the day after Adison was kidnapped." Nathan started walking toward the door. "Where is Adison?"

Alyx pointed up. "He's upstairs with the other two." She was about ask him to join, but it looked like it was using most of Nathan's strength to just stand. It hadn't taken her as long to find Nathan as it had to find Lynn, but she was sure the emotional duress of knowing Adison was in danger hadn't helped. As they reached the family room, she slipped him her knife. "If you watch these two, I'll go get your brother."

Nathan took the knife, nodding.

"What about the guard upstairs?" Stevens asked as he handed her the keys.

Alyx smirked. "I don't need a knife to be a dangerous wea-pon. It just helps." She turned away from the three men and ran up the stairs, taking them two at a time.

She had a boyfriend to save. And probably kiss. And then definitely yell at him for lying. *A lot.*

She saw the guard as soon as she turned into the hallway at the top of the stairs. The problem with that was that he saw her too. Alyx took off, running at him with an explosive sprint her track coaches would have been proud of. With perfect form, she took the momentum she gained in the sprint and applied it's force into bringing her off the ground, her right foot in front of her like she was getting ready to jump a hurdle, her torso bending forward over her knee, and her left leg bent off to her side. Had she actually been jumping a hurdle, she would have been wearing her track spikes, with the ball of her foot sporting seven 3/8 inch pyramid shaped pieces of metal she could use as a weapon. Since she wasn't, she tried to bring her toes up a bit further than she usually would to use more of her foot to apply force as she planted it in the guard's chest. The guard fell over backwards, but he was heavier, and much taller than the hurdles she jumped for competition, so she too fell to the ground. She had expected as much, so she was ready, tucking and rolling when she did, quickly jumping back up and returning to the guard. Then again, she had run hurdles long enough to know that what made you good at hurdles wasn't *never* falling, it was getting back up when you did because even the best hurdlers fell on occasion.

She leaned over the guard to hear him groaning. She had

probably fractured at least one of his ribs. "Are you going to get back up?" She asked him,

He shook his head, unable to answer since the fall had knocked the air out of him.

She patted his shoulder. "Good answer." She straightened, going to one of the doors that the guard hadn't been at. As much as she wanted to see Peter, she was certain he was going to be at least a little angry at her, and she really wanted to make sure all of the Generation members got out.

The door she opened revealed a young man who resembled the one she'd left downstairs. She was relieved to see that he not only was provided with a cot to sleep on, but wasn't left in chains like his brother had been.

"You must be Adison." She said. "I'm Alyx. Your brother is downstairs, and I believe he would like to see you."

Adison looked like he didn't quite want to move. He sat on his cot, just staring at the girl standing in the doorway.

"Come on." She urged, waving her hand at him to come. "I neutralized the guards. There's no one left to be scared of at the moment. But if we don't hurry, Hall will be back."

Adison reluctantly got up, slowly following. "When you say neutralize..." Adison trailed off as he entered the hallway, seeing the guard lying on the floor.

"This one probably has a broken rib. The one in the doorway downstairs probably has a broken nose. The other one, surprisingly, cooperated without me even threatening him. Nathan's making sure he remains cooperative." Alyx explained.

"He probably read the BOLO, and doesn't want to be the one that dies." Adison commented.

Alyx shook her head, as she unlocked the next door. "I haven't killed anyone. Sure, I stabbed a guys foot, and threw a knife at another, but to be fair, they kidnapped Lynn, and they attacked me first, so a little violence was justified. They may have been a bit unconscious, but they were alive. Even the assassin that chased us through the forest."

She opened the door to the room she was standing in front of, finding the member of the training program that she didn't know. "You must be Cameron." Cameron also had a bed, but there was also a shackle chaining his right foot to the wall. She held up the keys. "How would you like to escape."

Cameron sat up, watching Alyx as she came over with the key. "The CIA is looking for you."

Alyx glanced out into the hallway at Adison. "So I've heard." With Cameron released from his bonds, Alyx left the room. She didn't know how long they would have before Hall showed up, but she would need all of them released and ready to fight when he did.

Adison pointed at the guard groaning on the floor. "What did you do to him?"

Alyx shrugged, walking to the last door in the hallway, where she was certain she'd find Peter. "I kicked him. I can show you if you join track in the spring." She promised.

Adison looked like he wanted to be appalled, but he had

been kidnapped, and had been here the longest, so guaranteed, he didn't want to turn down learning something that might help him prevent the same thing happening again.

Alyx handed Adison the key to Peter's car. "Do me a favor. Go out to the BMW out front. In the glovebox is my phone. Call whoever you call in these situations."

Adison nodded. "If Nathan is here, that would be Peter."

Alyx pointed at the door of the room she was standing in front of. "Peter is here."

Cameron shrugged. "Call whoever you can for back-up." He looked at Alyx. "I'll go help Nathan."

"Thank you." She said. Cameron nodded, running downstairs with Adison, leaving Alyx to unlock the door.

19:48 PDT
Tracy, California
Hall Base of Operations

PETER LOOKED up as he heard the door unlock. He had been here two days already by his estimate. He had spent most of his last day going through his plan, trying to see if he could figure out where he went wrong. He never stopped to ask himself if Alyx was worth it, because he knew she was. His parents weren't right. His love for her didn't make him weak. He'd messed up somewhere else; he just didn't know where yet.

His only hope was that Alyx had taken the advise in his note, and had flown to London after her tennis tournament. She was probably still trying to adjust to the time change. She had barely fallen asleep, despite it being almost four in the morning, and she would be tired when her uncle woke her up in a few hours. But she was safe. That was what mattered. Except he knew better. He had seen the note. She had stolen his laptop.

The last of his hope was ripped away when he watched

the door open, revealing the tall, slender girl sliding in the door. She looked tired, but based on the groaning coming from the guard he could see laying on the floor just beyond the door, she had worked quite hard to open this door. "No. You shouldn't be here," he lamented. "You. Were. Safe. I told you to go to London." He complained, struggling against the metal that locked him to the chair he was currently in.

"When have I ever done what I was told to do?" Alyx quipped. "Telling me to do something almost always ensures I do the complete opposite." She walked across the room, showing him the key. "Besides, who would have saved you had I gone to London?"

"I wasn't supposed to need saving." Peter admitted as Alyx unlocked his right hand. "The idea was to give my laptop to Hall, and then this entire nightmare would be over, and you would be safe."

Alyx unlocked Peter's left hand. "Well in that case, you should have read me in on the plan. At the very least, your note should have told me *not* to steal your laptop off your table, leaving a taunt for Hall in its place." She reckoned.

"Payback for last summer. He showed me." Peter murmured.

"Yep. I also used Scarlett to start a rumor that you and I are secretly dating to make sure Hall assigned an agent to follow me, which he did. And that allowed me to trick said tail into following Chelsi in my car, while I followed him in your BMW, which led me straight to you." Alyx looked up from unlocking Peter's legs. "By the way, I borrowed your BMW."

Peter cradled Alyx's face in his hands. "I love you, but seriously, you are in danger, and I hate that you put yourself in more danger to save me."

"Good. Then you know how I feel now." Alyx said. "Also, we kind of need to go. I was hoping to be gone before Hall shows up."

Peter nodded, moving his hands from her face to grab her hand instead.

PETER WATCHED the chaos around him. The FBI was officially in charge of the crime scene. Neil McLean was guiding the scene, his agents taking statements, and looking quite productive for the media while he gave the interview. The victim's faces—they'd been promised—would be blurred out. But the FBI had been called in to see the Generation's response to law enforcement involvement. As McLean rattled off the cover story that the CIA had developed for the training mission, Peter could only hope they'd passed. When Wraith had shown up after Alyx freed them, he'd told Peter that the Training Division was considering terminating their program if they failed.

Personally, the only flaw he saw in their program was Dr. Wraith.

Peter couldn't help but watch as Alyx gave her statement to an FBI agent. He would have loved to be close enough to hear that statement. It would be interesting to hear her explain how she'd figured out that he was a spy, or how she'd connected him to everyone kidnapped. He knew she had a source in London that had told her about the BOLO, but everything else... She knew a lot she shouldn't.

There was even more that she should have known, but didn't.

Thane cautiously approached Peter. He and his dad had arrived on the scene slightly before anyone else, and Alyx had been ready for a fight, but it never came. Apparently her rescuing them was good enough for him. Training mission terminated. It had been Hall who called the FBI in. He blended in with the rest of the FBI agents, except for the ever so slight smile on his face. He looked like he won, even though he had technically lost. He never got the Generation's files.

Peter threw his arm around Thane, drawing him in. Thane looked at him startled. Peter had seen the way the other three had looked at Thane. To them he was a traitor. He had been there when each of them were kidnapped. Even if Thane had been tapped by his dad to help run this training mission, Peter couldn't help but think about the fact that Thane helping his dad was helping Alyx, and he couldn't fault him for that.

Derek Stevens involvement, on the other hand, did feel like a betrayal. Stevens had been on the football team with him and Cameron at West High School, and he was the closest thing Peter had to a brother outside of the Generation. To know that he had helped identify Alyx as a weakness they could exploit to get him to talk hurt more than Peter would ever admit.

"You are helping write the report of this exercise," Peter commented, looking at Thane. "How do you think our program fairs in it."

Thane sighed. "I don't know. I'll be honest, I think my dad asked me to participate on his team so he would have an argument for the potential of the program's effectiveness." Thane nodded towards Alyx. "And I think he just found another one."

"Do you know where she hid my laptop yet?" Peter asked.

Thane shook his head. He looked away as Alyx glanced over at the two of them. "But it looks like you might have an opportunity to ask her." Thane walked away, leaving Peter alone so Alyx could talk to him as she finished her interview and approached.

"So…" Peter started.

"So." Alyx replied.

"We probably need to talk. There are some things I should explain." Peter admitted.

"I would like that." Alyx told him. She pulled the sleeves of the sweatshirt she was wearing over her hands, folding her arms around herself to keep her warm. She glanced at her dad, who's eyes somehow stayed on her, despite the appearance of him being entirely focused on the reporter who was interviewing him. "I think it will have to be here though. I don't think my dad is going to let me leave."

Peter smiled at her, his hope for a future with her blooming as he noticed that she was wearing his jacket over her tennis uniform. He could only imagine how hungry she must have been. He doubted she stopped to eat after tennis, based on how long it had taken her to rescue him. "You ask me any question, and I'll answer it." Peter promised.

Alyx raised an eyebrow. "Why do I feel like Dr. Wraith isn't going to like that?"

"Because he won't." Peter admitted. "But you are a member of the Promising Generation, whether he likes it or not. Your credentials were never deactivated."

"Promising Generation. That's kind of a mouth full." Alyx commented. "But Promgen is much easier to say."

Peter shook his head. "We *do not* call it *Promgen*. Usually we'll just call it *the Generation* for short."

"I like Promgen." Alyx insisted, with a playful smile. Her smile faded, her face taking on a more serious expression. "I love you." She said softly. "I don't run into harms way for just anyone."

Peter wanted to tease, pointing out she had run into danger to save Lynn, who she'd barely met over the summer, but something about her tone told him not to. He just smiled at her, pulling her to him. "I love you too." He replied.

He couldn't help but look at her. Technically, this was the first time she had told him that she loved him in English, and it was the first time she'd said it first. But as much as he wanted to savor the moment, he couldn't.

He swallowed a laugh before it escaped, but he still made a noise.

"What?" She asked, a lightness returning to her voice. "Did I say something funny?"

Peter shook his head. "You've just never said *I love you* in English before." He smiled. "I think it's official now."

Alyx stepped closer. "It better be. Everyone at school knows. And I mean it."

"Good." Peter whispered. He leaned down, giving her a kiss. "Ich liebe dich."

Alyx smiled. "Ich liebe dich auch." She grabbed his hands. "In any language we say it."

21:13 PDT
Tracy, California
Corral Hollow Avenue

ALYX WAS silent as her father drove her home. She knew a lecture was coming, and she didn't want to say anything that would set it off before she had a chance to escape. Because the truth of the matter was, no matter what her dad told her, she didn't regret her decision. How could she? She'd rescued three teenaged boys with no personal harm to herself.

Alyx glanced over as her dad backed his Civic into the garage, seeing the bay where her car should have been empty. She wouldn't put it past her parents to intentionally make it difficult for her to get her car back from the Halls. It may have been her car, but she was still a minor, under her parents care, and they didn't really appreciate her doing things without asking first. If she didn't have a car, she was easier to control. Sometimes.

The second Neil shut the car off, Alyx unbuckled her seatbelt, sliding out of the open car door before her dad had even noticed. She had almost made it in the door to the house when her dad's voice stopped her.

"Alyxandrie Madelyn McLean. You are not running off before your mother and I have a chance to talk to you."

Alyx huffed, opening the door anyway, only to find her mom standing in the laundry room, arms folded.

She wasn't getting out of this.

"Before you lecture me about the importance of telling the truth, stop and think about the lies you've told me over the years..." Alyx started, focusing most of her attention on her mom.

Sarah looked at Neil with an exasperated expression. Neil just shrugged with a head shake. Neither of them were sure how to be good parents, especially not with a teenager like Alyx.

"If your father and I choose not to tell you something, we only do it from a place of trying to keep you safe." Sarah told Alyx.

Alyx threw her hands up. "How does not telling me that I had siblings keep me safe?" Alyx pointed to her head. "You have no idea how many times I thought I was crazy, because I remembered one of them, because I dreamed about one of them, but there was no way I had any siblings, because I'm an only child, and my parents wouldn't lie to me about something like that. I thought my parents wouldn't *lie* to me. After all, we pride ourselves on always telling each other the truth."

"You remember them?" Sarah asked softly, her voice on

the edge of breaking. She too, after all, had lost a sibling. She knew what it felt like to lose the sister she shared everything with. And when Alyx had lost her siblings, she lost her children.

Alyx rolled her eyes, pushing past her mom to go in the house. She ran up the stairs, straight to her room.

Sarah just looked at her husband, tears in her eyes. Neil entered the house, enveloping his wife in his arms. "Maybe it's time to come clean. On everything." He whispered. "She's clearly smart enough to figure it out."

Sarah nodded. "I'll go get the photo album. Do you have a copy of the report?"

Neil shook his head. "Maybe we shouldn't tell her that part. If she doesn't remember..."

There was a reason five-year-old Alyx started to block the memories of her siblings. Some of it was trauma. Some of it was guilt.

Sarah and Neil pushed their way into Alyx' room, finding her with music blasting as she laid on her bed, doing home-work. She had a perfectly good desk across the room she could be using. They knew this was a defense though. She rarely did her homework when she was at home. The only time they'd actually *seen* her do homework was when Peter was sitting at the table with her.

She was a good student, but she could be so much better if she just applied herself.

Neil turned the music off as Sarah took the photo album

full of family pictures to Alyx' bed, sitting down next to her.

"You were our third child." Sarah started. She opened the photo album. "Cole was born in 1990. He was such an active and happy child. Emily loved him, naturally. He was like a little brother. Finally she wasn't the youngest, and she started teaching him all the things Ally and I had once taught her."

Alyx sat up, looking at the pictures her mom was showing her.

"And then we had Analyn Grace in '93. If you could have seen those two..." Sarah trailed off, trying not to get too emotional. "They were both the best of friends, and the worst of enemies. Annie lived to drive Cole nuts. But whenever she was hurt, or scared, he immediately went into protective older brother mode."

"Then I was born in '95." Alyx added, pointing to the next picture, with her siblings holding her as a baby.

Sarah nodded. "Annie immediately loved you. She was thrilled to have a sister. And Cole was immediately protective. He may have only been five, but he was such a big helper. I sometimes think he hated me for sending him off to school. I only made it up to him by creating the Promising Generation and teaching him how to protect you even better."

"You guys created the Promgen?" Alyx asked.

"If that's what they're calling it now, yes." Sarah answered. "Your father and I were two of the CIA's top agents at the time, and he loved the things the two of us as well as Emily taught him. He also spoke French, of course, and easily started to pick up Russian. He had talent, and thrived at everything we taught him, so we started to include Annie. We quickly expanded the number of kids involved to most of the kids of the top agents at the CIA. You felt left out, and while you were learning French from me, you had to start learning Russian and Italian too. By your fifth birthday, you were just as advanced as any of the other members of the training program, besides your own siblings, but only because they taught you everything you knew."

"That's why I knew 2000 was important." Alyx said softly. "That's when they died. Isn't it?"

Sarah nodded.

"How did they die?" Alyx asked.

"There is a terrorist organization that had infiltrated our CIA task force, and somehow had gotten close to the Promising Generation. They didn't care that you were children. They saw you as threats to be eliminated."

"What are they called?" Alyx prodded.

Sarah sighed. "The Circle of Fifths." She turned the page, showing Alyx the picture she'd seen in her dad's desk. She brushed her finger over each of her kid's smiling faces. "We had Cassandra Mae at the beginning of 2000. When the Circle of Fifths attacked, and—" Sarah choked up, not able to finish the sentence. "We knew that both of you were in danger. But in order to hide you, we needed new professions, and we couldn't do that, and take care of Cassandra, so we faked her death, and one of my good friends adopted her."

Alyx fingered the picture of her and her siblings.

"We've kept a lot of things from you." Neil admitted. "But it was only to protect you. If the Circle of Fifths found you... and you didn't handle Cole and Annie's deaths very well. When you stopped remembering, we thought it best to just let you forget."

Alyx was still angry. And she wanted to argue. But she let them tell her about her siblings, and make their excuses. At least they were starting to open up to her. It was a start.

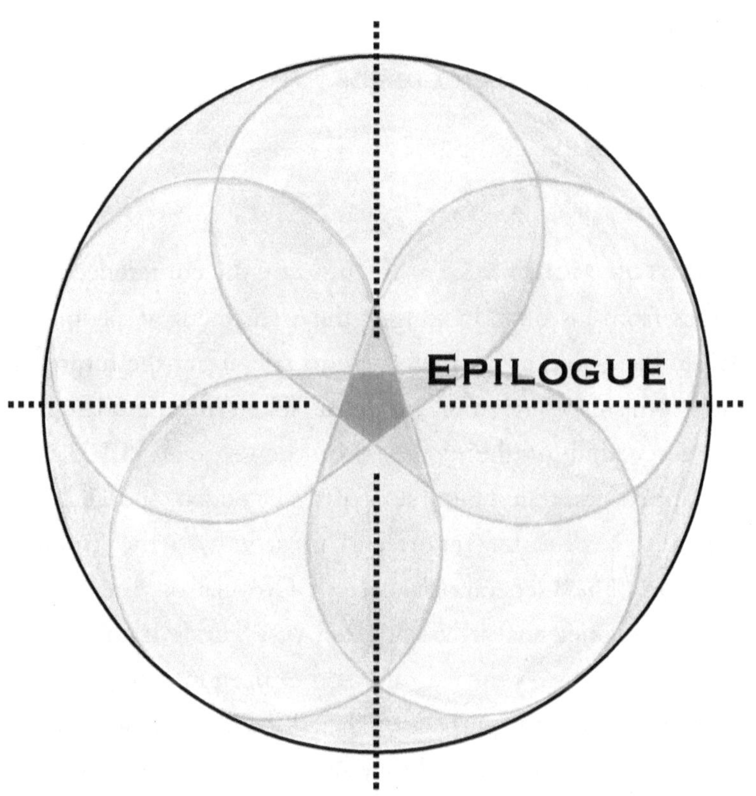

EPILOGUE

9:05 EST November 21st, 2011
Langley, Virginia
Office of the Director of the CIA

DIRECTOR MCLEAN sat at the head of the conference table
across from his desk, looking at the assortment of people he
had in his office, all of them here to talk about the future of
the Promising Generation Program. When his granddaughter
had rescued all of the members of the Generation Hall had
kidnapped, the training mission officially ended, and Hall was
required to write his report and present it to the Training
Division. The Generation's current CIA liaison Dr. Wraith
had complained that it wasn't a fair or accurate training mission, because he, as the liaison, had not been informed.

And that was the purpose of this Monday morning meeting.

Everyone who believed they should be involved in the future of the Promising Generation sat at this table, as well as a
few people who didn't know about the training program, but
as the Director of the CIA, he had taken the liberty to invite
them, such as his son—who was one of the founding members of the program—and his son's boss. In attendance, he

had his newly appointed Deputy Director of the CIA for Operations, Dylan Hall; the Associate Director of the CIA for Talent, Daniel Thornton; psychologist Dr. Ignatius Wraith, the current Program liaison; the Executive Assistant Director of the FBI's Intelligence Branch, Eric Brooks; Special Agent Neil McLean; and, of course, the Director of the Central Intelligence Agency himself, William McLean. McLean looked at everyone at the table. He already knew he was going to make some people at this table angry, and he didn't quite care.

"I was concerned about the training of our best agents' children in the Promising Generation, so I tasked Dylan Hall with testing their training. I think his report says all it needs to. Dr. Wraith is not doing the best job at training our best bet for the future. The group was jeopardized by their use of Social Media, and they haven't been provided training in proper counter interrogation techniques." He started. "Clearly something needs to change."

"And you think Dylan Hall can do a better job of training them?" Wraith challenged.

"I think Hall will make sure they are better prepared to be the field agents we need." McLean clarified.

Wraith pointed at the file he'd brought that detailed Hall's findings. "Hall says here that Peter Carlyle wanted to be found, and that it was his capture that ultimately led to the Generation members rescue." Wraith summarized. "I would just like to point out that I have had a very strong hand in Carlyle's training. Anything he does reflects on me and my training of him." He claimed.

Hall controlled a sigh and eye roll in an effort to maintain professionalism. "You clearly didn't read the file if you think that was what it says. Yes, ultimately it was Carlyle's capture that allowed for their rescue, but it was not because of Carlyle's actions. In fact, Carlyle failed to inform the other Generation members about his plans. He also left a note for Alyx McLean, resulting in her stealing the computer that was vital to his plan, and also the very thing that would ensure their failing the training mission. She also, may I point out, is the one member of the Generation who has not had any formal training under Wraith, and was the one who ultimately rescued all of the captured members." Hall corrected. "But sure, your training was completely flawless."

"Who, may I ask, trained McLean?" Thornton asked. He looked around the table when his question was answered by silence, realizing his error. "I mean Miss McLean, the young agent mentioned in the report." He added, trying to make up for the mistake of making it seem like he was addressing both his boss, and the FBI agent with the question. "How are we meant to refer to her?"

"We can simply call her by her first name to forgo confusion." Director McLean stated, to which Thornton just nodded.

"Alyx is not an agent." Wraith leered. "The Training Division hasn't approved her acceptance into the training program."

Hall just smiled. "Her file was never deactivated when her parents moved her away from the program, so she technically never quit. She doesn't need to be approved, which is why she has been training with them since she rescued the members." He turned to Neil. "As to who trained her, we should let her father speak to that."

Neil shook his head. "She has no formal training. She took a few martial arts classes. She's really good at using google, and can retain just about everything she reads, which is why she knows the FBI handbook better than I do."

"Would it be fair to say she has the training of an investigator?" McLean asked his son.

Neil shrugged. "Maybe from watching me, but she never received formal investigator training. She has always been naturally observant, and I have used outings in public as a way to hone the skill on occasion. I've asked her to pay attention to her surroundings, because I've seen the world we live in and how dangerous it can be for a young woman. At some point, she became adept at using google and other public source materials to improve her skills."

"Until recently, Neil has been assigned to the Criminal, Cyber, Response, and Services Branch, where he handled various criminal cases. While he was there, he had permission to get assistance from his daughter, in an attempt to cut down on the number of times she solved one of the cases as an anonymous tipster." Brooks reported. "So she may not be a trained investigator, but she definitely has the talent of one."

"Are you suggesting, director, that we train our agents to be investigators?" Thornton asked.

McLean shook his head. "No, what I'm suggesting is that our training is too narrowly focused. The truth of the matter is that we don't know where we will need the children of our best agents when they decide to join our agencies. We need to diversify their training."

"If you diversify their training, they won't be ready for the specialized missions we want to send them on immediately after graduation." Wraith argued.

"The program's graduates are spending at least two years continuing their education in some way, and most of them have been attending training at the Farm anyway. I see no reason to specialize their training if we are just going to send them to training like the rest of our agents." McLean asserted. "That is why I would like to move oversight from the Training Division to Operations, and invite the FBI Intelligence Branch to join. The students we have in the program may not be interested in only joining the CIA, and if they would fit better at the FBI, I don't see why we should dissuade them. It would also open the program up to the children of FBI agents who think they might like to join their parent's profession." He turned his attention to his son and his boss. "I've already spoken with Director Kelly, and he agrees with me, but said he would leave it up to your discretion, whether or not to join, as it will be under your purview."

Brooks nodded. "I think I will. Since Special Agent McLean was one of the people who founded the program when he was still at the CIA, I think it would be wise if I assign him as our liaison."

"Good." McLean grinned. "I will be contacting other agencies to see if there are any that would like to join us."

"If you're moving the program to Operations, who is the CIA liaison?" Wraith inquired.

"Ah, I did forget that, didn't I." McLean turned to Hall. "As you are my Deputy Director of Operations, it falls to you to chose who will be the CIA liaison."

"My son is graduating from High School in just a few months time, so I will be splitting my time between DC and California anyway, I figured I would have them just report directly to me. Neil and I can train them over the course of the next couple months, and with the older members being sworn in agents, they should be fully capable to handle the daily operation of the program on their own." Hall reckoned.

McLean turned to Thornton. "It looks like Wraith is yours to reassign. He is no longer needed to oversee the Promising Generation." He publicized, turning back to Wraith. "Thank you for your service."

Wraith turned a violent shade of red.

Thornton nodded. "I just lost my psychologist at the Farm. I could really use him there." He turned to look at Dylan and Neil. "I look forward to training the agents you send me. It will be quite interesting to see how they compare to our other recruits."

McLean looked around the table. "Well, unless there are any other concerns, I believe that will be all." Everyone stood up, starting to head for the door, Wraith the last among them.

13:10 EST November 23rd, 2011
McLean, Virginia
McLean Central Park

PETER WALKED down the pathway through the trees, holding his girlfriend's hand. It had been amazing how fast he had gotten used to the small things, like holding her hand at school, or catching her as she left the cafeteria to kiss her before class. Since she and her parents flew out right after school on Friday, he hadn't seen her since Lunch that day, and he had missed her every second, anxiously waiting for today and the date they had scheduled.

Alyx pulled the hand Peter wasn't holding out of her coat pocket, tucking her hair behind her ear. "So how are your parents?" She asked cautiously.

Peter looked down, kicking a rock on the path in front of him. He watched it skip down the path before answering. "So, I may have lied about them asking me to come visit for Thanksgiving." He admitted. "I just figured when I heard from Thane that you and your parents, would be coming to Virginia to spend Thanksgiving with your grandparents... I didn't think

I could spend an entire week away from you, so I may have used my parents as an excuse to follow you." He paused waiting for Alyx to get mad at him, but when she didn't, he decided to continue. "They don't know I'm here yet."

Alyx smirked. "So I take it I'm not meeting your parents."

"You're not mad I lied?" Peter asked.

Alyx shrugged. "Maybe a bit peeved, but when you make it seem as sweet as you did, it's hard to stay that way." She teased. "Besides, I've seen you every day for almost two months. I wouldn't have survived a week without you either."

"You are the strongest person I know. I'm sure you would have been fine." Peter corrected.

"Maybe." She shrugged.

Their conversation seemed silly, knowing everything they'd been through. Sure, everyone at school knew they were dating once they returned to school after escaping Hall, but they had maintained their own lives. Alyx still ate lunch with Thane, Carlie, Savannah, and Kaden. Peter still sat with his friends from football. If they brushed hands on occasion, or even exchanged a kiss on campus, that was the only indication they were dating. The biggest change was the fact that they had gone on a few more actual dates now that her parents knew they were dating, and Alyx was present at the Generation meetings, meaning they saw each other every day.

"Have you heard back from Oxford yet?" Peter asked.

Alyx bit her lip. Then, of course, there was Oxford. Oxford had been her refrain, her mantra for putting space between her and Peter. And when that hadn't worked, she decided throwing herself into solving a kidnapping was a good distraction. After all, Oxford was her future, and she couldn't possibly jeopardize her future for short term happiness. At the beginning, that's all she thought dating Peter could give her. They were just another teenaged couple that would never last.

"I didn't turn in my application packet," She admitted.

Peter stopped, their connected hands making Alyx stop as well. She turned to look at him, shock evident on his face. "Why not?" He breathed. "Oxford meant everything to you."

Alyx nodded. It did. But I made a decision, and if that means I don't attend Oxford, I'm fine with that."

"Alyx if dating me is—"

"Dating you wasn't the decision I made that stopped me from applying to Oxford." She assured him. She started walking again, dragging Peter with her. "I have this bad habit of jumping at the chance to do anything exciting, and I think I should take some time to decide what I want my future to look like before I go to school. Who knows. I'm graduating a year early. I'm going to take a gap year to figure out what I want. As long as I make sure my grades look good, pass my AP test, and graduate with honors, I could apply next October for any program I want."

"Hm," he hummed. "You wouldn't be thinking about becoming a spy would you?" He teased.

Alyx smacked his arm with the hand he wasn't holding.

"Ok, Mister *I want to be an engineer.*"

Peter shrugged. "I *have* been thinking about my future, you know. I like the life I'd have if I were an engineer. Could you imagine? I'd have regular hours. No emergency trips. No missions that would take me away from home months on end. I could be home every night and have dinner with our family. No missed sport games. No missed concerts or plays."

"Our family?" Alyx asked, picking up on the small detail he'd let slip.

"Yeah. Our family." He ran his hand through his hair. "I don't think I can imagine my future without you." He admitted.

She smiled, setting her head on his shoulder as they walked. Her future was a jumbled mess of possibilities right now, but what she'd come to realize the more time she spent with Peter, was that it didn't matter what college she went to, or what job title she held. What mattered was the people she kept in her life.

"Alyx, will you promise me something?" Peter asked as they walked.

"What?"

"Don't give up on your goal of going to Oxford. No matter what happens, and no matter what you decide to study." He insisted.

"I won't." She promised.

"Good." Peter said. "We will make something work. Long distance. Maybe I'll move to London to be close…"

As Peter rattled off different ways they could make it

work, Alyx couldn't help but think of the futures she saw for herself—all of them included Peter.

She wanted nothing more than to jump forward five years to be there.

21:42 PST November 27th, 2011
Tracy, California
McLean Home

ALYX SIGHED as she walked down the hallway towards her room. Virginia had been full of more memories than she'd realized. She'd started school there. She remembered the school uniforms, and the playground where she'd waited for her Aunt Emily to trek across the private school campus to pick her up. She remembered Emily helping her with homework, and her grandma making all her favorite meals. She even remembered packing her suitcase for their flight to London. She remembered how somber everyone was. She remembered the black dress her dad had helped her pack. She remembered wearing that black dress, and standing next to Kate at Ally's funeral.

What she didn't remember was her siblings. Any of them.

All she had were dreams, mere hazy memories of their faces. While her parents scrap books helped her piece together some of those broken memories, they didn't tell her everything, and despite their pledges of transparency, they still wouldn't tell her who had adopted Cassandra Mae.

She couldn't help but feel like she'd been robbed. She had always longed for that bond siblings had probably because she felt the hole it had left by losing the bonds she had until 2000. Emily had been the first person she had tried to use to replace the empty space left by her siblings' deaths, but the age gap eventually pulled them apart. Stephan had always felt like a brother, but he lived in England, and she only saw him over the summer. She'd always felt a kinship with Kate, but when Lynn had shown up, their relationship changed. Kate no longer needed a substitute sister; she had a real one: a twin. So when Alyx found out that she had her own sister, who was alive somewhere, growing up without her, it was painful.

People liked to say it was impossible to miss something you'd never had, but Alyx disagreed. There were a thousand possibilities of what a relationship with Cassandra might have looked like, and she missed every single one of them. She even missed the imagined relationship where Cassandra drove her nuts, and she sometimes wondered what it would be like to be an only child, because even then she had a sister to talk to about the hard things in life.

Yes, Virginia had been full of memories, and pain. But Peter had been there, and some how, that had made it better.

Alyx dropped her suitcase in the doorway of her room. It had been a long week—a week full of family, food, and homework. She was looking forward to taking a nice hot shower and burrowing in bed until 5:30 the next morning.

Unfortunately, Kalen Mckenzie and his uncle had other plans for her.

Kalen had been patiently laying on the roof of the house next door, waiting for the McLeans to get home. Jackson had finally decided the best way to convince Alyx to join him. It required him to psychologically break her before he could rebuild her into the agent that would best help the Circle of Fifths. Tonight was only the first strike in an elaborate fight for her sanity.

As soon as he saw McLean step into the doorway of her room, he hit send on his phone, letting Jackson know that she was in position. He watched through his scope as she paused, pulled her phone out of her back pocket, and answered.

"Hello?" She said.

"Miss McLean, we met at Feilds Ball in June. I have a job opportunity for you. I would like you to come work for me."

"Who is this?" She asked.

"Phillip Jackson." She could almost hear a sinister smile through the phone. "I believe we would make quite the team."

Alyx' eyes burned with hatred as she heard the voice on the other end make his offer. She recognized the voice. Worse, she recognized the name. Jackson had been the name of man she'd pulled her uncle away from after Lynn left with Hall. It was also the name on the note left for Hall when Lynn was kidnapped from him. Jackson was the name of the man who told Lynn he'd killed her mother.

It didn't matter what opportunity he wanted to offer her.

She didn't want to work for the man who'd killed her aunt. "I don't work for terrorists." She stated.

"We'll see." Jackson promised, hanging up.

Two seconds later, Kalen received a one word message, *Go.* Kalen squoze the trigger, sending one bullet into the door frame next to McLean, slightly adjusting his angle before sending a second bullet through her window. He sat up on the roof, a satisfied smile on his face as he picked his rifle up, collapsing the bipod with his arm. He gave a short salute to McLean across the chasm between them, then began climbing down the roof on the other side of the house.

Sarah and Neil came running up behind Alyx just after Kalen disappeared. They saw the two round holes in the window and immediately began checking their daughter for the entry wounds.

"I'm fine." Alyx assured. "Jackson wants me to come work for him. This was his warning shot." She walked away from her door, crossing the hall and closing herself in her bathroom.

While Sarah knocked on the bathroom door to check on her daughter, Neil searched for the bullets. He found the first one in the door jam right next to where Alyx had been. It was easy to justify that the shooter had been a poor shot, but any doubts about the shooter's ability vanished the second Neil found the second bullet hole: in the middle of the small teddy bear Alyx kept on her bed.

When they wanted to shoot to kill, they would.

Acknowledgements

This book would not exist if not for the culmination of countless people that have helped me tremendously over the last 10 years while I've been writing this book.

First, I'd like to thank my mom, who kindly told me I needed to rewrite. The first draft of this book was good, but not as good as what it became in the following rewrites.

Mikayli and Maddyx both also receive thanks for reading the first draft of this book. Your excitement for this book made the painstaking edits I've made since then worth it.

I would like to thank the family of Professor Jeff Metcalf for letting him spend his life teaching. He may be gone, but his legacy will live on in those he taught, me included.

Thank you Professor Lepa Espinoza, who encouraged and me helped me expand what I read in the Young Adult Genre. I can never forget to thank Mrs. Maslyar, Mr. Lee, Ms, Chamber-lain, and Mr. Carlo, who taught me to love reading, helped me become a better writer, and encouraged me to follow my dreams of becoming a writer.

I also owe thanks to my friends, writing group, and family for their constant encouragement, feedback, and support. You help keep me going every day, even when I sometimes want to give up. I love you all.

Keep reading for an exclusive first look at
the next book in

The PROMGEN files

OPERATION: LATENSIFICATION

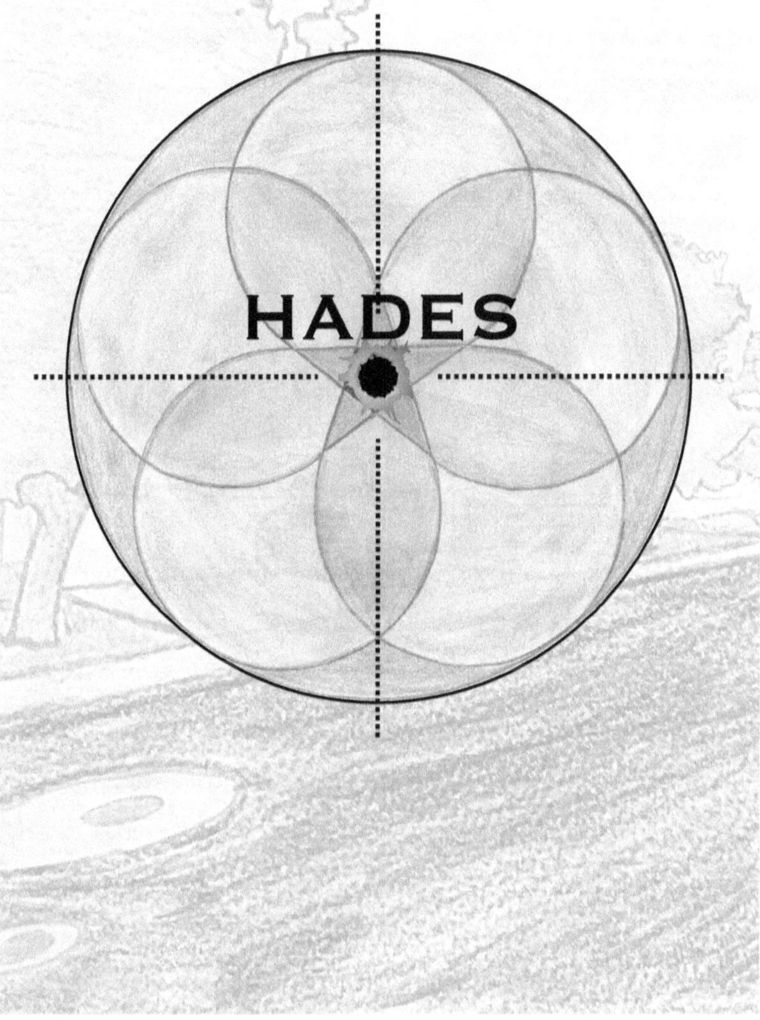

22:22 PST November 27th, 2011
Tracy, California
McLean Home

THE BLUE and red lights of emergency vehicles lit up the night, bathing the street in their strobe lights. A patrol car was parked, blocking off the street right at the bend. The officer belonging to the car was directing traffic to turn onto Ann Gabriel Lane.

Peter turned his BMW as directed, trying to see around the bend to where the McLean house was. It seemed like the emergency vehicles were congregated just down the street, but he didn't want it to be true. He needed it to be a coincidence. These emergency vehicles couldn't be congregated here for the incident Hall had called him to the McLean

House for. If it was…

Peter parked his car just down the street from where he had been forced to turn, pulling his phone out of his pocket to try to call Alyx again while walking back down the street toward her house. He swore as he got her voicemail box again. He hung up. It had only been a few minutes since Hall had called him, and leaving voicemail number five seemed like a bad idea. He could leave it at four.

Nothing stopped him from dialing her again.

The cop on the corner was too focused on turning cars away from the street. He didn't pay any attention to the pedestrian that walked around the corner, getting past his blockade.

Past the lone officer, and around the bend, the scene could only be described as organized chaos. There were two fire trucks and an ambulance. It looked like half of Tracy's police department were present with several patrol cars parked on the street. All of their lights were on, bathing the area in a dizzying blur of blood red and blue that could barely be distinguished by each other on the houses.

Everything was almost glowing purple.

Peter hung up as he got Alyx' voicemail yet again, letting himself take a refreshing breath when he saw that Tracy's emergency officials were focused on the single story house next door to the McLeans'. He watched as a gurney was rolled out of the house carrying a black body bag that was loaded into the ambulance.

Like a moth drawn to a flame, Peter left the sidewalk, crossing the street diagonally towards the house he had been in more times than he could count any more. He may have been allowing himself to hope Alyx was fine for the first time since he'd received the phone call from her uncle, finally explaining her not answering her phone with reasonable things, instead of his fears.

"Sir!" One of the police officers called. "I am going to have to ask you to return to your house."

Peter glanced at the officer, but kept walking. "I'm just trying to get to my girlfriend's house." He replied.

"Not through here," the officer insisted, sticking his arm out to stop Peter.

Peter pointed at the house that felt more like home than his own. "It's just right there. She just got home from Virginia. I told her I'd come by."

As the officer saw where Peter was pointing, his eyes told Peter everything he needed to know. "I'm sorry. I can't let you into an active crime scene."

The officer pushed him back towards the sidewalk he'd come off of. He was saying something more to him, but he didn't hear any of it. All he could hear was the echo of two words. *Crime Scene.* Two words was all it took to knock the air out of him worse than any tackle he'd survived in Football. Two words hurt more than every punch he had taken in the name of training.

The only time he'd felt a pain like the one he felt now had been when his mom had left him with his dad, and had stopped accepting his phone calls.

That day, he'd promised himself he would never let himself feel that pain again. That day had been the reason he had never let himself get close to anyone else. He didn't want to be hurt when they left.

The officer had succeeded in pushing him back to the sidewalk. "Where did you live. I can get someone to take you home."

Peter didn't answer. He was focused on where his real home was. FBI jackets were walking in and out of the Mc-Leans' House. He had been so focused on the local emergency vehicles, he hadn't noticed the black SUVs that were evidence of the heavy FBI presence. He recognized some of the agents walking in and out of the house. They worked with Neil.

Determined, Peter stepped off of the sidewalk again, shaking off the arm of the police officer who had still been standing in front of him. "Special Agent," he called. "I want to talk to Special Agent Neil McLean. This is his house. Where is he?"

One of the Agents broke away from the others, sticking his hand up. The police officer that had still been trying to grab Peter, stepped back, returning to what he had been doing before a persistent teenage boy had intruded on their crime scene.

Peter recognized the agent walking towards him as the agent Alyx had given her statement to after she had rescued him and the others from the house Hall had used to hold them, but he hadn't paid enough attention at the time to know his name. He had been focused on Alyx. Had he known that paying attention to his name then would help him get information about Alyx now, he may have made more of an effort.

"I'm sorry I didn't catch your name last time. I need to speak to Agent McLean." Peter said, oozing a confidence and authority he had no reason to. If his training was good for anything, it better be good for this.

"You are the boyfriend." The agent said. "Peter Carlyle."

Peter nodded his head. "Yes."

The agent stuck his hand out. "I'm Agent Carter. McLean is busy right now, but I can help you."

"Is Alyx ok? I just want to see her. I don't have to go inside, I just need to know she is ok. Maybe if she can come out for just a minute…"

Agent Carter nodded his head. "Alyx is fine. She is giving her statement right now, but if you stick around a bit, she can come out. Agent McLean mentioned something about having you take her to an uncle's for the night."

Peter nodded as he took a deep breath, not realizing he had been depriving himself of oxygen.

"Actually, he will be heading in with me."

Peter turned toward the voice, seeing Dylan Hall walking up towards the FBI agents. His voice was commanding, but Peter could still see the hesitation exuding from both the police officers and the FBI agents.

Hall stuck his hand out towards Agent Carter. "Deputy Director Dylan Hall. I believe Neil let you know I was coming."

"Of course." Agent Carter shook Hall's hand. "If you don't mind me asking, why is the CIA interested?"

Hall smiled. "For one, my sister is married to Neil, and I am the uncle Alyx will be staying with tonight. Second, Neil's father is my boss. We want to make sure this wasn't to get to him, especially since they just got back from visiting them. And I'm sure you remember Peter from the training mission."

Carter chuckled. "I don't think he's here for official reasons."

Hall shrugged. "Never said he was." Hall gestured for Peter to walk into the house, and the two of them passed by Carter and the other agents congregated out front to cross the threshold.

www.ingramcontent.com/pod-product-compliance
Lightning Source LLC
Chambersburg PA
CBHW030653190726
48286CB00008B/2792